ANATOMY OF A CRIME

SIBEL HODGE

"The truth is still the truth, even if no one believes it. A lie is still a lie, even if everyone believes it."

-Author Unknown

CHAPTER ONE

EPISODE 1
SLEEPING BEAUTY

I t doesn't start with a crime. The crime is the ending. Before it happens, there's a culmination of events. A journey of different pathways. A combination of thoughts and emotions and motives— fear, jealousy, love, hate, greed, anger, and revenge, to name a few. Decisions made in advance or snap choices that take a split second. Opportunities won or lost.

The crime is the trigger point, where everything that's gone before it manifests, sometimes with tragic and horrific consequences. That's the anatomy of a crime, and that's what I'm here to explore.

In the summer of 2017, two eighteen-year-old women went into Blackleaf Forest on the evening of the summer solstice... Only one came out alive.

The Crown Prosecution Service says that the murderer was successfully caught and prosecuted and is now serving a life sentence in HMP Ashmount. The defence maintains that the actual killer is still out there.

So what's the real story here? What happened on that night? Was the whole truth told at the trial? And if so, what would motivate one girl to murder her best friend?

Welcome to this series of *Anatomy of a Crime*. Just like *Serial* and *Criminal*, this podcast delves into true crime—mysteries, murders, and cold cases. I look at the lives of those who commit atrocities, their victims, and those who fall somewhere in between. I'm Lauren Taylor, an investigative journalist.

Or am I?

That name is a pseudonym, and I use it for two reasons. One, my work often leads me into dark corners of the world—places where I wouldn't want people knowing my real identity. And secondly, I think my anonymity gives me more opportunity to be candid about my thoughts and questions. But my name might not be the only untrue thing you hear in this series, because the truth can mean different things to different people.

But that's enough about me. This isn't about me. This is about the untold story here. In any crime, there are always unanswered questions. Anomalies that don't quite fit. Loose threads left dangling. Most of the time, those details might not be important, but this case has far too many to be ignored.

Media Clip from BBC Southwest Newsnight [January 2018]

—I'm standing outside Bournemouth Crown Court, where eighteen-year-old Caris Kelly was convicted of murdering Flora Morgan.

Kelly, who pleaded not guilty, will shortly be transported to Ashmount Prison to begin the life sentence handed down by the judge. The jury took just two hours to reach a guilty verdict. This case has attracted a lot of publicity, and cheers went up in the courtroom from a packed public gallery as the verdict was announced.

The Sleeping Beauty Murder that captured the attention of the nation happened in Blackleaf Forest on the outskirts of the picturesque Dorset town of Stoneminster on the twenty-first of June, 2017. Allegedly, Kelly, who was obsessed with witchcraft and satanism, drugged Morgan before strangling her in what the Crown Prosecution described as a 'ritualistic thrill kill'.

Melinda Cartright, QC for the Crown, told the court, 'The extent of the defendant's dishonesty knows no bounds. She is someone who's lied repeatedly and brazenly during the course of this police investigation and trial. We cannot rely on anything she says'.

The victim's mother, Willow Morgan, said in an impact statement to the court, 'Flora and I were very close. It's as if I lost part of myself when she was taken from me. There's not a moment of the day I don't think of her. I'd give anything to have her back with me—to hear her voice, her laughter, and to hold her tight. My daughter's life has been taken, and I implore the court to now give Caris Kelly the maximum sentence so she's never eligible for parole'.

My colleague in Morgan and Kelly's hometown of Stoneminster has been capturing the sentiments of local residents to the verdict...

—We all knew she was guilty. Right weird girl, Kelly was. No wonder, with their family like that. I'm glad she's been locked up. We can all sleep safe at night now.

—How could she do that? I'm just gobsmacked. I feel for Flora's mother. I really do. Willow Morgan has been so composed about all of this. I don't know how she does it. I'd be spitting feathers if anything happened to my kids.

—It's a tragedy, but I don't think the whole story has ever come out. There was no way Caris Kelly could get a fair trial. That's the trouble with rumours. They take on a life of their own. It was trial by media!

—Get these freaks out of Stoneminster—that's what I say. They don't belong here. Kelly never belonged here. Dirty, thieving, cunning little liar. This used to be a nice, wholesome town until this happened.

—I don't believe everything I read in the papers. And we've been inundated with you lot for months since it happened. We can't even walk to the local shops without getting harassed by the press these days. They're always skulking around! Hopefully, you'll all leave us alone now.

—Kelly's where she deserves to be. Evil little witch.

—This is what happens when outsiders come into your town, bringing their wicked ways. I've lived here all my life. I'm eighty now, and I've never heard the likes of it. I hope Flora's mum can find some peace now, knowing justice was done.

—My daughter went to school with Caris and Flora, and I always knew there was something not right about Caris. You know how you can always tell? There's something in their eyes, isn't there? I'm glad that witch has been sent down.

Dubbed by the tabloids as the Sleeping Beauty Murder, this case had everything the media could want to start a feeding frenzy, with claims of witchcraft, devil worship, and ritual killing, and, at the centre of it, two beautiful, photogenic women.

But as we journey through these episodes, you'll see there is far more to the official narrative than has ever been explored. At the heart of it lies deception and perception, rumours and myths, prejudice and investigative errors of judgement. At the end of this series, you might reach the same opinion as me, or you might see something completely different. This podcast is a medium to draw your own conclusions.

For those listeners who've never heard about the case, here's a brief rundown. On the twenty-first of June, 2017, Flora Morgan and Caris Kelly entered Blackleaf Forest around six p.m., with the intention of celebrating the summer solstice. Self-proclaimed modern witches, the two girls were supposed to be carrying out various rituals and spells, something that will be explained as we listen to other people's stories later on. They took with them several items to carry out the rituals—candles, wine, and a lighter. Around nine p.m., a local couple who were walking in the woods stumbled across the two young women in a clearing locally known as Witch's Hill. Flora was already dead by that time.

I'll let you hear from Liz Jenkins, one of those witnesses. I talked to her in person over a coffee in one of Stoneminster's artisan coffee shops.

—It was awful. You just don't expect to discover something so terrible, do you? My husband, Bill, and I are keen walkers. We've been in those woods thousands of times. It was just... Well, I still can't get it out of my head. It was so spooky. So bizarre.

Liz's face scrunches up with horror here, and I don't blame her. It's not every day you stumble upon a murder victim. Liz is in her late fifties and owns the small supermarket and post office in Stoneminster high street with her husband. She's lived in the town for the last twenty years.

—Can we just back up for a moment? Did you usually make a habit of walking in Blackleaf Forest that late at night?

—*No. Not at all. But the weather had been so hot that week. You know, the kind of freak weather Britain has when it's just so humid? We'd been everywhere trying to find fans on sale, but, as usual, they were sold out.*

We knew it was going to be too hot for us to sleep. Even with the windows open, there was no breeze. Instead of going home, we thought we might as well get some fresh air, so when we closed the shop up at just gone eight p.m., we drove to the forest. There are quite a few different entrances and car parking areas to Blackleaf, and we left our car in the south entrance, which is known at the Sika Trail car park.

—And at this point, it was still fairly light? The hours of daylight for that date show that dusk was at 10.09 p.m.

—*Yes. We reckoned we had about an hour and a half left for a wander around before it got too dark in there. It was the longest day, after all.*

There are so many trails in the woods. You can use the tracks already carved out by walkers or just head through the trees. We started off on one track, and we were just wandering around, chatting as we meandered through. And I had this idea that we could go for a paddle in the river near Witch's Hill. To be honest, I was... Well, it was so hot that we both felt like stripping off and getting in the water there and cooling off. So that's where we headed eventually. It was peaceful in there, until... well... until we found them.

.   .   .

Liz pauses for a moment, visibly shuddering at the thought of what she saw. After clasping her hands together in her lap, she takes a deep breath and carries on.

—Witch's Hill is at the northeastern end of the forest. It's not even a hill, actually, so I have no idea why it's called that. It's a clearing where the remains of an old stone cottage are. The building is just in ruins now, but that's where local folklore says a woman called Rose Hurst lived. Apparently, in the seventeenth century, she was accused by the villagers of Stoneminster of being a witch and was hanged from an ancient oak tree about three metres from her cottage. Behind the cottage, there's the river, which is usually a few metres deep. We found Caris and Flora next to the oak tree.

—And what did you see?

—At first, we thought they were both asleep. Or drunk. Both of them were lying on the ground. Um... next to Caris was a wine bottle. I saw the label, and it was the same one the girls had bought from our shop earlier that afternoon.

—What time did they come into your shop that day?

—They arrived at 5.03 p.m. and left at 5.14 p.m. I know because of the CCTV cameras inside. They bought the wine and a lighter.

—And how did the girls seem? Did you notice any tension between them?

—They seemed in good spirits. They seemed happy. Bill was on the post office counter in the corner of the shop, and I was serving at the till. It was summer, so we were busy with holidaymakers coming in. We get a lot of tourists in this area. But I did notice Flora and Caris particularly at one point when they were trying to choose a bottle of wine. When the customer I was serving left, I walked over to them and asked if they wanted any help. We'd had a new delivery of some lovely Australian wine in, and Bill and I had sampled a few bottles, so I thought I could recommend something to them.

Anyway, Caris said they wanted something with a fruity flavour. She was holding a couple of bottles in her hand, and Flora was leaning one elbow on Caris's shoulder, peering at the labels. They seemed comfortable in each other's presence. There didn't seem to be any tension between them.

I recommended a different bottle, a Shiraz, but it had a cork, and they wanted one with a screw top because it was easier.

—Easier for what?

—*Well, they said they were going for a picnic, so they didn't want to faff around with a corkscrew.*

—Did they mention where this picnic was going to take place?

—*No. In the end, they bought another bottle with a screw top that I recommended. It was called Fallow Creek.*

—In light of what happened later, is there any way the bottle could've been tampered with before it arrived at your shop and you didn't notice?

—*No. We always check produce thoroughly to make sure any seals are intact when we put them on the shelves.*

—Okay. What happened next?

—*They also bought a lighter. Flora put the items in the big bag she was carrying, the multi-coloured fabric thing she had. And then they left. And the thing that stuck in my mind later was that it all seemed so normal.*

—Did you know what was normal for Caris and Flora? Did you know them well?

—*I wouldn't say I knew them well. But this is a small town. And working in the only supermarket and post office for miles, you get to see a lot of the locals. Since the time the girls were about fifteen or so, I'd see them a lot together. So I knew they were friends.*

—And what was your impression of the two girls from interactions you had?

. . .

8

A troubled furrow crinkles Liz's brow. She looks as if she's struggling with what to say, weighing up how much she wants to share. Her gaze darts around the café. A young couple in the corner, holidaymakers by the looks of them, wearing hiking gear are studying a map spread out over the table. At the back of the shop, two middle-aged women sit, nursing a couple of Dorset cream teas that they haven't touched since we arrived. They've been too busy watching us to eat. I'm guessing they're locals, and after Liz glances at the women, she leans forward, keeping her voice low.

—*You know what small towns and villages can be like. People are always quick to gossip. Rumours fly around and gather speed without a grain of truth. And if people don't know the truth, they'll just make something up. I'd see Flora and Caris in passing sometimes or in our shop. They were always polite. Always said hi. Flora was a bit more outgoing, I suppose. She seemed more confident. Caris was... I don't know. Aloof, maybe? I mean, she was still well-mannered, but there was just something about her. Like she had this brick wall round her. I didn't see it when the girls were together. It was like Caris came out of herself more when she was with Flora. But when Caris was on her own, she was... well, there was some kind of sadness about her. She never really seemed there. It was like there was something going on deep inside her.*

It sounds strange. And I could be completely wrong about her. But I just thought something wasn't quite right with Caris.

—And plenty of people would agree with you. After all, she's been convicted of murdering a friend she was supposedly very close to.

Liz takes another look at the middle-aged women, whose gazes are crawling over us, before turning back to me again.

· · ·

—Yes. I think Caris was damaged in some way. But...

—But?

—I don't know. I'm not an expert on behaviour. It's not for me to say more.

—Did you know the girls' parents well?

—Willow Morgan, Flora's mum, is lovely. We weren't close friends or anything, but she would always take the time to chat when she popped into the supermarket. She had her own shop in Stoneminster, further along the high street to ours, called Ethnic Crafts. One of those hippie-type places. It sold crystals and incense and knick-knacks. Buddha's. Lovely handmade Indian soft furnishings. I bought a couple of bits and bobs from her myself. And I'd see her at the local business organisation's meetings, where we'd all get together periodically to discuss things. And we'd have a polite chat then too.

I really feel for her in all this. Bill and I never had children, but I can imagine how hard it's been for her. When I used to see her out and about after it happened, my heart just twinged for her. Some people blame her for what happened. How cruel is that?

—Why would they blame Willow?

—Because she encouraged Flora with all that witch stuff. Willow and Flora were always a little bit different. A bit hippieish, I suppose you'd say. Or some people would, anyway. Willow encouraged her daughter to set up an online website selling witchcraft things— spells, candles—witch boxes or something, they called them. Caris was involved in it too. I thought it was just harmless fun—a quirky business idea—and they seemed to be doing really well with it, but some people are too quick to judge what they don't understand. And some people are just plain jealous of others' success.

· · ·

Liz looks pointedly at the two women at the back, who still haven't touched their cream teas. They're far too interested in us to take a bite.

—*Again, it's not my place to say any more. I'm sure you'll be speaking to other people who were closer to them than me. But to answer your question about both girls' parents, what I will say is that Caris's dad, Ronan, had his problems.*

   —Can you elaborate on what those problems were?

   —*I'd rather not say.*

   —Okay. So let's move back to the night in question. You and Bill came across Flora and Caris in Blackleaf Forest and thought they were asleep or drunk?

   —*Yes. They were lying underneath the oak tree to the side of the cottage. Caris was sort of on her side. Her head resting on her arm, eyes closed. The wine bottle was near her hand, the screw top lid by her foot. But Flora... well, it was really bizarre. She was lying on her back, legs together, arms crossed over her chest. Around her body was a stone circle. Like someone had collected some stones from the ruins of the cottage. It was built with a mishmash of local Purbeck stone, and they were different sizes, but they'd been placed around her. Flora's... um... her eyes were also closed. And there were the remains of some candles on the ground that had burned out. They were also arranged in a circle. And there was a pentagram, drawn in the dusty ground next to Flora, like it had been marked out with a stick or something. It looked like they were both asleep at first.*

And this is why the press were quick to label this tragedy the Sleeping Beauty Murder. Flora was a stunningly beautiful girl, and from the crime scene photos, she did look as if she was simply sleeping in a serene pose. Of course, that label helped to fuel the flames of this case, and some of the outlandish headlines saw the tabloids flying off the shelves.

Sadly, Flora was dead by the time Liz and Bill arrived. The post-mortem report revealed Flora had alcohol in her system, along with ketamine, a drug used as an anaesthetic by medical practitioners and vets. It's also used illegally by people to get high, and it can produce psychedelic effects and hallucinations, causing people to see, hear, smell, or feel things that aren't really there. It comes in the form of white crystalline powder or tablets that can be dissolved in liquid.

But it wasn't the ketamine that killed Flora. She'd been strangled and then arranged in the posed position within the stone circle that Liz described. Caris also had alcohol and ketamine in her system.

—When did you realise there was something a bit more sinister going on?

—*Bill and I walked over to them. If they were drunk or asleep, we didn't want to leave them like that. First of all, I said their names out loud then asked if they were okay. I didn't get a response from either of them, so I went to Caris and kneeled down beside her while Bill went closer to Flora.*

We were saying, 'Hello, hello, can you hear us? Are you okay?' But neither girl answered. I touched Caris's shoulder, and she sort of moved a bit and mumbled something, but she seemed really out of it. Not with it at all. While I was trying to wake her up, Bill called out to me that Flora wasn't breathing. I know CPR, so I went over to Flora while Bill called for an ambulance. And I... well, I was pretty sure it was too late for CPR, but I tried. I tried anyway. For... for about ten minutes, I tried, but it was obvious she was gone.

—I know this is hard, and I want to thank you for sharing what was a very traumatic discovery. I promise I just have a few more questions for you.

What was happening with Caris when you were doing CPR on Flora?

—*Um... Bill was patting her hand, trying to get a response from her. Caris was mumbling again but still pretty incoherent. She had her eyes closed. Semi-conscious.*

—Did Caris wake up while you were waiting for the ambulance?

—*Once. Her eyelids kind of fluttered open, and her eyes were glassy and unfocussed. Her pupils were huge. I thought it was more than just alcohol then. I thought they'd been taking some kind of drug. That Flora had overdosed.*

—Did you see any drug paraphernalia around?

—*No. Nothing like that. Caris couldn't seem to really see us, but she said something. Two words, actually.*

—What did she say?

—*'It's him'. That's all she said. Then her eyes rolled back, and she was out of it again.*

The paramedics took a while to get there. The forest is on the edge of town, and then they had to leave the ambulance in one of the car parks and get to us on foot. I thought Caris might die, too, before they arrived. It was just awful.

And there are plenty of people in Stoneminster who've been pretty vocal that they wished Caris *had* died that night. The story generated so much hatred and car-crash fascination, with some people even calling for Caris to be burned at the stake like a witch in medieval times. But has the venom directed at Caris been an understandable response to having an accused murderer in their midst, or was it fuelled by the tabloid media's sensationalist headlines that have mired this case? Headlines that have possibly shaped people's opinions and stopped Caris from ever receiving a fair trial? We'll hear more about this later in the series.

—*Before the paramedics arrived, we were panicking, and then... then, while we were waiting for help to arrive, I heard something behind us. A crack. Like someone stepping on a stick. I thought I could hear breathing, as well, but it could've been my own. Or Bill's. We were both distraught, breathing quite heavily. The adrenaline was kicking in with both of us.*

At first, I thought it was the paramedics. So I shouted out to them, trying to let them know our location. Bill had his phone in his hand with the torch application on as a beacon, because it was getting darker then, being enclosed in the woods, and we were worried they wouldn't find us.

Bill was waving the phone around above his head. But it wasn't the first responders. They didn't arrive until a good fifteen minutes later. And no one answered us. That's when I started to worry someone else was out there.

—That must've been very frightening for you. Did you see anyone else in the forest?

—*No. Not when we were walking to Witch's Hill, and not when we got there. There was another car in the car park when we arrived, but we never saw who it belonged to. And I didn't hear anything else after we called out. Not until the paramedics and police really did get there. So we just assumed that it was an animal out there. Maybe a fox or something.*

—You recounted this at the trial and in your police statement. Your senses were obviously overwhelmed that night. As you said, you were panicking. You'd stumbled across something no one ever wants to witness. The adrenaline was pumping, and you were trying to save one girl and knew one was already gone. Both of you were alone in the forest, waiting for help to arrive, in a scary situation. It would be easy for your mind to play tricks on you. But looking back on things now, do you still believe it was an animal out there that night, or is it possible someone else was in the woods?

—*I really don't know. The police thought it must've been an animal. And Bill didn't hear it. But... and this is going to sound silly, but you know that kind of sixth sense you have when danger is near? When you think someone might be watching you? In the midst of everything going on, I had that. It felt like someone else was out there.*

—I have one final question for you, Liz. You've described what you saw at the scene in Witch's Hill. You mentioned the wine bottle, candles, the stone circle, and pentagram, but were there any other items in the vicinity?

—*I didn't mention the lighter, did I? The one they'd bought in the shop with the wine. It was on the ground near the candles. But there was nothing else I saw. I didn't see Flora's bag. The one she put the wine bottle into when they were inside the shop.*

And this is something I feel is a loose end. Liz and Bill's supermarket had security cameras, and I've watched the footage from that afternoon. Caris's and Flora's movements were exactly as Liz described. They seemed in fun spirits and are clearly seen laughing with each other, relaxed in each other's company. They bought the wine and lighter, and Flora did put them into her bag before exiting the shop. Presumably also in the bag were the candles they took to Witch's Hill. But here's the problem... that bag was never found at the scene. It's never been found anywhere. So what happened to it?

The police believe Caris hid the bag in the woods in an attempt to throw suspicion away from herself. Police conducted a cursory search for the bag in the surrounding woodland at Witch's Hill, but with a huge area to choose from within the forest itself, they weren't surprised it was never discovered. But I think it could mean something more compelling in this case.

I finish the interview with Liz then, thanking her for recounting what's still an upsetting discovery. And I think it would make sense at this point to set the geographical scene of Stoneminster.

It's a small, quaint town in Dorset with a fascinating history dating back to around 500 BC. It's full of picture-postcard cottages with thatched roofs and made from local Purbeck stone, and the centre boasts rustic streets of original cobbles worn smooth over the centuries. Some properties constructed during Elizabethan times in the black-and-white half-timber style of the era nestle in the nooks and crannies of the oldest part of town.

Located on ancient trade routes, it's always been a historical market centre and still hosts a regular weekly farmer's market. Ancient burial sites and artefacts from the Iron Age have been unearthed in open fields surrounding the town, and evidence of a stone circle similar to Stonehenge, although much smaller, was discovered on its outskirts.

There are about seven thousand residents, and the high street that runs through the town has a small selection of artisanal and quality cafés, gastropubs, and independent shops. Its charm attracts regular crowds of holidaymakers.

At the eastern end is an abbey. To the west, two miles along a country lane, is Blackleaf Forest, a three-hundred-and-fifty-five-acre area that's home to the county's finest conifers and ancient oaks, as well as a huge variety of wildlife. With the many tracks that traverse the woods, it's walking and cycling trails are popular with locals and tourists alike. There are numerous official and unofficial entry points into the forest and many different car parking areas for the multiple trail routes. We have a small map of the area up on the *Anatomy of a Crime* website, so if you want a more visual representation, press pause and scroll down the page.

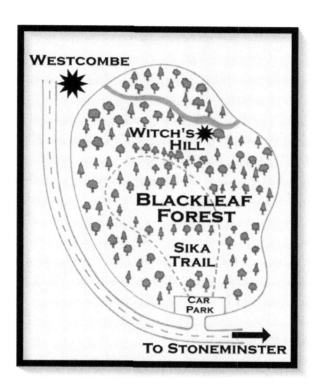

<< ▶ ‖ >>

There are no CCTV cameras in the town, so the only way of tracking the girls' movements after they left Liz's shop is through several eyewitness accounts.

Caris and Flora walked westerly, up the country lane, passing several vehicles along the way. When providing descriptions of the girls in their police statements, a few witnesses described the distinctive colourful bag Flora had with her.

But another witness saw something in the forest that night.

—It was, uh, about half eight at night. I was sitting there, like, in this tree. Well, not in the tree. There's this hollow bit. Mum always used to tell me when I was a kid, it was the black diamond tree, 'cause that's what it looked like. I mean, it doesn't have diamonds in it, does it? That doesn't make sense. It's just that there's this big gappy bit in the middle of the trunk, and it's all black in that bit. But it's a good place to hide. I mean, not hiding from people. From animals. And bats. They roost in some of the trees. I was there for the bats. And the owls. But what I saw wasn't a bat.

That is the voice of Damian Reece. He's a twenty-two-year-old resident of the nearby town of Dorchester, and as a keen nature enthusiast, he regularly visits Blackleaf Forest to study the wildlife. I meet him at his place of work, a historic stately home called Wentworth Hall fifteen miles away from Stoneminster. It's open to the public and boasts huge gardens and wide-open spaces with picnic areas. Damian is one of the gardeners employed by the owners.

There's a café on the grounds, and I offer to buy Damian a drink while we chat, but he prefers to sit on the grass away from the crowds of visitors.

—Was it unusual for you to be in Blackleaf Forest that late at night?
—Nope. I like wildlife, see? All kinds. I'm in there all times of day and night. Have you seen the sika deer in there? Oh, wow. They're so beautiful. They've got a shorter tail than fallow deer. And

they've got these white glands on their hind legs. They make these amazing noises. Groaning, clacking, screaming, whistling. They've got a really big variety of vocal sounds. They come out in the daytime and nighttime. But

night's also for the owls and the bats, see?

—So that evening, you were sitting in the hollow of the tree, bat watching?

—*Uh-huh. I was watching owls and bats. It's peaceful in there. I don't... I don't like too many people. I like being in the woods. Just with the wildlife. With the nature, see?*

—And what happened that night?

—*I'd been there about an hour. Hadn't seen no one else or nothing. I had me binoculars, like. They're daytime ones, but they have night vision on them too. They're called Night Owl. Pretty cool, right, because they're named after an owl, but they can see owls too. That's why I bought them. I liked the name. And they've got really good magnification. And the buyers' reviews were really good. I'd spotted Ollie, and I was watching her.*

—Who's Ollie?

—*Oh yeah, sorry. Ollie's an owl. A tawny owl. That's what I called her. I know it's a boy's name, but I couldn't think of a good name for a girl owl, see? Anyway, she had a nest just opposite the diamond tree. The tree's a perfect cover, 'cause when you're in the hollow, no one can see you. Which means Ollie can't see you, either. Well, she can, really. I mean, animals and birds know humans are there, don't they? But I wasn't disturbing her. I was all quiet and still. And I was waiting for her to go off and get food for her chicky.*

I had me binoculars on her, like, just waiting. I saw the top of her head pop up out the nest. I was thinking, Yeah, this is it; she's getting ready for a night of hunting. But then I heard something. Actually, Ollie heard it first. Did you know that tawny owls' ears are out of alignment with each other, which gives them amazing directional hearing so they can pinpoint their prey precisely? Pretty impressive, eh? And their eyesight is a hundred times better than humans... wow... right?

As you can hear, Damian gets a little sidetracked—he's obviously passionate about wildlife. His face is animated when he talks about it, and he's got this energy about him, his hands flying around in the air as he describes the various complexities of owls. But the more I talk to him, the more I realise that's just his personality, his quirk. But in my opinion, because of these traits, it's possible that the police and jury may have made an essential, prejudicial error of judgement about his story.

—What happened after you heard something in the woods, Damian?

—*No, Ollie heard it first.*

—And you heard something after her?

—*Well, she swivelled her head, searching for the sound. Do you know you can't see owl's ears? They're hidden. Amazing, right? I thought maybe it was a mouse or a vole. Maybe a rabbit or something she'd heard. But then I heard it too. And it wasn't a mouse or vole or rabbit. It was a bit of a crashing sound. Nah. Not crashing. Not then. It was kind of like swishing. You know when you're, like, running through the forest? Through the bracken? And it makes this swaying, swishing sound. It was like that. In the distance at first. Then it got louder. And Ollie got spooked then. She flew off then.*

—And what did you do?

—*I kind of poked my head out of the tree. Most of me was still inside it. Just my head looking out. Well, a bit of my head. Not all of it. And I saw something. A shadow at first. I mean, it wasn't dark then, like. Not properly dark. It was a little bit dark. Not proper nighttime. 'Cause you're in the woods, there's less light, see? That bit of the forest is pretty dense.*

—Would you say it was more like twilight?

—*Nah. Well... I guess, yeah. And the shadow was running through the forest. Getting closer and closer.*

I kind of froze. I didn't know if it was real at first. 'Cause, you know, animals can see things that aren't there. They can see spirits, can't they? And I thought it was a ghost at first. Or a spirit. Or something. I was scared. I kept waiting for it to come and get me. But then I thought it wasn't a ghost. It must be real. And it was.

He got closer to me. He couldn't see me, like. And the closer he got, I kind of poked my head back in the tree so I could still see him, but he couldn't see me.

I watched him. First, I thought he might be jogging. Some people do in there. Jog round the trails and that, like the cyclists, except running, you know, not on bikes. Exercise, anyway.

—But he didn't look like a jogger to you?

—*Yeah. I mean, nah. Sort of. He was wearing jogging clothes, like. Shorts and trainers, but he didn't look like he was just jogging for exercise. He looked like he was running from something, not just for fun. Although I don't think jogging is fun. It's pretty tiring. I prefer gardening for exercise. He kept looking back over his shoulder, like, in the direction he came from.*

—And where had he come from?

—*Looked like he came from Witch's Hill. I was about a mile away from there, but I don't go there. I don't go to Witch's Hill. Not ever.*

—As he got closer, did you see him more clearly?

—*Yeah. I only saw him quickly. 'Cause he came up alongside the tree, about seven metres from me, and he ran right past where I was hiding. Didn't see me there. I held my breath. Even though my heart was banging, like. It all seemed to happen really quick. He ran past, and he was still looking back over his shoulder.*

—Can you describe him?

—Yeah. Course. I'm used to describing animals and birds. Well, their markings and features. I make notes of their description in my head so I know who's who. I give them all names, like. So I'm good at that.

I reckon he was about six foot tall. He looked about the same age as me. Twenty-one, twenty-two, or something like that. He was quite meaty. Not fat. Not chunky. Muscley, like. Like he did weights at the gym. He was wearing green shorts and a green T-shirt, like the army, sort of. He had dark hair. Dark brown. It was short on the sides and longer on top. He had a big nose. A fat nose. Fat, like a hammer-headed bat. I mean, not quite like that, but you know what I mean.

—I'm not familiar with that type of bat. Can you elaborate a bit more for me?

—Well, it's got a long nose. Sort of hooked. Rounded at the end. It sticks out. But they're so cute, even though people probably think they're ugly.

—So the man you saw had a hooked nose?

—Nah. Not hooked. It was flat. Fat and flat. Like he'd had his nose squished. Like a boxer. You know when they get their nose broken? Or someone who plays rugby. I never played rugby. Or football at school. I don't like being touched by people. Too many germs. And sweat.

—And what else did you notice about him?

—He had red skin.

—Do you mean his skin was red because he was flushed from running? Or he had some kind of skin condition?

—I don't know. It was too quick to see if he had a skin condition. I'm not a doctor, like. Like some people have those reddy old acne marks, don't they? I've never had acne, but there was a boy in my class at school who had it really bad. When he got older, it stayed with his face, and his face was pretty red. He used to get called Pizza Face. Which wasn't very nice. I used to get called worse than him, *actually. Still do sometimes. But then there are a lot of not nice people out there. It's why I prefer nature, you know? Ollie never calls me a weirdo or freak. I think she likes me coming to visit, because she looks at me sometimes. Right in the eyes. And wow, you know she's studying you carefully and thinking,* Yeah, I like you. *And she appreciates me coming to visit her.*

I think he was just red from running.

—Was there anything else you noticed about the man you saw that night?

—*Not about him. But I noticed he had something in his hand. It was swinging and hitting the bracken as he ran by. It was a bag made of bright-coloured material. Purple and orange and yellow. A bit of green and blue in it too. Like the colours of a sun conure parrot. They've got almost all the colours of the rainbow on their feathers. And it seemed weird. It was like a girl's bag. And—*

Damian stops abruptly then as a family of four sit on the grass a few metres away. Their young son screams for a drink, throwing a tantrum while the mum hastily searches in her big bag for the required item to keep him quiet. The dad tells him to calm down and stop disturbing the other people eating their picnics nearby. Damian puts his hands over his ears to blot out the screaming, which creeps up decibel by decibel. Then Damian gets to his feet and walks off, stomping away towards the tree line of woodland that surrounds the estate, where there are no other people. I get up and follow him, and by the time I've caught up, he's sitting down again with his back to the people, looking into the trees. I sit next to him.

—*Sorry. It's loud, like. They're loud. I like it peaceful.*

—That's all right. I understand. Are you okay to carry on?

—*Uh-huh.*

—What happened after that?

—*Well, the man disappeared through the trees. He was going south, towards the Sika Trail car park. I never saw him again, like. I stayed there for about another ten minutes, but Ollie didn't come back. She was probably spooked. So I walked back to my car.*

—Where was your car parked?

—*In the Sika Trail car park. I saw another car there. A blue Ford. That was the only other one there. I thought it might be the jogger's, but I don't know.*

The blue Ford, in fact, belonged to Liz and Bill, who had entered the woods approximately fifteen minutes before the time Damian saw the man. The car Liz mentioned seeing at the car park belonged to Damian. No other vehicle sightings that are unaccounted for have been reported for that evening in any of the other car parks that serve Blackleaf Forest.

If Damian's story is correct, though, the person he saw could well have been involved in Flora's murder. He was carrying something that sounds identical to Flora's bag. He was acting suspiciously, running away from the area where Flora and Caris were found. So what happened when the police interviewed Damian, and how did this sighting get downplayed into insignificance?

—You told the police what you'd seen that night, didn't you?

—*Yeah. I heard about what happened with the two girls the next morning. Well, Mum did. She told me when I woke up. And I told her about the man. She went to the police with me, and I told them about it, like. I was there for hours. They asked me all sorts of questions and stuff. And we were going round and round and round,* and they was asking me if I'd done anything to those girls. If I'd hurt them. If I'd strangled Flora. Like they were blaming me. And I only went there to try to help.

Mum got a lawyer then. One of those legal aid people. She was nice. She was really sweet. They asked me if I'd give them my clothes from that night and have my DNA taken and stuff. And I said of course. I just wanted to help. They didn't believe me, though. They didn't believe I'd seen the parrot bag and the hammer-headed bat-nosed man.

—The police saw you as a potential suspect at that point, then?

—Yep. They let me go eventually, later that day. But they never believed what I said about what I'd seen.

There's more to hear from Damian, but I want to break off here and speak to Sarah Perkins, Damian's legal aid lawyer who represented him during the interviews with the police. With Damian's permission, she gives me her perspective on things. She's a busy lady, and I talk to her by phone.

—Yes, the police did consider Damian a potential suspect at first. Although his mother was with him, acting as an appropriate adult, he was still vulnerable, and she didn't quite know how to deal with it all. The police were pushing him hard, trying to make him confess to the murder. They thought they'd struck gold. Damian was a quirky loner who lived with his mother, and he'd admitted to being out there in the forest at the same time the murder took place. He fitted into their initial profile of who they thought the killer was.

Luckily, after several hours, Damian's mother insisted on calling the duty solicitor, which was when I got involved. They carried out forensic analysis and found no DNA on either Damian's person or clothing that linked him to Caris or Flora. They did, however, find *some DNA evidence on Caris Kelly. Then, of course, as more details emerged about the case, the police's theory became that Caris was responsible. That she'd staged everything.*

—And what do you think about Damian's version of that night? The sighting of the man running through the trees?

—*Damian was never going to be a credible witness for the police, which I think is completely inept on their part. It doesn't matter whether someone is on the autism spectrum or not. Damian is a sweet and harmless man, and while he does tend to overanalyse or overly explain certain things, I found him to be believable, detailed, and completely earnest in his descriptions of that night. But the trouble with the police setting their sights on fitting the evidence to match their theory means that other avenues of enquiry weren't properly pursued. From what I can tell, they never even tried to trace the man Damian saw.*

The police have refused all my requests to speak to them about the case and ask them why, in particular, they never followed up Damian's sighting. In future episodes, I'll dig further into this man's identity, but let's get back to Damian. His lunch break is almost over, and I can see he's itching to get back to work.

—You said you never go to Witch's Hill. Why is that?

—*I used to go there. Before I saw some stuff up there. Near Rose's cottage. You know she was a witch?*

—I know that's what the local folklore says.

—*There's something out there. At Rose's cottage. I've seen it. Her ghost, I reckon. I was about fourteenish. Or maybe fifteen. Don't know. Something like that. Back when I first started going in the forests by myself. First, it was to get away from people, see? Then I realised how magical it was in there with all the flora and fauna. I*

26

don't mean flora like Flora, the girl. I mean the trees and vegetation. Then I found the wildlife, and I had to keep coming back. Been going in there all the time ever since.

I was wandering about in the woods that day, and then I spotted a roe deer. I was following it. Silent, like. Wow, it was beautiful. And then I came across the ruins of the cottage. Rose's cottage. Just the walls are still there. Some of the walls. A bit of the walls. Inside, the walls are black. Like someone's set the stones on fire at some point.

I wandered through what would've been the inside of the cottage, crunching over the fallen stones and the flora that's sprouted up over the years. And then on the other side is the river. I sat on the bank for a while and was watching a green woodpecker. Didn't know the story about her being killed then. Not the woodpecker, Rose Hurst. Didn't know what the place was or used to be. Didn't know she'd been hanged from the ancient oak in front of the cottage where they found Flora and Caris. The real Flora this time, not the vegetation.

And then I kind of felt something. It was weird, see? I had this kind of feeling someone was watching me. My hairs went up on the back of my neck. I felt this shiver go over me. It was like all the times at school when the bullies were waiting to pounce on me when I was sitting on my own, trying to mind my own business, eating my lunch quietly. And they'd sneak up behind me and try to steal my lunch or my backpack or call me stuff. So I had that same feeling, like. Maybe I was tuned into it, you know, because of the bullies before. Or because I can read the wildlife normally, and something was disturbing it.

I was still sitting there, looking around me. Couldn't see no one. But I didn't like it, so I got up and looked around some more. It was silent. I mean, really silent. No bird noises. Nothing. And they know when danger's about, don't they? Eyes in the sky. Even when you think it's silent in the woods, it's not. There's all kinds of chattering and rustling and tweets and scuffling and scratching, see? So it all felt wrong.

I didn't go back through the cottage ruins. I walked down the side of it. And then I got to the oak tree, and I heard this noise. It was like something creaking in the branches. Swinging. Like the noise a rope makes if it was swinging from the branches. Creaking on the wood. Like the noise the rope must've made when Rose was hanged there. But there wasn't a rope. There was nothing. I was really spooked then. I started looking into the trees. But it's all overgrown with woodland there. The trees are thick. No trails there.

So I started running through the trees, and I could feel something on the back of my neck. Like someone breathing down the back of it. It was summer, but it felt like cold breath. Icy cold on my neck. And I could hear it too. Breathing. Heavy, like. It wasn't me. It wasn't my breath, I swear. And then I saw something in front of me. This shadow. A black shadow. The shape of a woman.

It was kind of shimmering there, ahead of me. And I was so scared, instead of running, I just stopped and froze and stared at it. And the shape changed. She got more real. Not just the shape anymore, it actually became a woman. She had this long red hair. Curly. Her eyes were just black sockets, but her face was young. Her skin was smooth. I was staring at her. Just standing there, holding my breath. And she was looking right at me with those socket eyes. And my eyes were pinging out, 'cause I thought I was going mad. The kids at school always called me mad, and I thought then I actually might be. And she started whispering something. She was whispering my name. She knew my name! But it sounded like my nana. It was my nana's voice. But it couldn't have been her. She was dead by then. She'd died a couple of years before. But she... this shape thing with the orb eyes said, 'Damian, you're not alone. You're my tiddlywinks'. Then she sort of drifted up into the treetops. And then she was gone.

—That must've been an unsettling experience. Did the word 'tiddlywinks' have any significance for you?

—*It was scary! It was so weird. My nana used to play tiddlywinks with me when I was a kid. It was the only game I wanted to play. All the time, like. And I liked it so much she used to call me her little tiddlywinks. It was a nickname, see? It sounded like Nana, but it didn't look like her. And I was so scared, I just ran. I went home and didn't say anything to no one about it then, 'cause people already thought I was a weirdo, and I didn't want them to take me away from my mum and lock me up somewhere, like in a mental hospital.*

After that, I didn't go in the woods for a while. And when I did go back, I never went to Witch's Hill.

—Did you ever tell anyone else about seeing Rose's ghost that day? Later on?

—*Yeah. I told the police after the murder. I knew I couldn't not say anything anymore. I was trying to help them. But they didn't believe that, either.*

There have been numerous sightings over the years of what's supposed to be Rose Hurst's ghost around Witch's Hill. Many strange occurrences have also been reported near the cottage. I'll be exploring more about that in future episodes. And I have no doubt Damian believes what he's just told me. His mannerisms, his arm gestures, and facial expressions seem completely genuine as he recounts these events.

The fact that Damian told the police he'd seen Rose Hurst's ghost might also explain why Damian's sighting of the man on the night of Flora's murder was never taken seriously by them. But what about Liz's story? She also thought there was someone in the vicinity of Witch's Hill when she and her husband were trying to help Flora and Caris. And although what Liz heard was about

29

forty-five minutes after Damian says he saw the man running away from the area, did the man come back? And if he really did have Flora's bag, why did he take it? Could it have been a trophy? It's well-known that certain killers like to take items from their victims.

This suspicious man has never been traced. At the very least, he could've been a witness. At worst, he was a suspect who might've had a reason to want Flora dead. It's something important to ponder as I wrap up this first episode.

But what do you think? I'd love to hear your views on what you've heard so far, so please leave your comments on our website.

Thank you for listening to *Anatomy of a Crime*.

Until next time...

Carolyn C • 1 day ago
I remember hearing about this murder when it happened. What a bitch! Kelly's where she belongs. Hope she rots in hell.
^ | ˅ • Reply • Share ˃

Tootie1 • 1 day ago
Who was the man in the woods? How come I never heard anyone talk about that before? What else didn't the police investigate? I always thought the case sounded not quite right.
^ | ˅ • Reply • Share ˃

LuLZ → Reply to Tootie1 • 1 day ago
Did you listen to Damian? He's obvs not right in the head, is he? He's the village idiot! No wonder they didn't take it seriously!
^ | ˅ • Reply • Share ˃

Dollyrug → Reply to LuLZ • 1 day ago
My son's on the spectrum, and he's NOT a village idiot!!! You're the idiot for thinking that. You prejudiced bigot!
^ | ˅ • Reply • Share ˃

W*34* • 1 day ago
The jury found her guilty, so she must be. Kelly killed Flora because she was into devil worship. I bet you'll find she was one of those psychos who've been chucked out of a mental institute and put back into the community. They're dangerous and should be locked up.
^ | ˅ • Reply • Share ˃

Kiki99 → Reply to W*34* • 1 day ago
Seriously? You don't think juries or police ever get things wrong? Look at the Oval 4, the Birmingham 6! Barry George in the Jill Dando murder, Colin Stagg with the Rachel Nickell murder, and Angela Cannings who was convicted of killing her children. All miscarriages of justice. The legal system often gets things wrong. I haven't heard anything about devil worship yet. Keep an open mind!
^ | ˅ • Reply • Share ˃

XOXO • 2 days ago
I want to know what happened to Flora's bag. It couldn't have just disappeared into thin air. If a man was seen carrying that bag away from the scene of a murder, then it should've been investigated. He could be a serial killer who likes to take trophies.
^ | ˅ • Reply • Share ˃

Crimejunkie → Reply to XOXO • 1 day ago
Agreed! Doesn't sound like investigated properly. Can't find any other crimes with a similar MO in recent years. Serial killers are

31

actually a very low percentage of killers out there. Not like in films and TV.

Most victims know their killers. Maybe Caris did bury the bag, but I want to know more before I make a judgement.

^ | ˅ • Reply • Share ˃

Serra568 • 2 days ago
I had a similar experience to Damian when I was a child. I was visiting this old house on the Isle of Wight, and it was supposed to be haunted. I saw this shimmering white apparition and heard it whispering my name. But it was my dad's voice, calling me, and he'd died. I heard it quite plainly.

^ | ˅ • Reply • Share ˃

Jester → Reply to Serra568 • 2 days ago
Yeah, my dead tortoise spoke to me once. It said, 'Oi, get off the grass, that's my patch!'

^ | ˅ • Reply • Share ˃

327856 → Reply to Jester • 1 day ago
Ha ha!

^ | ˅ • Reply • Share ˃

Leano • 2 days ago
Kelly's totally guilty! I'm glad the police got her off the streets. She's a danger to the public.

^ | ˅ • Reply • Share ˃

MrBiggs • 1 day ago
I remember all the media around this case at the time, and I thought then that there was no way Kelly would get a fair trial. I mean, you'd have to be living under a rock not to have heard about all the witchcraft and devil worship thrill kill things they said, and

the jury must've all known about it, too, and formed an opinion beforehand.
^ | ˅ • Reply • Share ˃

Comstock → MrBiggs • 1 day ago
The jury is supposed to be impartial.
^ | ˅ • Reply • Share ˃

MrBiggs → Reply to Comstock • 1 day ago
And the keyword is 'impartial'. Is there ever such a thing? We're all biased in some way. We all have preconceived ideas or beliefs about things. We're all brainwashed by the media, whether people admit it or not. And that's my point. Is there ever such a thing as an impartial jury when they're just human? A selection of everyday people, like you and me. Look at the comments on this podcast, and you'll see what I mean.
^ | ˅ • Reply • Share ˃

MrSam • 2 days ago
Love your podcast! Greetings from Singapore!
^ | ˅ • Reply • Share ˃

CHAPTER TWO

CARIS (Aged 15)

That suffocating feeling clawed over me again. A throbbing pulse in my head boomed through my ears. The walls closed in on me. I was trapped, and I couldn't breathe. My throat constricted, my airway getting smaller and tighter. I wanted to break out of there, to get in the open air and suck in lungfuls of oxygen.

Not again. Not again. Not again.

Head held high, I hurried past the lockers into the girls' bathrooms, trying not to stumble over my feet. *Breathe. Breathe.*

The cubicle doors were open. No one was inside. I walked to the sink and clutched the edge as I took a deep breath and held it. Blowing out slowly, I concentrated on myself in the mirror. I repeated the slow inhales and exhales, staring at my reflection until my vision blurred, trying to ground myself.

I didn't recognise the girl staring back or even know if the real Caris had ever existed. Who was she? Where was she?

I pictured myself crawling onto Mum's lap when I was young,

my arms latched around her neck. I heard her voice saying, 'Your name means "love", my sweet girl.'

Flames and heat exploded in my head as the visions overpowered me: smoke drifting up from our caravan, dancing in the air, calling up to the Great Goddess and the Universe to claim what they wanted to steal away. Screams filled my ears, echoing around me, piercing my heart. Someone grabbed my arms, pulling me back, then running, away, away, away.

I closed my eyes, trying to shake off the memories, my cheeks wet with tears.

I wasn't love. I was the opposite. I couldn't push the darkness down. I couldn't contain it. It gnawed through me, a parasite demanding to be fed.

The toilet door creaked as it swung open. I darted into a cubicle, locked the door, leaned my back against it, and stared at the graffiti scrawled on the wall opposite.

Lynn 4 Jack: I shagged Paul Bath
Blobby is a fat bastard
Caris Kelly is a slapper!!!!!

My jaw tightened as I heard someone go into the cubicle next to me. The main door opened again, and the voices of Dawn and her friends filled the air, talking about me, slagging me off.

I clenched my fists at my side, digging my nails into the palms of my hand. My body shuddered with effort. I tried to hold it in. Until I couldn't any longer.

CHAPTER THREE

NOW

Two days after the first episode airs, I go back to Blackleaf Forest. I've already been there several times, but I feel drawn to it somehow. I have so many questions brimming inside, and good researchers immerse themselves in their subjects, take time to walk in the footsteps of those they're investigating.

I leave the quaint two-bedroomed cottage I've rented in Stoneminster through Airbnb and head on foot along the country lane to the Sika Trail car park. At the exact point Caris and Flora entered the woods proper, I stop and look around me, wondering again what was going through each girl's head on that fateful night.

Taking the trail that Caris reported they followed, I become immersed in the beauty of the plant life around me. My feet crunch over dead leaves, and the sounds of birds fill the air.

When I get to Witch's Hill, I observe the scene of the crime with a critical eye. Between the front walls of the cottage and the oak tree where Rose Hurst was hanged is a circular clearing that used to be Rose's physic garden, where she cultivated her potions and herbs. It's just a dusty patch of land, devoid of any vegetation, approximately five metres in width. Strangely, nothing has grown there since Rose's death, even though the area surrounding its eastern edge is the most densely populated part of the forest, flora and fauna wise. Here, ferns grow to chest height, and ancient trees cast dark shadows as they loom over you, sentry-like, their trunks entwined with thick brambles. Dense, untamed vegetation sprawls across the forest floor like a carpet, smothering the roots and soil. There's something eerie about the clearing, as if death has left its mark and permanently scarred the land, like a constant echo of previous violence. I can imagine at night that the darkness transforms the trees into sinister skeletal shadows of twisted men and hunched women.

Although the walls of the cottage have crumbled, they're still over two metres high in places, and any view from the river to the clearing or oak tree is further impeded by the shrubbery and weeds reclaiming the building as their own, rising up through the remains of the ground in the interior. Thick ivy clings to the moss-covered walls like gnarled fingertips grabbing on for dear life.

I press my hand against the cool bark of the oak tree and wonder what things it's witnessed, what stories it could tell, before heading towards the river to sit on the bank.

I think about Caris and Flora splashing in the water on that hot summer's day before carrying out their spell ritual. I hear their laughter ringing in my ears.

I don't know how long I sit for, staring into thin air, lost in planning the questions for the people I hope to speak to in my head, before a sound snaps me from my thoughts and seems to echo in the silence.

My gaze darts around the river, behind me, and into the dense woods. I stand and survey the area as a shiver passes through me. It could be nothing. An animal or bird foraging, or someone walking or cycling in the distance. But goose bumps scatter on my skin as I get that unnerving feeling that someone out there is watching me.

I listen for a few minutes, ears straining, my heart rate spiking as I expect someone to crash through the forest and hurtle towards me. For a fleeting second, I think the ghost of Rose Hurst is about to appear. But I don't believe in ghosts. My imagination is running away with me; that's all. There is no unseen threat.

Silence follows. No stirring of leaves. No cracking of twigs. Clouds pass overhead and the sun disappears. A cool breeze drifts over my skin. An icy feeling claws at my insides. I don't want to hang around anymore and hurry away from the area, my gaze constantly scanning my surroundings. Even though I tell myself I'm being stupid, it's not until I get to the car park that I finally breathe freely again.

I head back to the rental cottage, and even before I get to the front door, I spot something sticking partially out of the letter box. I slide my finger and thumb onto the corner of it and ease the item out. It's a colour photo of me sitting in the coffee shop in the centre of town, talking to Liz when I first arrived. It was taken through the window, and whoever was behind the camera had zoomed in on my face. Around my neck, they've drawn a noose in thick black marker pen.

It seems as if I've ruffled someone's feathers.

I glance up and down the street, but no one's around. That doesn't stop the wriggling of unease in my stomach.

I unlock the cottage's door and push it open. As I stand on the threshold, my gaze darts around the cosy lounge and the kitchen beyond through the open doorway in case the photo isn't all that's awaiting me.

No one's downstairs, but I leave the front door half-open just in case, ready for a quick getaway. I head into the kitchen and grab a sharp knife. Then I stand at the bottom of the open wooden staircase in the lounge, looking upwards, listening to the sounds of the boiler ticking away on the wall at the top. My heart hammers as I take a step onto the first rung. If anyone is waiting for me up there, they already know I'm here, so instead of taking my time, I rush up the stairs to the landing.

To my right is the small bathroom, its door open. I can see no one's inside. Further along the corridor to the right is a spare bedroom. The door's partially open, just as I left it, but I can't see all the way inside. To my left is the master bedroom I've been sleeping in.

Left or right?

I duck into the master and jerk open the small cupboard door. It's empty, apart from the hangers and spare blankets and pillows I haven't bothered to use. I kneel in front of the bed and lift the valance sheet. Nothing there but dust.

One place left to hide, if someone wanted to.

My head tells me I've had enough of being scared now, but my heart and stomach say otherwise as I stride along that hallway to the spare bedroom and push back the door so it hits the wall. No one's lurking under the beds, and nothing has been disturbed.

I exhale a shallow breath as I run down the stairs, shut the front door, and lock it.

My stomach clenches as I wonder what to do about the sinister delivery. Leave? Stay somewhere else? How big is the threat?

It doesn't take long to make a decision. It's not the first time I've been threatened, and I'm not going anywhere. If someone's trying to send me a message, it means there's something to hide.

CHAPTER FOUR

EPISODE 2
WITCHES AND TROLLS

—T he theory formed by the police and prosecution was that Caris had drugged Flora by putting ketamine in the wine bottle, and after Flora had passed out, Caris strangled her and arranged her body in the stone circle. They then believe Caris hid Flora's bag somewhere in the woods and also drank the ketamine-laced wine so she'd have an alibi of sorts.

Of course, it was, and still is, a ridiculous theory. Why would Caris kill her best friend? A friend she was incredibly close to. A friend who was more like a sister to her. There was no evidence prior to that of any problems between the two women. No arguments. No jealousies or rivalries. And the idea that it was a ritualistic witchcraft murder, as the police labelled it, is quite honestly preposterous.

Welcome back to *Anatomy of a Crime*. That was the voice of

Annabelle Sherbourne, a criminal solicitor on Caris's defence team. Caris has never given an interview to the media about her side of the story, although plenty of journalists have tried to visit her in prison. And to be honest, I'm not surprised she's declined. The press vilified her, and I don't believe Caris's version of events has ever been properly investigated. Annabelle has informed me that depending on how I handle this podcast, Caris may or may not grant me an exclusive interview. Unless or until that happens, I'll crack on.

I speak to Annabelle by phone, and she's made it clear she will only give brief details about the case. If Caris wants to tell her full story to me at a later date, then that must come directly from Caris.

—Before I say anything else, I want to tell you that although Caris is unable to listen to this podcast in prison, I'm keeping her informed of the content. Unsurprisingly, after the way she's been portrayed, she doesn't trust people. She wants to see what angle you take before she makes a decision about whether to talk to you or not.

—I can assure you that there is no angle. All I'm after is the truth. Maybe we should start with why Caris and Flora were at Witch's Hill that evening.

—There's a big misconception about witches. There always has been. I'm not an expert, so I'm not going to go into the ins and outs of it, but to put it succinctly, witchcraft or Wicca is the same as any other belief. For Caris, it was essentially about celebrating life, nature, and healing. It was the summer solstice, a date that's very celebrated in many belief systems, including Wicca and paganism. And Flora's and Caris's intentions were to go to Witch's Hill to do a celebration ritual. But as soon as the police honed in on the words witchcraft and ritual, they blew it all out of sane proportion. It was a smoke screen by them that gave credence to their ritualistic-murder angle and muddied the waters.

—What was the ritual Caris and Flora were going to perform?

—First, there was a cleansing opening. They went into the river behind the cottage and swam in it. Afterwards, they arranged a stone circle and lit candles. They incanted some words. A spell, if you like. Then they celebrated by drinking the wine. But neither of them knew it was laced with the ketamine.

—What happened to the bottle of wine between when the two young women bought it and when they drank it?

—After Caris and Flora left the supermarket, they walked along the country lane towards the forest. When they got to the nearest official entrance for the forest, known as the Sika Trail section, they entered through the gravel-lined car-parking area. One family who'd been cycling in the forest that day were returning to their vehicle at the time and saw the girls head into the woods, but the parents were distracted because their daughter had spilled a drink down her clothes, so they were busy mopping it up and noticed Flora and Caris only in passing. However, two other witnesses saw Flora and Caris as they headed further into the woods. A couple of holidaymakers walking their dog passed them and did observe Flora's bag, which subsequently went missing. They described the girls as laughing and joking around with each other. And later on, another sighting of the girls was at around 6.15 p.m., by a couple who were cycling along one of the trails. At that time, Flora and Caris were heading northeasterly, in the direction of Witch's Hill. None of these sightings have ever been contested by us.

Before Flora and Caris went into the river, they put Flora's bag—which contained the ritual items—beneath the oak tree at the front of the cottage. Then they went into the river behind the remains of the cottage. Caris has always maintained that someone else must've been in the woods, watching them, and that this person took the wine from the bag, unscrewed the top, poured in the ketamine, then screwed up the top again and replaced the bottle. Have you been to Witch's Hill?

—I have.

—*And so you know that if you're in the river behind the cottage, you can't see the area around the base of the oak tree where the bag was.*

Flora and Caris were in the water for around thirty-five minutes. They'd stripped down to their bikinis and were bathing. It would've been impossible for them to have seen someone tampering with the wine bottle from their position.

Shortly after they'd drunk the wine, Caris started feeling strange. And this is where it gets very hazy for Caris. She still can't remember what happened after that. She has no clear memories. She was unconscious for most of the time and possibly suffering from hallucinations at other times.

—The court transcript said that at one point, Caris thought she saw the ghost of Rose Hurst. She described a dark shape swirling around the base of the tree. And at another moment, she thought she saw a dragon.

—*Yes. And she vaguely remembers being unable to move, but she just has fragments of recollection. The rest is blank. And that was due to the ketamine, which frequently renders people semiconscious or unconscious and can induce hallucinations.*

Ketamine is extremely powerful—it's not called a horse tranquiliser for nothing—and when ingested, effects can happen quickly without the person realising something is wrong and can commonly last for forty-five to ninety minutes. When mixed with alcohol, the effects can be magnified and cause further complications, such as death. It can also cause other experiences, like feelings of detachment from your body, confusion, clumsiness, slurred speech, blurred vision, anxiety, panic, violence, inability to move, and lowered sensitivity to pain. Often, people who've had it in their systems have no recollection of events at all. It's also known as a 'date rape' drug, in the same way Rohypnol is, due to its anaesthesia properties, and victims may become completely unconscious and suffer from memory loss after having their drink or food spiked.

—Some people would say Caris is a cunning killer who invented a story about someone else in the woods to throw the scent off herself.

—Caris has always maintained her innocence. She's a victim in all of this, just like Flora.

—One thing that never made sense to me was that the prosecution claimed Caris drank the ketamine-laced wine *after* she'd killed Flora as an alibi to prove she'd been affected by it, as well, and create the invention of another person's involvement in the murder. But there was no way for Caris to know that someone would find them out there that night. It was only really luck that Liz and Bill stumbled across the girls.

—*I'm glad you brought that up. It doesn't make sense, does it? It never made sense. Even though Blackleaf Forest is a popular spot for tourists and locals, Witch's Hill is off the beaten track in a densely wooded area. Although it's mentioned in some local folklore books about historical witchcraft in Dorset, it's not listed on any ordinance survey or tourist information maps, so it's not unusual that specific, secluded spot doesn't get much traffic.*

The prosecution believed that Caris drank the wine because then she could claim she'd been spiked, as well. They maintained that if Flora and Caris hadn't been found that night, Caris would've woken up after the ketamine wore off, called the police, and claimed she'd been unconscious the whole time of the murder, and a blood test would prove it.

—If Caris is innocent, and someone else spiked the wine, it means that person had to have known they were out there. Who else knew Caris and Flora were going to Witch's Hill that night for a ritual?

—*That's one of the problems. We couldn't find anyone who said they knew what Flora and Caris were going to do that night, apart from Flora's mother, Willow. It's not something the girls discussed with other people, as far as we know. Certainly, Caris didn't tell anyone. It seems unlikely Flora did, either.*

—So, that would mean if someone else *was* there, someone who laced the wine and took Flora's bag, it would've had to have been either a chance encounter, or the girls were being followed. It makes more sense for the girls to have been followed, because I doubt people randomly carry around ketamine in the hope that they can drug someone.

—*I would hope not. But I have come across date-rape cases where that's exactly what happened. Our theory is that they were followed by someone. They may have been followed for some weeks or months without either of them knowing.*

—Flora's post-mortem report noted high levels of ketamine and some alcohol. And then she was strangled, her hyoid bone fractured, but no bruising had appeared around her neck.

—*Oftentimes, manual strangulation doesn't produce any sign of external bruising.*

—But there was also forensic evidence found on Flora's body. On her wrist, she wore a bracelet, which had two strands of Caris's hair caught in it, which had been pulled out by the roots.

—*Yes. Which is probably one of the things that helped convict Caris. The prosecution's version was that Flora was lashing out at Caris while she fought for her life when Caris was allegedly strangling her. But our contention has always been that it could've got there in any number of ways. We believe the hairs got transferred prior to the murder. But there's also always the possibility Flora's fingers could've caught in Caris's hair earlier, when they were both drugged and hallucinating, and pulled it from the roots. Or someone could've planted it there.*

—What about the skin found beneath Flora's nails? Caris's skin. And the scratches on Caris's right forearm that correspond with Flora's nails. It's a common defence mechanism in stranglings for the victims to try to grab or prise away the perpetrator's hands or arms.

—Caris has never denied those scratch marks came from Flora. But our position is very different. Those marks happened earlier in the evening, after the two girls had finished bathing in the river, when they climbed out onto the bank in front of the cottage. If you've been there, then you'll know the bank is quite steep, approximately one and a half metres in height. Caris scrambled up the bank first, and as Flora was coming up behind her, Flora stepped on a rock in the mud and lost her footing. In an attempt to stop Flora falling, Caris reached out to her, but Flora's fingernails caught Caris's arm. Flora's bracelet could've also caught Caris's hair at that time.

Juries love forensic evidence, though. They think it doesn't lie. But the hairs and scratch-mark evidence in this case were taken completely out of context, which hurt our case immensely.

—There were no other signs of trauma on Flora's body, were there?

—No. She wasn't sexually abused. There were no marks or bruises or injuries other than the scratches.

But don't forget, though, that Caris had no motive, and the prosecution's theory of that was very tenuous. If you take away the easily explained DNA evidence, then there's no case against Caris. However, we do believe that the 'thrill kill' motive expressed by the police and prosecution may well be true.

—In what way?

—A thrill kill is a premeditated or random murder motivated purely by the offender's desire to experience the sheer excitement of the act. These types of murderers are usually psychopaths who rarely feel remorse for their actions. The major commonality between people who commit such crimes is that they usually feel inadequate and are driven by a need to feel powerful. There are many previous murders across the globe that have been dubbed thrill kills by the police and media, and some serial killers fall into this category.

The victims of thrill killers are generally strangers—sometimes the killer may stalk them beforehand to increase the thrill of the hunt.

—Which would fit your theory of Caris and Flora being followed or watched for some time before the murder?

—*Exactly. And according to some Home Office statistics, the proportion of murders in which the victim isn't known to the killer has nearly doubled in the last decade. A worrying part of this trend is thought to be down to thrill killing.*

The term isn't just a twenty-first-century buzzword. The murder of a fourteen-year-old by Richard Loeb and Nathan Leopold way back in 1924 is described as a thrill kill. One of the infamous thrill kills in the UK was the horrific murder of toddler James Bulger by two ten-year-old boys in 1993.

But the ritual Caris and Flora were performing had absolutely nothing to do with death or devil worship or sacrifice, as the press bandied about, and everything to do with a celebration of life and nature. Their beliefs in witchcraft were not about black magic but, again, to do with healing and harmony.

And although there has been a rise in so-called 'thrill kills', the statistics show that these are usually killings by a stranger to the victim. There was absolutely no reason for Caris to kill someone who meant the world to her.

—For me, the motive has always seemed questionable, as well. But as you mentioned, ketamine produces hallucinations. If Caris vaguely remembers seeing a strange shape, something she thought was the ghost of Rose Hurst, and a dragon, what else did she hallucinate that night? What if the drug brought on some kind of hallucination that made Caris believe she was fighting off a demon or some other attacker, when in fact, she was attacking Flora?

—*Caris didn't put the ketamine in the wine. She never saw Flora put it in there, either, before they started drinking it, and Caris is adamant Flora would never have done that. So someone else had to*

have laced the bottle with nefarious intent. If—and this is purely
hypothetical—if Caris, under the influence of that drug through no
fault of her own, was hallucinating that Flora was some kind of
monster or attacker and killed Flora under those circumstances, then
at the very least, the coroner should've declared Flora's death as
death by misadventure. At the very most, Caris should've been
charged with manslaughter, not murder. But we maintain that Caris
did not kill Flora in any circumstances, be it accidental or otherwise.

—What's your opinion about Damian Reece's police
statement? About his sighting of a man less than a mile away from
Witch's Hill that night.

—*We thought Damian was a credible witness. We still think he*
is. But the problem was that the jury didn't find him credible. People
with autism often have a fixation on particular subjects or ideas, or
they have a unique linguistic expression. Damian's description of
the man he saw was rooted in comparing him to animals or birds,
and, sadly, I think the jury interpreted this as completely
nonsensical or unbelievable. Unfortunately, there's still a lot of
stigma and misunderstanding about how people with autism
function or express themselves. And while Liz did give evidence at
the trial and stated her belief someone else was in the area at the time
she and her husband found Flora and Caris, of course, she didn't
actually see anyone.

—And that was approximately forty-five minutes after
Damian's sighting. And it seems unlikely the man seen running in
the opposite direction was the same one still hanging around
Witch's Hill when Liz and Bill arrived. So maybe what Liz heard
really was an animal.

—*Or an accomplice to the murderer who was still hanging*
around the area. Or even the ghost of Rose Hurst. We'll never know,
will we? The only person who knows for certain is the real killer.

—Did Caris ever file an appeal against her conviction?

—*Yes. But, unfortunately, you can only appeal a conviction if you're granted leave. If it's refused, as Caris's application was, that's the end of it, unless something new emerges and the Criminal Cases Review Commission agrees to refer a conviction to the Court of Appeal.*

I end the conversation there. I think I've got all I can from Annabelle, and I want to explore possible motives further. I want to delve into the young women's lives and find out about them through other people's eyes. For that, I tracked down people who actually knew Caris and Flora.

—*That Caris girl was mental. A real bad'un. Do you know what I caught her doing one day? Killing a bird! Smashing its brains out on the grass verge with a rock! I mean, that should tell you everything you need to know right there.*

I looked out of my window and couldn't believe it. I was speechless. This poor little blackbird, lying next to the road, and her —that Kelly girl—crouched beside it, hitting it over and over again. She looked crazed. Mad. Well, she must've been mad. Thought she was a witch? Pah! The devil is more of an accurate description of her.

There was a pentagram drawn up at Witch's Hill where they found Flora, wasn't there? They're always using pentagrams in devil worship and animal sacrifice. She was just evil, that one. It's no wonder, really, with her dad like that, and them being gypsies. They're always trying to con people, especially the elderly, like me. I'm glad he's gone now too. The council should never have let them come here in the first place. If they hadn't, that poor lovely Flora would still be alive.

· · ·

That is the voice of Bea Pearce. She's lived in the same house in Stoneminster all her life. It's a local authority-owned two-bedroomed property on an estate a twenty-five-minute walk from the centre of town. In 2012, when Caris was thirteen, she and her dad, Ronan, moved into the house next door to Bea.

—Let's go back to when Caris and Ronan arrived in Stoneminster. What do you remember about them?

—*He was a scruffy so-and-so. Shaggy, dark hair. Tanned skin. He always looked a mess. Caris was well turned out, better than him, anyway. Her clothes were cleaner and all, but she always had this look about her. She never smiled. She never really spoke to me, either. She was a feral thing. He'd say hello in passing, but they weren't interested in being neighbourly, which suited me fine, really.*

—What did you know about them? About where they'd come from?

—*Everyone knew they were gypsies. Those Irish ones who go round trying to tarmac people's drives and then rip them off. Or try to sell people lucky heather and then curse them when they don't buy it. A few years back, an army of them turned up overnight on some waste ground near Dorchester. You should've seen the rubbish piling up round their site. It was a pigsty. Like Steptoe's yard! And all their little brats roaming around everywhere, starting fights with the local kiddies, stealing things from people. And they're driving around in their big cars and trucks that must cost a fortune. So where are they getting the money from, hmm? I bet they were nicked too. It took the council months to evict them.*

—What did you know about Caris and Ronan specifically?

—*Apparently, Caris's mum had died in a caravan fire, and after that, there'd been some family falling out with their gypsy clan. They'd left their Traveller group and were rehomed here by the*

50

council. Of all places! You can't trust them, can you? They're always getting up to all sorts of criminality.

—So you didn't know them well, then?

—I knew all I wanted to know, thank you very much. They were druggies. They liked to smoke that cannabis. I could smell it wafting into my house when the windows were open. It reeked! I might be old, but I'm not stupid. I know what it smells like. And he never went to work. He was on benefits, sponging off the taxpayers. Of course, Caris was going to turn out like she did with that as an example. I mean, she took everyone for a ride, didn't she, that girl? I'd see her flouncing off to school in her uniform, looking all normal, but what was really going on in that house? She was probably devil worshipping right next door to me! I wouldn't be surprised if they put some kind of gypsy curse on me, because after they moved in, I had trouble with my drains. Nothing ever happened before, until they showed up. Then they were blocked up every single month. Sometimes twice a month!

—Let's go back to the incident you described earlier, when Caris was killing the bird. What did you do when you saw it happening?

—I was in two minds about it. By the time I realised what was going on, the bird must've been dead. And I was a bit scared of confronting them. She might've bashed my brains in while I was asleep! So I didn't say anything to her or Ronan.

—Did you ever see any other incidents that gave you cause for alarm?

—Not like that, no.

—How old was Caris at the time of the bird incident?

—Probably about fifteen. I feel really quite sick about it now. If I'd known what she was going to do years later, I would've told the police. I could've warned them. Not sure if they would've listened, but still, it's on my conscience now.

—Did you ever see Flora visiting the house?

—No. Never. Who'd want to go into a house with druggies and a devil worshipper?

So what can we ascertain from Bea's story? First, it sounds like there was animosity between the neighbours. And it's quite telling of the prejudice or pre-conceived ideas about Caris and Ronan's background. They were indeed part of the Irish Travellers community, or gypsies, and historically, such groups have faced discrimination, prejudice, and persecution.

I'm still trying to trace any other members of Caris's family or extended family who can give me a better understanding of Caris's early life before she and Ronan arrived in Stoneminster. Gypsies are notoriously secretive and insular, and I doubt I'll have any luck. It may not even be relevant to this podcast, but I think it might help put things in context.

Whether there was a falling-out between Ronan and his family after Caris's mum, Mary, died is unclear, but it seems that was the catalyst for Caris and Ronan to be rehoused in Stoneminster, and the pair ended up on the council estate built in the sixties on the edge of the town, away from the quintessential chocolate-box part of Stoneminster.

But back to Bea's story about the bird, which I can't get out of my head. Was that an early warning sign that something wasn't right with Caris's mental health? We've all probably heard by now how killers often start living out their fantasies by practicing on animals. Was that a prelude of things to come? An omen of what would happen?

For now, though, I want to speak with people who spent more time with Flora and Caris. One of the teachers who taught both girls has agreed to talk to me. She's now retired from Stoneminster High School and wishes to remain anonymous because she's worried about Caris's family targeting her in the future. I speak to her by phone, and her voice has been digitally altered to further hide her identity.

—*You're sure you won't reveal who I am? It's just that I'm aware the family are gypsies and can mete out their own kind of justice to people.*

—I always respect a source's right to remain anonymous, but it's possible someone could work out who you are from what you tell me.

—*That's why I'm going to be very careful about what I say. But I think you should know about it. Okay. Here goes. I'll try and start at the beginning.*

—Wherever you feel comfortable.

—*I worked at Stoneminster High for quite a while, so I saw a lot of both girls. Flora was well-liked, but she was never one of the popular crowd. She got on with everyone, but she was definitely away with the fairies. Even though the kids wore uniforms, she always stood out a bit. She had her own style. Some people would probably call it shabby chic, but it just looked slovenly to me. Hippieish, like her mother. She'd have a feather clip in her hair or a lotus flower necklace. Those colourful bags with Om signs on them. That kind of thing. And she always smelled of incense or patchouli.*

And she could be a bit intense. She was always trying to pressure the staff to donate money and time to her ethical causes. Always trying to raise awareness about waifs and strays in Africa or God knows where. Academically, she was an average pupil. If she spent as much time on her schoolwork as she did to her various social ventures, she would've left school with better qualifications.

Then Caris joined the school. She was very different to Flora. Caris was sullen and moody from the beginning. Standoffish. She'd sit at the back of the class and just stare at you with this defiant attitude on her face. She didn't want to interact with anyone else, either. And she had this anger bubbling under the surface—you could tell. I could see right through her. Caris had no respect. She was clever and manipulative. And Flora was easily led by her.

—It must've been quite hard for Caris, starting a new school when she was thirteen, where everyone had already established friendships. Especially as she'd come from a Travelling community, where they tend to be very close-knit.

—I suppose so. But she didn't really make an effort, either.

—Did you know about her background?

—Yes, I read the report. Apparently, the gypsies don't go to school. I suppose their excuse is they're always travelling, but I think it's just laziness. Gypsy children run amok, and most of them are illiterate. And there's no smoke without fire, is there? The public don't want them around for good reason. There's always a criminal element about them, and they live off land for free that doesn't belong to them.

Caris was quite good at English and history. But she was way behind in most subjects, and she didn't bother trying to catch up, either. So both her work and her attitude was a problem.

—What else did this report say? Did it give any reasons why Caris and Ronan had moved to Stoneminster?

—All I knew was that Caris's mum had died. And there'd been some tension in their... community, and that Ronan Kelly had applied for rehousing by the council.

—So it's possible that Caris wasn't sullen or angry or standoffish? That she was, in fact, grieving for her mum and maybe missed the support of the gypsy community, as well? And she was having trouble keeping up with the schoolwork that she'd never been taught before?

—I wouldn't say so, no. I've taught kids for years, and you can just tell the ones who are going to grow up to be trouble. Oh yes, at that age, their real personality starts coming out, shedding its skin.

—Did anyone offer Caris support?

—I don't think it was support she needed. It was some discipline.

This raises red flags of concern with me. It sounds as if Caris was hurting. She'd lost her extended family and her mum and was thrust into a new way of life, a new area, a new home, a new school. That's a lot of stress for a thirteen-year-old girl to handle. And before I can question her further on this, the retired teacher hastily adds something, her voice sharp and defensive...

—I want to make it clear that there were never any outright concerns for Caris's welfare. She came to school clean and tidy. She did most of her work, even if it was often atrocious. But she was just... There was something wrong about her.

Anyway, a month or so after Caris joined the school, I saw she was pretty thick with Flora. They were together all the time. They had most of the same classes together, ate lunch together. And I'd see them in town at the weekends. I think they lived in each other's pockets after that.

—Did you ever see any arguments between them? Any animosity?

—No. That's not what I wanted to tell you. It was Caris's artwork that was... It was always quite dark and moody, but when she was about fifteen, it changed to something frankly quite disturbing. The class was given a title of 'the Body', and they had to design a piece around it. Caris's has stuck in my head ever since. She'd made a collage of all these photos. She had X-rays of a skull and neck. But the skull had a knife wedged into it. There were pictures of hospital trolleys and empty hospital corridors. Scalpels and various surgical instruments. Even gruesome pictures of post-mortems. It was all shades of grey and black and white and red. The red was the areas of paint spattered across it all, as if it was supposed to be blood. It was really chilling. It looked like something from a horror film.

—But, surely, that's just art? Just an expression? And teenagers are notoriously morose and morbid.

—That wasn't all. Her English language assignments became very... let's say prophetic at that time too. Again, some of the subjects she covered in her stories were quite dark, often about witches and death and murder. But this one was troubling. It raised my hackles so much that I took a copy of it. Here, I'll read it out to you. It's a poem.

'In darkness shines the fires of hell, the devil's calling me to sleep. To take the soul from where it fell and drift down to the chasmic deep. I try to stop. I try to leave. But there is no more last reprieve. With the hands around its throat, it dies inside. It dies. It chokes. Taking life without within, there's nothing left from where it's been. Nothing is what nothing wants. It hurts forever. It will always hunt'.

Chilling, don't you think, after what happened to Flora? She was choked to death. And all this mention of the devil and death. Caris was obsessed with it.

—I think any kind of art is subjective. There are many things that can be read into those words. Crime authors, for example, write about twisted things, but it doesn't mean they're twisted.

—But art is the expression of the soul. The creative mind of an artist puts forth into action their feelings, beliefs, and character. I think this was a sure sign of what was to come. And I bet she was the one responsible for all the animal mutilations that were happening in the area for a year or so after she arrived in town. There were so many horrific incidents around here between 2012 and early 2014. Several horses were stabbed or had their hides scored with pentagrams, and in some cases, their eyes, teeth, and genitals had been removed after death. Those that didn't die of their injuries had *to be put down. Then there were the pets—six cats and three dogs found with their stomachs slit open and their organs removed. It was demonic, and no one was ever caught for it. But I just knew in my heart it was her. She was practicing what was to come. All that sadistic brutality in her had to be fulfilled some way, didn't it?*

I've found no evidence to suggest a woman was involved in any of these mutilations, but the vile acts were emblazoned all over the press at the time of Caris's arrest, making connections that she was involved in them based on what seemed to be wild speculation. But does what Bea saw with Caris and the bird make it more likely Caris *was* responsible for them?

This anonymous teacher has said all she intends to and ends the call. It's possible she's reading a lot into what seems to be pure conjecture. So, wanting to find out more, I speak to Paul Bath, another teacher from Stoneminster High School. I meet him at one of the village pubs, and we sit in the garden that overlooks the village green and the ethnic shop Willow Morgan used to own. I don't know if it's an age-distortion thing, but when I was at school, my teachers seemed ancient. Paul looks to be in his early thirties. He's dressed more on the students' wavelength in skinny jeans, a checked shirt, and Converse.

—You taught history to Flora and Caris, didn't you?

—Yes, I did. Flora and Caris were both good at history. They were both fascinated with local history, actually, particularly local folklore about witchcraft and magic. But just because people have an interest in something, it doesn't mean they're satanists or devil worshippers. I like gaming, but it doesn't mean I'm going to shoot up the town because I've spent a couple of hours playing Call of Duty!

—What was your impression of them both?

—I thought they were nice girls. They were obviously close friends too. You could tell that when you saw them together. Flora was probably more academically gifted than Caris, and Flora was very imaginative. Fantastic at art. Caris excelled at creative writing but didn't make much progress in her other subjects, apart from art. In fact, they were both very creative. I think... I'm trying to work out how best to say this... I think this is quite a closed community. There aren't many people of different ethnic backgrounds here. Walk around this area—not just Stoneminster but Dorset in general—and you won't find much diversity. And I think there was an unfair prejudice about Caris from the start. I think she's always been misunderstood, and that started as soon as she joined the school.

—Do you mean misunderstood by the staff or pupils?

—Unfortunately, both, and it was really down to her heritage. There are various different groups within the Travelling community, and it's believed that Irish Travellers became nomadic in the sixteenth or seventeenth century. Roma Gypsies, who originated from India about a thousand years ago, migrated across Europe. Then you have the so-called crusties, hippies, and New Age travellers, who, for many reasons, choose to live away from conventional society.

Gypsies were ruled as an ethnic group in England under the 1976 Race Relations Act. In 2000, Irish Travellers were also granted this status. But even with this ruling, the popular opinion or attitude to gypsies has made little difference to how they're perceived.

At first, Caris didn't want to be here, and that was kind of obvious. She was a lost soul, and I felt incredibly sorry for her. Do you know what happened to her before she got to Stoneminster?

—I know that her mum had died. It's been mentioned there was some family falling-out between their community before Caris and Ronan were rehoused here when she was thirteen. I'm still trying to track down any of Caris's family.

—Her mum was killed in a fire in her caravan. I saw a report from a Traveller social welfare group that liaises between Travelling communities and officials—social services, the police, etcetera. They act as intermediaries between the parties because there's a lot of mistrust on both sides of the coin. A lot of prejudices on both sides. And I'm not saying some of that's not valid. There are bad apples in every basket. But anyway, I'm digressing here. So, the report mentioned the fire, which the police believed was an accident as a result of a poorly maintained gas hose connected to the kitchen's gas supply, where the gas bottle started leaking into the caravan. And when Mary lit a match to light the hob, the whole place exploded. And it said that after Mary's death, there had been some kind of dispute between the Kellys and another gypsy family. After that, Ronan upped sticks with Caris and left the Travelling community and got rehoused here.

When Caris arrived, to me, she seemed like this very sad little girl. She'd never been to school before. She'd lost her mum, her friends, her family, and she was all alone in a new place, trying to live in a house and put down roots for the first time. And at thirteen, that's a nightmare age for any kid dealing with the normal hormonal, teenager angst, let alone all these life-changing events. People didn't give her any credit for the huge adjustment issues she was going through. They just thought she was uncooperative and a bit of a troublemaker.

—It sounds like a really hard situation to be in. When I think about just the usual struggles I was going through as a teenager at that age, they're nothing in comparison to what must've been going on in Caris's life. What kind of trouble did she get into?

—That's just it. She never really caused any trouble, but she got that label from one of the teachers, and it just stuck with her anyway.

A short while after Caris and Ronan arrived here, some of the kids found out about her mum's death, and all these rumours started going around about Caris, saying that she'd killed her mum in a fire.

*I don't know who started it, but you know what rumours are like—
they turn into the plague, especially in small towns. Caris was
taunted a lot. Had comments thrown around at her. No physical
bullying I was aware of, but some kids just kept on and on, making
digs, calling her names, wearing her down. She was of gypsy origin,
and they thought she was a murderer at that age, so you can imagine
what kind of things she got called and how she was shunned by
people. In every school, there's a social hierarchy between the
students—the popular crowd, the troublemakers, the academics, the
teacher's pets, geeks, the uncool, social outcasts, and the ones who are
bullied.*

—How did Caris respond to her tormenters?

—*She ignored them. She would get this expression on her face.
This blankness in her eyes. She'd sit there and just let the words
bounce off her. Or she'd walk down the corridor with her head held
high, and it was like they didn't exist for her. Except, that was an act.
Inside, she was hurting deeply.*

*I could see what was happening, and I'd give the other kids an
earful if I caught them taunting her. But kids are clever, aren't they?
They usually did it when there were no teachers around.*

*I often asked Caris if she was okay. If she was settling in all
right, adjusting. But whenever I asked, she'd clam up. Go into
herself. Retreat. And that was the thing about her. She was a tough
nut. She never let anyone see her weaknesses. She never let them
know she was suffering. She created this armour around herself. But
they still carried on doing it. And there's a herd mentality, isn't
there? Not just in school but in life in general. One person thinks
something, encourages that belief, and others just believe it and pile
on the torment.*

—And what was Flora like?

—*She was a sweet girl. Very passionate about the underdog. She
cared deeply about things most kids her age wouldn't have given two
thoughts to. She used to collect donations for the local food bank,*

arrange food hampers for the elderly at Christmas, and she and Willow used to go to different human rights demonstrations locally. I remember seeing her at an anti-war march in Dorchester once. Flora didn't feel the need to impress others to fit in.

I started at the school about a year before Caris arrived, and at that time, Flora mostly hung around with a girl called Leanne, although I think their friendship waned when Flora and Caris got to know each other. And I think it was natural for Flora and Caris to gravitate towards each other. Flora was a bit of a hippie. She was interested in Wicca and paganism—or witchcraft, if you want to call it that. And I guess that was her mum's influence. Willow Morgan is a homeopath; she had a New Age ethnic shop in town then. So Flora was really into nature, herbal remedies, that kind of thing. And when you think about it, some gypsy culture has a lot of similarities. They're slap-bang in the middle of nature where they live outdoors. They often use natural remedies for things passed down from generation to generation. So although both girls were on the fringes of their peers—maybe ostracised in Caris's case—they both had a lot of similarities between them. And they were both interested in the same things.

But I never believed the thrill kill motive. The lead detective on the case was on TV all the time, milking it for all it was worth. I think he just hyped it up. Wanted the publicity. A lot of people involved in the case got famous from it—not just police, but the reporters too—and I bet their careers got a big boost off the back of it. People have always been morbidly fascinated with crimes and criminals, and he played up to that.

Did you see the photo that the papers kept splashing on the front covers? The one of Caris where the headline said, 'Wicked Witch of the West Arrested'? It was just a tiny fragment of a second where they caught Caris off guard, and it portrayed her as being evil and remorseless. Caris became the story, because killers are always more exciting to readers than their victims, aren't they?

61

I remember the photo he's talking about. Anyone who read about the case three years ago will remember it too. It shows DCI Richard Lewis, the senior investigating officer in the case, leading Caris from a police van into Weymouth Police station. She's hunched over, her hands cuffed behind her, her face distorted into a contemptuous snarl. Her eyes are wild and feral, her long dark hair matted around her shoulders as she tugs at her handcuffs. She looks deranged and dangerous, like an escaped wild animal. Except, as Paul says, this is a tiny snapshot in time, an unreal representation of Caris used to revile her to the public. And if you search deeper, to a video on BitChute of the events leading up to that photo, you'll find Caris's expression is a reaction from being kicked in the leg purposely by a young male reporter behind her. No doubt that reporter's colleague was ready with his finger on the trigger to capture her reaction. They say photos don't lie, but I disagree. She wasn't an escaped animal; she was a cornered, frightened girl, surrounded by a press pack of wolves manipulating her reactions while baying for her blood.

—When did Flora and Caris become friends?

—*I think it was a month or so after Caris arrived. I saw them hanging around together all the time. I remember being glad they'd both found kindred spirits.*

—And what do you think now? After everything that happened?

—*It's tragic, obviously. But the Caris that was created by the rumours and media wasn't the real Caris I knew. I don't think for one minute she was a cold-blooded killer. And I know that's not the popular consensus around here. I mean, I know anyone's capable of murder in the right circumstances, but I just can't see it. I didn't see any cruelty in her. Despite all the rubbish in the press about Caris, I didn't see any mental health issues or jealousy or anything else.*

I tried to speak to the press and give them a more balanced view of what Caris was like, but they weren't interested in the truth. I think someone else must've murdered Flora, and Caris was the scapegoat.

—Any ideas who would want to hurt either Flora or Caris that way?

—*Plenty of people hated Caris, for all the reasons I've told you. But as far as I knew, no one hated Flora with that kind of venom. If someone else did it, they must be really sick in the head, and with psychopaths, sometimes there are no reasons. At least, not reasons that seem normal to us.*

—Were you aware that a man was seen in the woods that night, near to Witch's Hill? A witness saw him running away from the area about half an hour before the girls were discovered.

—*Seriously? No, I wasn't aware of that. The press certainly didn't put that angle in the papers, did they? But of course, they wouldn't. They were all fixated on Caris because she fitted a profile they fabricated about her being into devil worship and witchcraft. Who saw this man?*

—A local guy. But his statement was never taken seriously because he's autistic. And because of something else he told the authorities, about a supernatural experience he'd had at Witch's Hill years before, where he thought he'd seen the ghost of Rose Hurst. As a historian, and someone interested in local folklore yourself, have you heard of other similar sightings over the years?

—*Yes, indeed. You know, Dorset has a history that's wrapped up in mystery and intrigue, sorcery and superstition. About fifteen years ago, a witch's bottle was found not far from here under a wall in a field. It was an amazing discovery because you don't find many of them. It dates back to the seventeenth century, and it was in pristine condition. It still contained some of the original fluids inside.*

—What kinds of fluid?

—*Salt water, animal fat, and nicotine. I know, not very pleasant. It was considered powerful to ward off evil spirits and protect animals, particularly cattle, against distemper, which was a common problem at the time.*

Witches have been a fixture in our imagination for centuries, and from Snow White to The Crucible, *that perception has been a mixture of fear, evil, beauty, sexuality, and power. Maybe that perception was borne from the bloody persecution of witches in the historical global witch trials.*

—Do you think the story about Rose Hurst's ghost is just one of those cautionary tales parents tell their children to stop them from going into the forest alone? Or an old wives' tale?

—*Absolutely not. Plenty of people believe she came back from the dead to haunt the area.*

Paul delves into the messenger bag at his feet. He pulls out a book and puts it on the table. The title is *Dorset's Folklore and Witchcraft*.

—*I thought I'd bring this with me, because I knew you'd ask about the witchcraft angle. This book was written in 1992, and there's a whole chapter about Rose Hurst from a local historian who researched her background.*

I won't bore you with too much stuff, but superstition has always been steeped in history. In 1675, when Rose was accused of being a witch, there were huge witch trials going on all over the place— Salem Witch Trials, the Pendle Witches, etcetera. Witchcraft hysteria broke out, and people were employed as witchfinders to hunt them out. The sixteenth and seventeenth centuries marked a horrific episode in European and American history with the wild accusations, inept and unfair prosecutions, and the executions of hundreds of thousands of people accused of practicing witchcraft. In Europe alone, between forty thousand to fifty thousand people were found guilty and executed. The majority were women. Essentially, most of the people accused were healers, midwives, women who lived alone, that kind of thing. A lot of people were accused of things just through petty jealousy. If you'd had an argument with your neighbour over a land dispute, accuse them of witchcraft and get them hanged, problem solved. If a woman had an affair with your husband, accuse her of witchcraft and get her out of the way. If your cattle caught distemper, it was because a witch had put a curse on them. If your child had a birth defect, it was because of a witch's curse. On and on it went. Some of the claims were ridiculous. And people just believed it. Not to mention the witchfinders were paid handsomely for finding witches. And once you were accused, that was it. You were damned if you were and damned if you weren't. Either way, you were killed.

—So who was Rose Hurst?

—She was a local healer. Her mum was a healer before that. Her dad died of pestilence. Her mum died when Rose was twenty-three, and Rose carried on living in the cottage at Witch's Hill, on the very outskirts of what was then the village of Stoneminster. She grew vegetables, had chickens, caught fish, was self-sufficient pretty much. And she had her physic garden, and she carried on being the local healer for the village. Most people were too poor to afford doctors in those days.

So one day, a woman called Agnes Applewood called on Rose and said her husband was having an affair with a girl who worked in the local tavern. She wanted Rose to make her husband fall back in love with her. Rose did a spell, using a candle, a mirror, and some clover and honeysuckle. She then told the woman to go home and take something belonging to her husband and wrap it in black sacking and bury it in the garden until the next full moon. Then

Agnes was supposed to put some basil and bay leaves in a flagon of wine and give that to her husband to drink. After that, Agnes was supposed to wake up the next day, and her husband would only have eyes for his wife.

But he died that night in his sleep, after the wife carried out her ritual. Whatever he died of, it was definitely not witchcraft. But Rose was accused of being a witch and hanged at the oak tree outside her cottage. Then the area became known as Witch's Hill, and her cottage was left to fall to ruins as the forest claimed it back.

—I'm getting a sense of déjà vu here. The wine and herbs are chillingly similar to the wine and ketamine. Burying an item is similar to the police's theory that Caris buried Flora's bag in the woods.

—*Again, that was something the media pounced on, claiming Caris carried out her obsession with witchcraft and Rose Hurst in a satanic killing fantasy with Flora.*

—Have there been any other sightings of Rose's ghost, apart from Damian's version?

He opens the book, flips a few pages, and reads aloud.

—*Absolutely. This is from 1865. 'Wealthy local landowner, Alder Parkford, whose ancestors have owned Parkford Lodge for centuries, was taking part in a partridge shoot in Blackleaf Forest when he became separated from his hunting party and found himself at Witch's Hill. A strange feeling came over him. He felt as if he was being observed, but no one was in the vicinity. He felt an icy-cold breath at his neck and heard creaking noises coming from the oak tree. The noises became louder, and as he hurried away from the area, he saw a shimmering black shape between the trees. He was transfixed. Frozen to the spot. And the shape gradually morphed into a young woman with long red hair. Her skin was pale, but her eyes were just black orbs in their sockets. She was staring at him through the trees, and he couldn't move for some minutes. He said the shape started speaking, calling him by name. But the voice he heard was that of his dead wife. Eventually, the shape disappeared, and he departed from the area at speed'.*

There are loads of similar sightings listed in this book, but I'll give you a later one. This is from 1987. 'The family of four were cycling in Blackleaf Forest when they stumbled across Witch's Hill. As holidaymakers, they were unaware of the local history, and as they explored the ruined cottage, their fifteen-year-old daughter, Gina, complained of a sinister feeling that someone was watching them. Although they couldn't see anyone in the vicinity, and the rest of the party felt no such presence, they decided to leave. As Gina's parents and brother cycled on ahead, away from the area, Gina screamed and came to a sudden stop. She shouted to her parents that there was a woman in the trees, but they couldn't see anything. Later, Gina described it as a shadow of a woman with long red hair and black eyes, and she heard the voice of her dead grandmother'.

There are lots more like this, but you get the gist. And this isn't an isolated phenomenon. There are plenty of strange reported sightings of unexplainable things all over the UK. The Beast of Bodmin Moor is a myth resulting from many sightings of a phantom, panther-like black cat with white-yellow eyes. The Loch Ness Monster is another famous example. Nearby Athelhampton House, in Dorchester, has long been associated with the ghost of a masturbating monkey who roams the halls. Strange, but true. In fact, the house was featured on the TV show Most Haunted in 2002.

Many bizarre and weird creatures, UFOs, or unusual, unexplained, and mysterious phenomena crop up all over the globe.

—I'm sure there will be plenty of people listening who think that anyone reporting such experiences might be considered crazy.

—Well, it's interesting that, contrary to popular belief, auditory *hallucinations—where people report hearing voices or phantom melodies, hearing their names being called, or someone speaking around them—are fairly common. Hearing the voice of a deceased loved one is often reported by people recently bereaved. And if you think people who've had those kinds of experience are suffering from mental illness, evidence from the last couple of decades suggests that healthy people also experience hallucinations. According to mental health surveys, approximately one in twenty people hear voices or see visual hallucinations at least once in their lives.*

I find the stories fascinating. But are they relevant to this case? While I'm not sure I believe in paranormal or supernatural occurrences, I think it *is* relevant, because I'm not convinced Damian's account of the man he saw in Blackleaf Forest was dismissed solely because he is autistic. I think the fact he also reported seeing Rose Hurst's ghost could've been an influencing factor, making anything he said seem far less credible. But if others have seen an apparition in Blackleaf Forest similar to the one Damian described, surely that means his story about the suspicious man should hold more weight.

So I think it's time to do something the police failed to do in their investigation. I want to try to see if this man is really out there, and to that end, I had an idea that required Damian's help.

Thanks to the help of a facial-reconstruction expert, we now have a computerised E-FIT likeness of the person Damian saw. Unfortunately, as this happened three years ago and Damian only saw the person for a very short time, he's not absolutely certain the likeness has been captured completely accurately. He says he'd be able to identify the same man if he saw him again, although putting a picture together piecemeal was a struggle for him. But it's a start. The image is now on the *Anatomy of a Crime* website, so please check it out and get in touch if you recognise him.

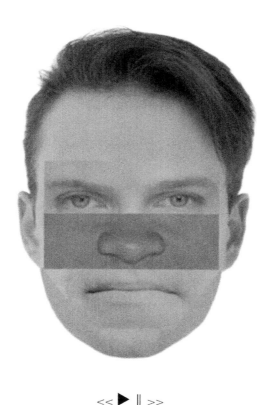

Paul Bath has shown us a different version of Caris, one that may be unpopular in the local community. It seems that superstition's not just reserved for history, and there was plenty of superstition surrounding Caris and this case. Superstition that may have blinded people or tainted the facts. Before I leave Paul, I want to ask one more question.

—What do you think happened that night in Blackleaf Forest?

—*I don't know. But what happened after that was a witch hunt.*

Now the witchcraft angle is out there, I want to explore it more from the point of view of others who say that modern witchcraft is as far away from the devil-worshipping tropes as you can get, and like paganism, it's a form of ideology or religion that promotes nature, nurture, and healing, rather than anything dark and destructive.

Self-identified witches suggest that the practice has ballooned into a robust, global community. The rise of social media has perhaps added to its popularity and helped witches come out of the closet. If you check out the hashtag #witchesofInstagram on the Instagram social media platform, you'll find over four million hits.

Elsie Hyde is a well-established Instagram witch known as the Amethyst Witch. She has over a million followers and gives tutorials on how to use crystals, read tarot cards, and cast spells, but she also does guided meditations and talks about healthy eating and all kinds of subjects relevant to the twenty-first-century spiritual woman. Elsie lives in London, and I speak to her on Skype.

Elsie looks every inch the contemporary witch. She has long black hair with purple streaks in it. Her heavy, dark eye makeup is artfully applied, her long nails shaped to a talon-like point and painted a glittering purple colour. She wears a rainbow-coloured tie-dyed smock over leggings.

—Can you describe what it means to be a modern witch?

—*Sure. It's the same as any religion or belief with offshoots and different groups. So while one group may follow certain practices or* rituals or beliefs, another one might follow something entirely different.

I don't consider it a religion, although some do. And there's no set path for everyone. People can follow or believe what they want to. For me, it's very much an individual path and practice that uses magic and spiritual rituals to bring me closer to nature, the Great Goddess, the Universe. It's about understanding and creating a harmony between ourselves and nature. Celebrating femininity. It's about love. Peace. Spiritual enlightenment. Destiny. Life. Reclaiming your inner strength. Lighting up your inner goddess. There are so many elements to it, but essentially, it's about positive things. Ninety per cent of my followers are women, and I think women find it an empowering lifestyle or practice to follow.

Spirituality is now firmly ensconced in mainstream culture, and there's a growing interest in all things mystic—tarot cards, crystals, astrology, energy healing, to name a few. And with many millennials already practicing yoga, meditation, mindfulness, and New Age spirituality, is it any wonder the practice of witchcraft has undergone a major growth in recent decades? Most of my spells and rituals revolve around herbal healing and using the benefits of the plant kingdom. I can hardly keep up with orders for my spell boxes and crystals and merchandise. In the past, spells, herbs, and even curses would have been passed along by word of mouth, but now we have the internet.

There's a massive change in attitudes from people now. Witchcraft isn't seen as evil, sacrificing devil worship anymore, and people want to find out about how it can improve their spiritual daily lives. They're embracing this in a fantastic way. At the end of the day, we should all want love and harmony with our fellow humans and species. There's so much negative energy going on in the world right now. Too many wars, too much hatred and fear. We need to embrace the old ways of spirituality and harmony so we can coexist in our earthly home. We may have different skin colours or religions and whatnot, but we are all one. To me, this is modern witchcraft in a nutshell.

—Before this case was splashed over the press, had you heard of Caris or Flora?

—When I read about the case, I was just so disgusted over the whole witchcraft stuff the media were portraying. This wasn't about witchcraft—at least, not real witchcraft. It was about selling papers! It was nonsense what they were saying about devil worship and ritualistic killing. Just total nonsense.

I knew Caris and Flora from their Instagram page. Five years ago, I set up my own merchandise store. I have a clothing brand, my jewellery designs. I sell crystals and spell boxes, and several of my bestselling books on spells and witchcraft. Caris and Flora had set up something similar to me—an online website selling spell boxes and other merchandise, like crystals and tarot card readings. Their business was called Pretty Little Witch Things, and that was the name of their Instagram account too.

Flora contacted me via my website for some advice, and we emailed each other. We followed each other's business pages on Instagram, gave each other shout-outs and stuff. I wanted to help them as much as I could with setting up the business and marketing to people, because we're all in this together, right? One person's success doesn't take anything away from another's. There's enough to go round. And they seemed to be doing well with it. The trouble is, though, when some people see you doing well, they get jealous, don't they? And that jealousy becomes toxic. I get a lot of trolls who either hate me or my ideals, and they inject their spitefulness into my life while they hide behind their keyboards with fake names. Some are religious nuts who think I'm the devil. Some are other people in the same business who want to attack me because they see I've built up my brand to be a success. Some are just... They need to get a life. They think it's big and clever to spread hatred about, but I don't waste my time on them. I don't feed the trolls. I don't comment. I delete their posts or emails. No one needs that negative energy in their lives.

Elsie rolls her eyes dramatically and shrugs her shoulders. A white cat with only one ear and one eye jumps up onto her lap. She strokes its head and pulls kissing faces at it.

—*This is Merlin. He's a rescue cat. No one wanted him because they think he's ugly. But beauty is more than skin deep, isn't it, baby?*

She rubs her chin over his head, and his vibrating purrs reverberate on the video call.

—*Flora and Caris were having the same problem at one time with a troll. You know, they were really clever girls. They worked in Flora's mum's shop when they were at school, doing weekends and school holidays, but when they were fifteen, they came up with the Pretty Little Witch Things business idea and set it up. So before Flora was killed, their business had been going for three years. But I saw some of the comments on their Instagram page. There was one person who used to post a lot of hatred, just after they first went online. This troll had a profile name of @InsRule, and they kept calling Flora and Caris bitches and whores. And they said something like 'I've got the power. You're just nothing'. Just really nasty stuff like that. Someone on a massive ego trip or jealous of them. Of course, they deleted the posts.*
　　—Did they report it to anyone?
　　—*They blocked the account, and that seemed to stop it.*
　　—So they never told the police?

—The internet is this amazing thing, but who polices it? The police don't have time to investigate crimes in person, let alone on the internet. @InsRule might not have even been in the same country. The same continent. No, they didn't make a police complaint as far as I know. I told them to just ignore the troll and delete, delete, delete.

It strikes me here that if Caris Kelly really is innocent, as she's always maintained, maybe we've stumbled on a motive. Did someone hate the girls enough to murder one and ruin the other's life? It seems far-fetched, especially as this trolling happened three years before the murder, but it's worth exploring more. And for that, I go back to Annabelle Sherbourne, Caris's defence lawyer.

—Did Caris tell you about the account belonging to @InsRule who was trolling them on their business Instagram page? I've never heard any mention of this at the trial.

—She did tell us about it. But the account doing the trolling had been shut down by the time of the trial.

—But surely, that still should've been exposed to the jury? Doesn't it establish a possible motive for someone else to have been involved? You mentioned earlier that your theory was that someone might've been following or watching Flora or Caris for some time, so couldn't an abusive online troll have fitted in with that theory?

—You have to remember that Caris was granted legal aid for her defence. With the massive budget slashes in legal aid funding, criminal solicitors and barristers are juggling hundreds of cases for a lot of fixed-fee payments that often amount to less than the minimum wage. Many criminal solicitors these days are finding it hard to make the business of representing those accused of crimes financially viable enough to stay

afloat. And for all those hundreds of cases we're chasing up, it generates many thousands of witnesses, pieces of paperwork, evidence, lines of enquiries to pursue. We have limited time and resources to devote to preparing each case, and we're constantly wasting time chasing up vital disclosure documents from the Crown Prosecution, who very often fail to disclose to us until the last-minute essential evidence and information that we need to provide a proper defence.

Did you know that the police and CPS fully comply with their statutory disclosure obligations in less than twenty-five per cent of cases? Which means sometimes exculpatory evidence is never passed on to us. Our justice system is in dire straits.

Yes, it's possible we could've put in a request to Instagram to provide a historical IP address for the trolling account, but we didn't feel that was the best use of our efforts in Caris's case. Someone who was trolling their Pretty Little Witch Things Instagram account for a few months when they were fifteen didn't seem particularly relevant.

Annabelle is reluctant to discuss their defence team's strategy further, but before I go, she tells me Caris still hasn't decided whether to speak to me and tell her side of the story for this podcast. I hope she changes her mind, but no one can force her.

As I hang up, I think back to what the anonymous teacher from Stoneminster High School said, which may now take on more significance. While I think her analysis of Caris's poem and artwork may be way off the mark in acting as some kind of prophecy of Caris's evil nature, I do think there's something in the timing of it. If Caris and Flora were being trolled by someone abusive and threatening online when they were fifteen, it must've been deeply upsetting to them both, maybe very scary. And was Caris's schoolwork around that same time a reflection of her worries about it? It's possible, but unless I can speak to Caris, it will remain an unanswered question.

So for now, I've tracked down one more person who thinks that Caris's interest in witchcraft wasn't as innocent as the Amethyst Witch and Annabelle have described.

—I saw Caris in the woods one day. I used to walk in there sometimes on the trails when the weather was nice. I was kind of a big lad. Well, fat, really, so I used to go off the beaten track a lot where people couldn't see me trying to exercise. I was embarrassed about my weight and didn't want to get laughed at for trying to make an effort.

One day, I was up at Witch's Hill—near the cottage—because not many people went up there. I had a stitch, so I'd stopped walking, and I was bent over double, in the woods to the east of the cottage a little ways. I was trying to breathe and massaging my side. And I heard this talking. It was a girl's voice. She started saying all these weird words, about invoking spirits and calling on Lucifer to protect her. I was curious, so I crept through the trees to see what was going on. And it was Caris there.

That is the voice of Rob Curran. He was a resident of Stoneminster until the age of sixteen, when he moved with his parents to Southampton. He also went to Stoneminster High School and was two years above Caris. I speak to him by phone.

—What was Caris doing when you got closer?

—It was so weird. There was this pentagram drawn in the dirt just next to the oak tree by the cottage. And there were stones laid out in a circle around it. Like a sacrificial altar. Inside the centre of

the pentagram was a candle. She was sitting on the ground, just outside the pentagram. She kept lifting her arms in the air and kind of moving them in a circle over her head and then pressing her palms together, like she was praying.

She started mumbling some other words. I couldn't hear them; they were more whispered. But I could see her lips moving. And I was thinking, What the hell is she doing?

—Did it seem like some kind of ritual?

—Yes, I guess. Some kind of spell or something. But that wasn't the end of it, because afterwards, she was chanting stuff, and she picked up this thing... ew, it was horrible. She was sideways-on to where I was watching, so the thing was hidden at first. Then she twisted around to the side I couldn't see and picked up this thing from off the ground. It was meaty. And bloody. I could see blood on it. I was a bit too far away to see it properly, and she had it cupped in her hands. Then she lifted both hands high in the air, like she was thrusting this thing to heaven. Except I don't think she was praying to God. Because she kept saying 'Satan' and 'Lucifer'. And then she brought this meaty thing back down and put it in the centre of the pentagram, and she picks up this knife that must've also been on the ground to her side and starts stabbing it repeatedly.

I was kind of crapping myself, but I was also kind of... fascinated, mesmerised. I'd never seen anything like it before.

I held my breath and just carried on watching. Her face... It was all scrunched up with this really intense anger. Her eyes looked proper evil. It was so scary. She would've been thirteen at the time, and there was this little girl, doing all this weird, angry stuff. And all the time she's stabbing this thing, she's chanting about protection and invoking retribution.

I could hear the music from that film Psycho *playing in my head. You know the scene where the woman gets stabbed in the shower? And* The Exorcist *film too. I was expecting any minute now she's going to be spitting pea soup and her head's going to spin round and that. I had a vivid imagination when I was younger.*

It went on for about five minutes. Then she said some more words that were whispered, and I couldn't hear them. And she goes over to the oak tree and digs a hole at the bottom of it with this stick. Then she buries this thing in the dirt, covers it over, and leaves. And I'm still just... stunned. And curious. I wanted to know what it was she was attacking. So I went over to the tree trunk and dug it up.

—And what did you find?

—It was gross. Really gross. Disgusting. It was a heart. An actual heart. It looked about the same size as a human heart. But it must've been an animal's. I mean, it couldn't have been human. Could it?

I thought... Oh my god... She must've been doing some kind of devil worship or dark witchcraft. But the thing was, at school, she seemed really quiet. This happened before she started hanging round with Flora, and I'd see her walking around on her own with a kind of blank look on her face. She gave this impression of being this little shy, quiet girl. I mean, I heard all the rumours about her. I knew she was a gypsy, and they get up to all sorts of stuff, don't they? Gypsy curses and superstitions and that. But she... yeah, she made out she was this hard-done-by fragile girl, but after I saw what she did, I thought she was more like Carrie. You know the girl from the Stephen King film? Carrie the psycho who killed her classmates because they bullied her?

Before I saw that, I'd tried to talk to her a few times. Ask her if she was okay and that. I felt a bit sorry for her when she first joined the school, because she seemed a bit lonely. But after that... well, I just steered clear of her. I didn't want to give her any excuse to slash me up. And look what happened in the end with Flora. She got too close to her, and she was killed.

—Did you ever report what you'd seen that day? Especially in light of the animal mutilations going on around that time?

—No. The thing is, I was bullied at that school too. And I was a

shy kid, anyway, because of my weight. I had no confidence. I just kind of tried to blend into the shadows so I wouldn't get picked on. So I didn't tell anyone, because then I'd be the centre of attention. And I didn't want it to get out to Caris that I was the one who'd told, because I was scared of her after that, as well. I wasn't sure she was responsible for the mutilations anyway. I feel bad, but I just... I just kept quiet about it.

I wish I hadn't now. I wish I'd told someone. Maybe things might've been different if I had.

I think it's unlikely what Rob saw was a human heart. But just to be thorough, I've researched any suspicious deaths or murders around that time where the victim was missing their heart, and I found none. It's far more likely this would've been from an animal. Pig or sheep hearts can be bought easily in butcher's shops and supermarkets.

Or could there be yet another correlation here between the animal mutilations going on in the area around that time? Were the missing organs from the pet cats, dogs, and horses used for witchcraft or devil worship? Don't forget, a pentagram was carved into some of the horse's hides. It's possible, but at this stage, it would just be further conjecture and coincidence. And although from Rob's story, it seems he witnessed some kind of spell or ritual, was it actually black magic? Devil worship? There are many historical myths and legends surrounding the use of hearts in witchcraft, and I'm going to share a quick insight from Tania Purcell, the curator of the Museum of Witchcraft in London. With over four thousand objects in their collection, she's an expert on the oldest and largest array of items relating to witchcraft, magic, and the occult. Here's what she had to say...

• • •

—In 1841 in Lancashire, a seagull's heart was pierced with four pins to reverse a curse Leonard Potter believed he was under. In 1886, a fox's heart with two nails in was used by Dora Barnham to protect her from witchcraft. In South Devon in 1902, a cow's heart was pierced by nails and pins by Allan Stanard as a way to protect his cows from someone he believed had bewitched them. A sheep's heart pierced with iron pins was used in 1913 to exorcise and punish a witch. These are just a few examples that are now exhibited in our museum and all originate from a time when it was commonplace to believe in witches. Historically, various, and often bizarre, methods were used to protect people against malevolent spells and magic. From time to time, these talismans, or charms, thought to provide counter-witchcraft measures have been found in houses. Mummified cats have been discovered in roof spaces or behind hearths and lath and plaster walls, or above door lintels in many Dorset cottages. But it seems the favoured charm was a bullock's heart stuck with thorns, pins, or nails. One was even found in a Dorset police station. And while most were probably installed during the paranoia of the sixteenth- and seventeenth-century witch trials, the practice did continue for a long time afterwards, in some cases until the mid-twentieth century.

It's not uncommon for some pagans to use animal parts in rituals and ceremonies. Thousands of years ago, many of our ancestors did exactly that. And animal parts, including hearts, have been used in all manner of religions and beliefs from devil worship, shamanism, voodoo, Santeria, even some Christian communities, to name a few. Commonly offered up as a sacrifice or as protection, animal hearts and, in some gruesome cases, human hearts have been used.

So was this ritual Rob described Caris carrying out a spell for protection? Or was it something more sinister? Either way, I think it's time to leave the witchcraft angle there. I want to get more of an impression of Caris and Flora and what their personalities were like.

—*Caris had a really violent streak. She attacked me for no reason. It was in the toilets at school, and she just started on me out of the blue. She was coming out of the cubicle, and I was by the sink, washing my hands, minding my own business, and she just flew at me. Screaming, calling me a bitch. Punching me. Someone else had to drag her off me. She was mental! It was like she was possessed or something.*

That is the voice of Dawn Bowden. She was in the same form class as Caris at Stoneminster High School, and the incident she describes happened when they were both fifteen. Dawn has moved away from Stoneminster and lives in Cornwall, and I chat to her on the phone.

—There was nothing that provoked the attack?
   —*No! Absolutely nothing. A teacher came in then. She must've heard all the noise. But I don't think she wanted to get punched by Caris, either, so she ran off to get one of the PE teachers, Mr Stamp. He was the one who pulled Caris off me. I had a broken nose and a black eye. My clothes were all ripped. Caris got dragged off to the headmaster, and I went to hospital. She ruined my nose, the cow! It was always wonky after that, and I couldn't breathe out of it properly. I managed to get a nose job on the NHS, though, which sorted it out. It's perfect now. But still, I've got psychological scars from it. I'm not surprised she ended up doing what she did later. Everyone knew she was a nutter. Those*

pikeys are always like that. Fighting each other. Ripping everyone off. They've got no morals or laws, have they? They just think they can do whatever they want.

—What happened after that incident?

—*Caris got excluded for a few weeks and moved to a different form after that, and we didn't share any more classes together. My mum tried to sue the school for damages. The governors were probably worried about being set on by gypsies if we won a case against them in court, so they offered my mum and dad a settlement. The cheek of it was that the school was trying to get me to leave after that and move to another school.*

—And did you leave Stoneminster High then?

—*No. Where else would I go? The next school was miles away, and there was no way I was going to take a bus to get there or pay for a school bus. And besides, why should I move? She started it. And I'd lived there all my life. She hadn't.*

—Did you have any other altercations with Caris?

Dawn pauses here for a moment. When she speaks again, I detect a slight shift of hesitance in her voice that's barely there. It's most likely unconscious.

—*No. I'd still see her around at school, though, but I kept out of her way after that. It was obvious she was always going to be trouble.*

—Did Caris ever give a reason for attacking you?

—*No.*

—Did you ever find out the reason?

—*Well, the headmaster, Mr Ford, said she didn't say a word about it. She didn't apologise to me, either. He tried to make her, but she wouldn't. I'm glad she's in prison, where she belongs. Don't know why Flora hung around with her. I reckon Caris got her claws* into Flora and was influencing her in all this witchcraft shit. Sorry, didn't mean to swear on air. I won't do it again.

—Did you know Flora well then?

—A bit, I suppose.

—She was in the same year as you and Caris, so did you have any classes together?

—Yeah, a few. Look, I don't want to sound rude, but Flora was on another planet to most of my mates. Every time we saw her, we'd kind of do a quick getaway, because she was always trying to collect signatures for petitions about saving whales or grasshoppers, or whatever, or handing out leaflets about boring crap like not eating meat. She was one of the nerdy, weird groups of people you always get at school.

—Did you belong to any particular group?

—Not really.

—But you'd lived in Stoneminster all your life, and you'd known a lot of the local kids at secondary school for a long time? Presumably most were from the town and from your primary school?

—Yeah. But I wasn't one of the popular girls with fake hair and fake nails, if that's what you mean. I wasn't one of the princesses. That's what we called those girls. You know the type. Think they're better than everyone else and look down their noses at us and think all the boys fancy them. But last I heard, most of those girls were fat and ugly now and working in Starbucks or Tesco on the checkout, so there you go.

—Did you think Caris was a 'princess'?

—Ha! Not me, Chief, no.

—What did the rest of your friends think of Caris?

—The boys wouldn't go near her. Neither did anyone else, except Flora. Everyone knows you can't trust those pikeys. Gypsy curses and selling lucky heather and ripping people off with their fake tarot card readings. Conning old people by pretending they're

83

from the gas board and need to check a leak and then stealing their life savings. Caris always walked round with a face like a smacked arse, like she was better than everyone else.

—What did your friends make of the attack on you by Caris?

—Oh, they all thought she was a psycho too.

—So why do you think Caris influenced Flora?

—Because Flora just bobbed along for years in her hippie clothes with her little do-gooding causes, and then suddenly, Caris comes along, and they're thick as thieves and up to all this weird witchcraft stuff. Caris was mad. I bet she manipulated Flora into all sorts of things. Caris led her up to Witch's Hill on some pretext about this summer solstice ritual and then strangled her. But if you swim with sharks, you're going to get bitten, aren't you? What else is there to say?

Was Flora influenced by Caris? Was it the other way around? Or were they just two similar people who found each other and became friends? Although Dawn's description of Caris and her background are quite telling, I also get the impression Dawn has been evasive and defensive with some of the questions I asked, and that makes me think there's perhaps more to the incident than she's told us.

For me, this little snapshot of Flora's and Caris's lives has left me with more questions about Caris's behaviour than answers. Was Caris a sadistic animal killer? Someone who practiced sinister animal-sacrifice rituals? Or was she a modern witch who wanted harmony with nature and the earth? Was she bullied relentlessly and that led to some kind of mental health issues that manifested in the murder of her best friend? Or was she an unpredictable and violent bully herself? Was she subjected to prejudice because of her ethnicity and just completely misunderstood? Was the troll just a harmless annoyance in the girls' lives, or did this troll have a deeper impact on Flora and Caris? And who was the man in Damian's story? Can we trace him, three years after the event?

Don't forget to check out the E-FIT picture on the website. If anyone recognises this man, please get in touch. And do keep your comments coming. Let me know what you think so far.

Thank you for listening to *Anatomy of a Crime*.

Until next time...

DottyP • 2 days ago
It was plain to see Kelly had mental problems from the heart she was stabbing in the woods and the bird she killed. And all those other animals she mutilated. That's wicked. I'm glad they stopped her when they did before she went on a killing spree.
^ | ˅ • Reply • Share ˃

8768 → Reply to DottyP • 2 days ago
Don't forget the pentagram. That's a sure sign of devil worship.
^ | ˅ • Reply • Share ˃

Bojo → Reply to 8768 • 1 day ago
No, it's not! Pentagrams are misunderstood. Just like Caris has been, I fear. To some people, they symbolize the 5 elements of life. Some people see it as a sign of mathematical purity. In Medieval times, some people thought it symbolised the 5 wounds of Christ and used it to ward off evil spirits. During the upheaval of the Christian Church in historical times, people who didn't conform to its strict views were executed and everything associated with

Paganism, including the pentagram, were thought to be evil and tools of the devil.
^ | ˅ • Reply • Share ˃

CoolWitch → Reply to Bojo • 1 day ago
I hear ya! The inverted pentagram was used by the Church of Satan as its logo and is usually depicted inside a circle with a goat's head inside the star. Which is probably where the association with devil worship came from. BUT... Wiccans and Latter-Day Saints also use inverted pentagrams in their rituals and ceremonies. I think the reason Caris gave for the scratch marks on her arm and her hair on Flora's bracelet were plausible. They were best friends!
^ | ˅ • Reply • Share ˃

LOL369 • 2 days ago
When Caris killed that bird and mutilated those animals it shouldve been a proper warning. If they hadnt stopped her shed probly be a cereal killer. Thats how Jeffrie Doormer started and look what he did!!!
^ | ˅ • Reply • Share ˃

HXHOP → Reply to LOL369 • 2 days ago
Are you a psychologist then? Or just an armchair expert?
^ | ˅ • Reply • Share ˃

LOL369 → Reply to HXHOP • 1 day ago
Everyone know that. Its a fact!!!
^ | ˅ • Reply • Share ˃

HXHOP → Reply to LOL369 • 2 days ago
How would you know? You can't even spell!
^ | ˅ • Reply • Share ˃

DottyP • 2 days ago
She was obviously a violent psycho. Look what she did to Dawn.
Beating her up in the toilets! Kelly probably made up that stuff
about being bullied herself. Gypsies are notorious thugs, criminals,
and liars.
^ | ˅ • Reply • Share ˃

Wall1919 → Reply to DottyP • 1 day ago
The pentagram gave her power after praying to the devil to invoke
his spirit. That's what she was doing in the woods, sacrificing the
animal heart, getting devil power. What other organs from those
poor animals did she sacrifice?
^ | ˅ • Reply • Share ˃

Dino12 • 2 days ago
I can't believe she killed that poor, defenceless bird. Wicked!
^ | ˅ • Reply • Share ˃

WhatsUP → Reply to Dino12 • 1 day ago
Do you eat chicken?
^ | ˅ • Reply • Share ˃

Dino12 → Reply to WhatsUP • 1 day ago
Yes. Why?
^ | ˅ • Reply • Share ˃

WhatsUP→ Dino12 • 1 day ago
There's no difference between killing a chicken in an abattoir that's
had its poor throat slit, or been boiled alive, just so you can eat it,
and killing a blackbird!
^ | ˅ • Reply • Share ˃

Dino12 → Reply to WhatsUP • 1 day ago

You fucking animal rights people get everywhere! It's got nothing to do with this.
^ | ᵛ • Reply • Share ˃

Colonel Mustard • 3 days ago
Psycho witch! Should've hung her like they did in the olden days. Bring back the death penalty.
^ | ᵛ • Reply • Share ˃

.

Lollyrugs → Reply to Colonel Mustard • 2 days ago
Totally agree with you. Might be a deterrent. And it would solve the overcrowding in prisons that the taxpayer's funding!
^ | ᵛ • Reply • Share ˃

Hayter • 3 days ago
Gypsies picked on my elderly mum. They threatened her into having her drive tarmacked and then tried to charge her a lot more money afterwards. She was scared to death that if she didn't pay them they'd come back and beat her up. These were big, hefty guys. I reported them to the police, but nothing ever happened to them. Even the police are scared of them. Conning, thieving bastards.
^ | ᵛ • Reply • Share ˃

.

Charlotte → Reply to Hayter • 2 days ago
They conned my granddad into letting them into his house to read the electric meter.
He was old and confused, and when they got inside, one of them distracted him, and the other stole money and family heirloom jewellery from the bedroom! They never got caught! Scum!
^ | ᵛ • Reply • Share ˃

Jester → Reply to Charlotte • 2 days ago

Wow, you and Hayter are tarring all gypsies with the same brush. Or should I say, tarmacking them with the same brush? There's good and bad in everyone.
^ | ˅ • Reply • Share ˃

Pepperz • 4 days ago
Great podcast! Listening from Canada. I think Caris's innocent. Who was that man in the woods? I believe Damian's story!
^ | ˅ • Reply • Share ˃

CHAPTER FIVE

Caris (Aged 18)

I slipped my denim jacket over my shoulders as I stood beside Dad, watching him sleeping on the sofa. The pinched lines on his face had softened in his unconscious state, giving him the appearance of the care-free man he used to be, and he had a smile on his face that told a thousand stories. The fun smile he'd had when I was sitting on his shoulders at about seven years old as he ran around the campsite, pretending to be a horse, my squeals of laughter trailing behind us. The patient smile when he'd taught me how to play poker as we sat at the fold-up table outside our caravan one warm summer's evening. His effervescent smile as he danced an Irish jig with Mum, both of them laughing as they moved faster and faster before collapsing into each other in a sweaty heap. The studious smile he'd had when showing me which plants could heal or harm and pointed out the edible or poisonous mushrooms and herbs in the woods. The proud smile after I presented dinner for our extended family, using the recipes Mum had taught me to cook over an open fire when I was eight.

Those smiles didn't exist anymore when he was awake. And appearances were always deceptive.

I turned away, slipped out of the house, and walked up the front path, pausing in front of the lavender bush I'd planted next to the gate three years before. I picked some flowers and rolled them between my palms, crushing the scent into my skin before cupping my hands to my nose and taking a deep breath. I sensed Bea watching me from behind her net curtains as always, my smile hidden behind my hands. *Let her look and watch. Let her think she knows everything.*

I slid my hands into my jacket pockets as my shoes pattered on the pavement. I let my mind drift to the new spell box I wanted to create using the lavender for a peace and serenity spell.

I was so deep in thought, blocking out the people and sounds around me as I walked down the high street, that I didn't see Mr Bath coming out of Liz's supermarket until it was too late to avoid the collision. His elbow banged into my side as he rushed out of the door, carrier bag in hand, staring down at his phone.

I stumbled slightly before I came to a stop and rubbed at the throbbing spot between my ribs that had taken the brunt of the impact.

'I'm so sorry.' His eyes widened with concern. 'I didn't see you there. Are you okay?'

'Um... yeah, I'm all right, Mr Bath. It was an accident. Don't worry.' I rested my hand over my rib and ignored the pulsing skin.

He held his phone up at me with an embarrassed smile. 'I was distracted, reading a text. Sorry. I feel really bad now.'

'It's okay.' I smiled at him. 'Really.'

'Glad to hear it. And please call me Paul. We're not at school anymore. How's life going with you? History lessons aren't quite the same without your and Flora's inquisitive minds.'

I looked into his eyes and wondered what he'd think if I just unleashed my troubles on him. Would he still be looking at me like that? With a concerned expectancy? The way he'd always looked at me when I was his pupil. He was the only teacher who'd ever really listened to me or seemed to care. There was a split second when I wanted to pour out my soul. Would it feel good to talk to someone other than Flora? Would he judge me like the rest of them? We were both adults, and I wasn't a schoolgirl anymore... Was there anything wrong with letting myself go?

I stared into his blue eyes, hesitating, feeling some kind of subconscious connection. What if I took a step in another direction? What if I really was good enough for once?

His eyes searched mine, waiting for an answer, and the possibilities disintegrated into the ether, like they always did. I didn't trust him. Didn't know if I ever could. 'Life's good, thanks.'

'Listen... Do you want to get a coffee or a drink?' He tilted his head towards the pub on the green opposite Willow's shop. 'As a way of an apology.'

'Sorry, I can't. I'm meeting someone.'

'Yes. Of course. Well... It was good to see you. Take care.'

'You too.'

He smiled as I turned away and walked on down the street, thoughts of spell boxes now replaced with Mr Bath. Paul.

When I got to the abbey at the far end of town, he was waiting on a bench outside the wooden gates that overlooked the sprawling fields below. He was smoking a cigarette in that hurried way of his, his right foot tapping up and down. He glanced around at a woman walking her dog, heading away from us, before turning his head in my direction and grinning.

'You're late.' He tapped his watch.

I shrugged and sat beside him, watching a hawk circling in the air above the fields in front of us.

'You know what I was thinking about the other day?' he asked.

'What?'

'I was thinking of changing my name to Dylan. Always liked

that name. Kind of funky, eh? And Dylan was that spaced-out cat on that kid's programme, *The Magic Roundabout*. Ha ha, that was funny, because all the characters were doped up to the eyeballs, and the parents pretended they didn't know what it was really about.' He glanced at me.

I raised an eyebrow at him. 'I haven't got time for a deep, meaningful chat.'

'Stop being so boring. You know where I'm coming from, the amount you get through. Still, not much else to do in Stoneminster, is there? The oldies are always moaning about all the drugs going on and "Ooh, the youth of today are so out of control!" But they're having a laugh! They were the ones teaching kids about junkie animals on TV! And what else is there to do in this boring shithole? Drink or do drugs. Or both. Or go to the seaside with their bucket and spades? Ha! Think not.'

'Have you got it or not?' I dug my hand into my jacket pocket and cupped my fingers around the folded pound notes. I slid them out and placed the notes on the bench between us, my hand covering them from view.

'On the outside, this place looks like this super-quaint town on the Jurassic coast—oooh, scary dinosaurs—and the tourists flock here because it looks all mega postcardy, but it's the same as anywhere else. Same as any other town anywhere in England. Bored kids with nothing to do. And lots of drugs floating around behind closed doors. You know what I think—'

'Hurry up, *Dylan*. I need to go. Have you got it or not?'

'All right, all right.' His head darted around again, looking up and down the path. He took one last desperate drag on the cigarette, threw it on the ground and smashed it out under his heel.

No one was around now. Just us and the birds. Families were at home, eating dinner, deciding what to watch on TV. People were getting ready to go on dates and see friends. A twinge of loneliness burned in my core, and Paul's kind eyes from earlier flashed into my head for a moment.

He pulled the packet from his pocket and held it out to me. 'There you go.'

I lifted my hand from the money on the bench and took the packet.

He quickly snatched up the cash and stood. 'Well, it was nice *chatting*.' He smirked and strode away.

CHAPTER SIX

LOVE

What is love? I used to believe all that stupid fairy tale bullshit when I was little. But now I see it's nothing like the films. Nothing like the pathetic cheery family crap on TV.

You're supposed to love your parents, love your partner, love your kids, love yourself—and that last one's the biggest load of happy-clappy rubbish out there. It's an illusion. Love is something else entirely, and I never really got that until I met you.

I love the thrill. Love the chase. Love the watching and waiting. Love the excitement. Is that the meaning of the word? Or maybe love is taking what you want and then giving it up, knowing you can have it again at any time you want. Reliving it in your head until it takes on more and more meaning and the emotions consume you day and night. They fill your imagination with possibilities you never dared to dream before. Love might be silence from all the noise. The quiet space that only exists in your head when people who 'love' you finally shut the fuck up. Does love make you a god or goddess, all knowing, all seeing? Does it give you choices that were never there before? Does love really mean pain and darkness? Is it tortuous? Can it make you bleed out with anger and viciousness and hate?

I thought you were different. Thought you were like me. Thought we'd understand each other. Have a connection. But you were fake too. Do you know how many times I've wondered if I love you, as I listened to your voice, watched you dance and chant your weird words and browse the supermarket shelves, or followed your swaying walk?

Now I know love doesn't exist. It's not real. But I love that I'm not the only one out there who thinks the same.

CHAPTER SEVEN

EPISODE 3
RUMOURS

—D awn was one of the bullies at school. Everyone who was there knows that. She was one of the hard girls and hung around in this little clique. Most of the time, she didn't do anything really physical. She just mouthed off a lot, making comments and slagging you off, trying to wear you down. She was always the same. I went to junior school with her, and then we ended up at secondary school together too. Unfortunately! She made my life hell.

I had really bad eyesight from when I was young. I had to wear these horrible thick glasses. My family couldn't afford nice ones, so I got the national-health glasses. The cheap, ugly things that made me look even uglier. Dawn and her mates just kept on and on, calling me names, having constant digs. I put up with it for years. Tried to ignore them. But in the second year, I'd had enough. So I told my mum what was going on, and she marched up to the school. Told the headmaster, Mr Ford, but he was a useless waste of space. He said he was going to do something, and *he called Dawn into his office. Told her to stop with the verbal bullying. But I think he was scared of her family or something. They've got a reputation round the town. Dawn's dad was in prison for GBH for a few years, and her mum was always getting into arguments with other parents. Her mum actually hit one of the other kid's mums at our school's netball match. Dawn was playing, and she tackled this other girl really viciously and got sent off the pitch. Then Dawn's mum was shouting about how it was victimisation. And the parent of the girl Dawn had kicked in the shin on purpose was really upset and annoyed and told Dawn's mum her daughter was a bully. So Dawn's mum then hit her! Can you believe it?*

Dawn's brothers went to the same school, and they were just as bad, except when they bullied the boys, they would get physical. I remember this overweight boy at school. I can't remember his name, but Dawn and Dawn's brothers used to call him Blobby, because he was... you know... a bit fat. They were so horrible to him. That was what the whole family were like. Just nasty and vindictive. And the parents used to let Dawn and her brothers do whatever they wanted.

So, anyway, after my mum went to see the headmaster, he told Dawn to stop calling me names. Which she didn't. She just got a bit more clever at it, I suppose. If I walked past her, she'd whisper the name-calling to me so only we could hear, instead of shouting it out like normal. She'd sit at the back of the class with her mates and throw things at me when the teachers weren't looking. She'd barge into me and knock me into walls if no staff were around. It was just this drip, drip, drip of harassment, and I couldn't see a way out of it. At one point, I was so low, I almost thought about killing myself because of it.

That is the voice of Leanne Welland, and this is the other side to the story that Dawn told us in the previous episode. Leanne moved away from Stoneminster to go to university in London at eighteen and never moved back. I talk to her by phone.

—I'm sorry that happened to you.

—*Thank you. People always say sticks and stones may break my bones but names will never hurt me, but they obviously haven't been subjected to the constant wearing down. They don't realise how much name-calling can affect you. It's psychological abuse. You hear about more and more kids now taking their own lives to escape, don't you? When you're that age, your image and emotions and self-esteem are really fragile. Dawn made my life hell. But I didn't want to come on here to talk about me. I wanted to refute what Dawn said. That incident... in the toilets. It wasn't like that at all.*

I was actually in the toilets when it happened. In the cubicle at the end. Just before I went in there, I saw Caris go into one of the other cubicles. Then a few seconds later, Dawn came into the toilets with her mate Tina, who was another bully. She was Dawn's little lapdog.

I heard the tap go, like one of them was washing their hands. Then they started talking about Caris, calling her all sorts of names —pikey, slag, gypo, dirty bitch, that sort of thing. They said Caris had killed her mum. That Caris had set fire to her mum's caravan and that she was, you know, just a psycho. And that her dad stole from everyone and was sponging off the state because he was on benefits. On and on, they kept going.

I held my breath. I mean, they knew other people were in the cubicles, because the doors were shut, but they didn't care. And I... this is going to sound awful, but I didn't want to get involved. I had enough problems with Dawn and her crowd as it was. From the cubicle next to me, I heard this kind of shuddering breath, like Caris was trying not to cry, but it was really quiet, like she was trying really hard to keep it in.

Anyway, I heard the door to the toilets go, and Tina must've left. But Dawn was in there, the tap still going. And I was just waiting silently for Dawn to leave, as well, so I could get out of there. And as I was waiting, the cubicle door next to me opened, and then I heard a commotion. Slaps on skin, grunts, Dawn telling Caris to fuck off. At one point, it sounded like they were both on the floor, grappling with each other. I heard the sort of noise a punch makes. Dawn was yelling and screaming, but Caris didn't say a word.

Then a teacher came in and kept making useless noises. It was Mrs [name redacted]. And I know she wants to remain anonymous, but hard luck. I'm sure she was the one who spoke to you in the other episode. She had no idea about kids. She should never have been a teacher. She was ancient. Completely out of touch with the real world or the real problems kids get through their teenage years. She should've been dealing positively with ethnic or cultural diversity, but her idea of diversity was having a curry on the school canteen menu instead of fish and chips. She thought education was all about barking orders at kids, and if you weren't one of the academic ones, she thought you were a waste of space and would never amount to anything and labelled you a troublemaker or a dunce.

I spoke to her once when I was being bullied, because she was my form teacher then. I was a shy and anxious kid, and it took a lot of courage to finally tell someone at the school what was happening. And she just told me to man up and deal with it myself! Seriously, that's what she said. She was nasty. She was a bully herself, really. I think she liked the power trip of being a teacher. But like most bullies, when faced with having to deal with someone stronger than them, she backed down. Like with Dawn, because Dawn was bigger than Mrs [name redacted], and Dawn's family was hard, so that teacher, she used to let Dawn get away with things. No one messed with Dawn's family.

. . .

Just for information, I've redacted the name of the teacher Leanne mentioned to respect her wishes for anonymity.

—Mrs [name redacted] was shouting at Caris to get off Dawn, but I could still hear them fighting. So Mrs [name redacted] went off and got Mr Stamp, and he broke it up. But Dawn totally deserved it. It was time she got a taste of her own medicine. She'd been digging at Caris for years. She'd go on and on and on. Same sort of things as with me—the name-calling, whispers, spiteful mutters, the looks. Throwing things at her, writing abuse on her locker, tripping her up in the corridor, breaking into her locker and ripping up her homework or stealing her textbooks. One time, Dawn emptied a tin of tuna inside Caris's bag so it stunk the place out. And after that, everyone started calling her horrendous things. Fishy Fanny, Smelly Cu—I don't want to say that word, but you can imagine.

—I can imagine indeed. I remember being that age, and there's no scorn and vitriol quite like that of teenagers. And you stayed in the cubicle the whole time?

—Yes. I didn't want to get punched in the face. I didn't want to get my glasses broken and end up with a pierced eye from the fragments. I just stayed there until everyone had left. But I was secretly cheering on Caris.

Then, after the murder, Dawn was suddenly being quoted in the papers about how Caris had bullied her at school. She told them all this ridiculous stuff that just never happened.

—You were friends with Flora and Caris, weren't you?

—Yes. Flora and I started secondary school at the same time. We were in the same form, and we sat together from day one, so in the first eighteen months after we got there, we were quite good friends. She was really sweet, and we hung around at school and sometimes outside school, as well, at that time. But we weren't really into the same things. I was more academic. I was in the chess club and debate team, and I didn't really like the outdoors, because I get a lot of allergies. But Flora was really into nature and crafty things and a lot of social causes. She spent her time either making things to sell in Willow's shop, or she'd be getting signatures for petitions to ban weapons or collecting money for charities. And I wasn't into the spiritual side of things that she was—the paganism and witchcraft things. So before Caris got there, we were kind of drifting apart anyway. But Caris was into a lot of the things Flora was, so they just became close.

I'd still sit with them sometimes at school, in the lunch breaks when they weren't outside on the playing field, but I became friends with some of the other people in the clubs I was in, so I didn't spend a lot of time with them that much after the second year at school really.

It was Dawn that started the rumour about Caris killing her mum in the fire. Dawn was going round, telling people that story pretty much as soon as Caris arrived. And people believed it. Dawn was also telling everyone Caris would put a curse on them and kill them, which alienated Caris even more. No one even wanted to go near Caris. So as well as calling her names, Dawn went a few steps further and purposefully tried to get everyone else to shun Caris, and it worked. They didn't want Caris round their house, because they were afraid she'd steal things off them or get her gypsy family to do something to them. I know what they say about gypsies, and I'm sure some of them are bad, but some of them aren't. You can't write off a whole group of people as being the same.

One of the reasons I wanted to get away from Stoneminster as soon as I could is because it's so small-minded. So prejudiced about things or people who are different. On the outside, it looks like a warm, welcoming place, but if you dig deeper, there's a lot of sourness. The locals keep to themselves and think outsiders are distrustful.

When Caris wasn't with Flora, like if they had different classes *together, she was always on her own. Caris was quiet. She also kept to herself. I suppose some people thought Caris was rude or arrogant because of that, but I don't think that was the reason at all. I think she just felt out of place, like she didn't fit in with anyone apart from Flora. She came out of herself away from the rest of the kids. With Flora, she was always relaxed and seemed happy. Laughing, joking. They were so comfortable with each other. It's kind of like they made each other whole. And when Caris was on her own, she was always rigid and tense, as if she was waiting for the next blow, whether it was physical or psychological. Do you know what I mean?*

—I think I do.

—*I thought Caris was really sad about her mum dying. My dad died when I was nine, so I knew how she must've felt. I think she put up this front. She wore this aloof mask, as if nothing could touch her. I think it was a protection mechanism from getting hurt, because I tried to do the same kind of thing. That's supposed to be the best way to deal with bullies, my mum always said. Don't show your weakness. Don't show that they've got to you, as it just makes them worse. Caris didn't show it. Apart from that one time in the toilet, and by then it had been going on for years. She let her mask slip for a few seconds then. All the anger and upset burst out. And Caris was the one who got the blame for it, because no doubt Mrs [name redacted] told the head Caris had started the fight.*

—Do you know if Caris told the headmaster what had really happened? That Dawn had provoked her and had been bullying her for some time and starting rumours about her?

—*I don't think she ever did. She stayed silent and took her punishment. And to be honest, I don't blame her. Probably, she thought it wouldn't do any good. It was obvious some of the teachers didn't like Caris too. Mrs [name redacted] was just one of them. Caris probably thought she wouldn't get any support. That no one would believe her. I know how that felt, because Mr Ford didn't give me any support about my bullying, either. He didn't really care about support for students. He was just worried about exam stat results, because the school inspectors kept breathing down his neck. I don't think Caris's needs or struggles were ever investigated, much less flagged up for support or help. She was let down by the system who painted her as a troublemaker, a degenerate, instead of as a victim of Dawn and her friends.*

I never saw Caris let any of her anger or sadness slip again after that. But I suppose some people thought that mask she wore made her look up her own arse or trying to be hard or insolent or anti-authority... I don't know. People thought she was evil in the end. But I never saw that in Caris.

I left school at sixteen to go to college and get my A-levels so, you know, I didn't really see Caris and Flora much after that, and it wasn't like we were close friends or anything by then.

—Did Dawn or anyone else ever bully Flora?

—*Not that I knew of, no.*

—What did you think when you heard Caris was arrested and later convicted for killing Flora?

—*I didn't believe it then. And I still don't believe it. There were so many rumours going round after the murder about Flora and Caris. One minute, it was the witchcraft thrill killing thing, the next that Flora and Caris were in a lesbian relationship and Flora wanted to end things with Caris, so Caris killed her. The other thing was that Caris was jealous of Flora.*

—Do you think Caris and Flora's relationship was more than just friendship? Do you think there was any truth to the rumours that they were in a sexual relationship?

—*I don't think there was truth to any of the rumours about her, no. But even if they were lovers, so what? Although plenty of people in small-minded Stoneminster would've hated gay people as much as they hated ethnic minorities. You know what it's like in these places. If you're the slightest bit different, you're always an outsider.*

I listened to your first episode and heard what Damian said.

Why was that never made public knowledge in the press? He saw a man running away. That's got to be connected, hasn't it? I always thought the way Caris was supposed to have killed Flora seemed too elaborate. There were too many variables that could go wrong, if that's what she'd planned. Like, how would Caris know she wouldn't overdose herself with the ketamine? How could she guarantee she'd be found like that, if her alibi was supposed to have been she was drugged too? Why would she arrange Flora's body in a stone circle? There are much easier ways to kill someone.

No, I think someone purposely spiked their drinks and waited until Flora and Caris were unconscious. But I have no idea what the motive would be. I can't believe Flora would've had any enemies. She was just too sweet, really.

And I've been looking at the E-FIT picture. It's weird, but there's something about it. About him. *Something that looks familiar. I just can't quite work out what.*

I think Leanne's story has given us a completely different impression of Caris. A more sympathetic view of what she might've been going through in her teenage school years.

Is the other aspect Leanne has mentioned—the rumours of a lesbian relationship between Caris and Flora—anything to do with what happened on the summer solstice in 2017? Could the real motive have been that Flora was intending to break up with Caris, and Caris killed her to stop that happening? It's possible.

On the other hand, I agree with Leanne that the way Flora was killed and the staging of the scene seems too elaborate, especially for a domestic-type murder, where it's more often a result of years of abuse and is committed in the heat of the moment. There would be far easier ways to kill Flora, particularly making it look like an accident, if a relationship turned sour was the reason for the crime. And when you factor in the suspicious man at Blackleaf Forest that night—a man who seems familiar somehow to Leanne, which could mean he was a local person, then does he cast doubts on whether Caris is as guilty of this crime? Had he been watching the girls, like Caris's solicitor, Annabelle, believes? Stalking them? And if he *was* a local, he would've found it easy to blend in so he became unnoticeable.

There's one other story I want to share with you. Everyone so far has confirmed that Flora and Caris were, at the very least, close friends or, if you believe the rumours, lovers. But surely all friends have their falling-outs, their disagreements. And I've found one person who witnessed something that may show things weren't always rosy between the girls.

Andrew Strytch is a solicitor who works at Ryder & Co, a local firm. I meet him in his office on the second floor of a shop in Stoneminster's high street, above a florist. Even though he's twenty-nine, he looks more like a middle-aged country doctor than a young solicitor, dressed in corduroy trousers and a tweed jacket, his cheeks ruddy. He specialises in conveyancing and wills. But it's not his legal expertise I've come to pick his brains about.

—Did you know Caris and Flora well?

—*I knew who they were, but I didn't know them well. Flora's mum, Willow, had the shop just along the high street. The New Age shop. My girlfriend liked some of their wares and bought a fair few things from there—oil burners, candle holders, some Indian-style cushions, and the like. Willow also had her homeopathy practice in an office at the rear of the premises, and I was seeing her for a small ailment that the doctors couldn't seem to clear up. I was sceptical at first, but whatever was in the little tablets she gave me certainly did the trick. So I'd been in the shop when Flora and Caris were working there at weekends and in summer holidays. It was perfectly legal, I hasten to add. Children under the age of sixteen can work a certain number of hours. Flora and Caris were always welcoming whenever I went in.*

—You saw an altercation between Flora and Caris, didn't you? Can you tell me what happened and when this was?

—Yes. It was May or June time. About three years before the murder, so they would've been fifteen, I suppose.

He stands up and goes to the sash window in his office that overlooks the high street, beckoning me to join him. From this view, you can see the village square of cobbled stone, where the weekly market takes place, and a pub called the Fox and Hounds directly opposite, with its Elizabethan architecture still intact and an outside garden area of rustic-style picnic tables contained inside a picket fence. Next to the pub is the small, central village green with a war memorial surrounded by a circle of benches. The farmer's market is in full swing, with rows of stalls and sellers shouting out their wares to entice the growing crowd of shoppers who bustle around.

Andrew opens the window and looks directly downwards. You can see the entrance to the florist below and a small brick wall that separates it from the Chinese takeaway next door on the left. Next to the florist on the right-hand side is what used to be Willow's shop, Ethnic Crafts.

—They were standing down there, in front of the Chinese takeaway. I heard them first. Their raised voices carried upwards because it was a hot day, and I had the window open.

I can't remember a lot of the exact words—it was a long time ago now—but I can recall the gist of it. Flora said she was going to tell someone something. Caris was telling her not to. It went back and forth for a bit in the same vein, the voices getting louder. Caris said something like it was nothing to do with Flora, and that she should keep quiet about it. Flora just kept saying it wasn't right and she had to go to the police. That's when I got up and looked out of the window. Caris's face was bright red, really angry.

The police station is further up the road. Flora tried to walk off in that direction. Caris grabbed her arm and yanked her back and said, 'If you do that, it's the end'.

And that was it, pretty much. Flora shook her arm out of Caris's grip and walked away, in the direction of the police station. I don't know where she went afterwards, but I kept wondering what it was about. I also remember religiously poring through the local papers after that argument to see if anything ever came to light about something to do with Caris, but nothing ever did. Not until the murder.

—And what did Caris do after Flora walked off?

—She stared after Flora for a while, watching her walk away, clenching and unclenching her fists. And then she went off in the opposite direction.

—But you have no idea of the real subject of the conversation? What Caris wanted Flora to keep quiet about?

—No. But it stuck with me, especially the words she used: 'If you do that, it's the end'. After the murder, it seemed a bit strange, like maybe Flora knew something about Caris and wanted to report it, but Caris definitely didn't want it getting out. Personally, I've never believed this 'thrill kill' theory put out there by the police. What makes more sense is that Flora knew some kind of secret about Caris that she wanted kept quiet, and Caris 'ended' Flora's life because Flora was about to tell it three years later.

—After the murder, did you tell the police what you'd seen that day?

—Yes. But they didn't think a minor tiff that happened three years earlier was particularly relevant. They were bullheadedly fixed *on their thrill-killing scenario. Particularly when the witchcraft angle came to light.*

As I leave Andrew, a thought strikes me. Something that the anonymous teacher at Stoneminster High School said about Caris changing when she was fifteen, around the same time as this argument, seems possibly more important now. Maybe Caris's morbid artwork and the poem she wrote really were prophetic. They could've been the expression of a dark secret Caris was carrying around. A secret known by her best friend that she wanted kept quiet at all costs. But the argument between them was a little too vague and ambiguous to make any significant conclusion. And is there another angle here?

Remember the troll @Insrule, who was giving the girls abuse on the Instagram page around that same time? It might've been those threats that Flora wanted to tell the police about.

Or could this be connected to the animal mutilations going on at that time? Was Flora aware that it was Caris doing those unspeakable things and wanted to report it?

Maybe we'll never find out the answers. And for now, we're going to leave Flora's and Caris's school days behind. These events happened years before Flora's murder, and although I think they're essential to building up the overall picture and background, I want to speak to some people who had interactions with or observed the girls in the years closer to the murder.

Another angle I want to explore is what Caris's neighbour Bea told us about how she frequently smelled cannabis from Ronan and Caris's house. Even though Caris has always denied any drug use in her past, was she really an addict? And if she was, Flora could well have been smoking cannabis with her on a regular basis, and the murder was really drug-related. Either a hallucinogenic trip that had devastating consequences or an accidental overdose.

Pam Everton is a retired nurse and now spends her free time volunteering for a local group called Helping Hands. She's got four rescue dogs and three rescue cats, along with several rabbits and ferrets that were unwanted pets and now live in large cages in a conservatory overlooking her garden. And after receiving an excited licking-and-sniffing-fest welcome from her menagerie, Pam herds the dogs into the kitchen so we can talk in her lounge without any interruptions.

—You've got quite the collection of animals here.

—*Oh, I know! You should see it in here when I let all the ferrets and rabbits out for a run round the house. It's bedlam! But that's just me. Caring is in my nature, I suppose. That's why I do the volunteering. I don't have kids or grandkids to look after so... this is the next best thing.*

Sometimes, I take one of the dogs round to see the people I care for. Like a therapy dog. That's a real treat for some of them. A lot of them can't get out now, you see. They're too old or immobile, so they like having a dog to make a fuss over.

—These are the people you go and see as part of the Helping Hands volunteer programme?

—*That's right, love. I might be retired from nursing, but I can't really give up looking after people. Social Services are woefully underfunded. Well, every NHS service is these days. People in need would be lucky to get a weekly visit for an hour! Sometimes Meals on Wheels will go in daily, but they're just there to deliver food. There are a lot of people that need proper daily help, but they just don't get it. So when I retired, I joined Helping Hands.*

There's about forty of us. I just cover Stoneminster with another few ladies, and that's a job and a half in itself. Originally, I told them I'd do ten hours a week, but as I said, some people need care for quite a few hours a day. They need washing, feeding, a bit of help cleaning or tidying up. It's criminal, really, that these elderly or disabled people are just left to fend for themselves.

There's been several times when I've visited one of my lovely people and they've been on the floor all night long! They've had a fall and can't get up. So, I usually do about thirty hours a week, because there are just not enough volunteers to go round.

—And you used to visit Ronan Kelly, Caris's dad?

—Yes. That was between 2014 and 2017.

—Why did Ronan need assistance from Helping Hands?

—It was his GP that suggested it, knowing Ronan would be lucky to qualify for any funded social care. Ronan had a degenerative disease. A condition that causes inflammation and weakness in muscles, along with swelling and pain. It can also cause trouble swallowing or breathing.

He was diagnosed back in 2012, actually, shortly after he got to Stoneminster. I suppose he had proper access to a GP for the first time when he was here. Before that, he was part of the Travelling community and kept putting things off and putting things off. They're very wary of going to medical professionals, you see.

He was very proud. The type of man who never wanted to ask for help. A stubborn old goat, really, bless him. I think it was Caris who made him go to see the doctor. They ran some tests, and he got the diagnosis. By the time I saw him, he was going downhill rapidly. He couldn't walk very far because of the pain. It was difficult for him to wash himself or cook a meal. Just generally looking after himself was a big struggle. He never went out of the house by then.

It was Caris who was looking after him, but she was just a tiny slip of a girl. It's scandalous that the government think a teenager should be pretty much his full-time carer. But that's the way it is now. And wait until the NHS is sold off and the American companies get their hands on it! It'll be sky-high insurance premiums, and people on low incomes just won't be able to afford any kind of help or treatment.

—So what did you do for Ronan when you visited him?

—*I'd come in after Caris went to school. After she'd done him his breakfast. About nineish. Then I'd give him a sponge bath, get him clean and into some new clothes if she hadn't already done that. Make him some lunch or a cuppa and have a natter with him. As you can tell, I like a natter, so that's no hardship for me.*

At first, he didn't really want me there. He didn't want to accept my help. He wanted to struggle on his own. So he was a bit offish with me in the beginning, but I'm used to that. Some of the elderly can get a bee in their bonnet and get quite feisty sometimes. And I could understand he'd gone from being this strong, outdoor type of man to a shell of what he was. But I'm a stubborn one too! So I told him straight how things were. That he couldn't go on like this and that it wasn't fair on Caris leaving everything to her. And that I was there to help him, whether he liked it or not.

Pam chuckles and has a cheeky sparkle in her eye. She's brimming with the energy of a woman half her age.

—Would you say you got to know Caris and Ronan quite well then?

—*Ronan, certainly. He was a rough diamond. A loveable rogue. He opened up when he knew he wasn't getting rid of me that easily. Caris was good at keeping the house clean and doing the laundry and ironing, but I felt really sorry for her. For all the responsibility she was carrying on such young shoulders. So I'd always put a load of laundry on. Do a bit of ironing while I was chatting to Ronan. If I had time, I'd sometimes whip up something easy for their tea. A bit of soup or a sandwich. I think Caris and Ronan probably lived on beans on toast otherwise, poor loves.*

I spent a lot of time there talking with him while I was doing my bits and bobs, but I didn't know Caris well, as I'd leave before she got home from school to go and see more of my regulars. Then it would start over again with the new person. Wash them, cleaning, get their tea on the go. I didn't see much of Caris unless I popped over at the weekends or the evenings, just to give them a cake I'd made or some sausage rolls or something like that. I do a big baking batch on a Saturday and whip it round to my people. I was fond of Ronan, though.

—Did he talk about his background much?

—*He was quite a private person. Caris was the same, because whenever I did see Caris, I made a point of asking her if she was okay. If she needed any help too. And she always said no. Always said she was fine. She was polite and sweet, but she didn't open up in the same way Ronan did.*

There were all these rumours going round town after they got here. How Ronan had started the fire in the caravan that killed his wife. Or how Caris had started it. Probably one of their vindictive neighbours that spread it about. You probably know who I'm talking about.

People should start worrying about their own lives rather than spreading gossip about other people. Often it's the ones that spout off about charity and do-gooding who are the least charitable people out there!

I take people as I find them. I don't listen to rumours or judge people on their appearance. I like to make my own mind up. And the things said about them were just ridiculous. The problem is, there's an unquenchable appetite by the public for the most horrendous stories. And when one person commits a crime, others feed on it. And you only have to look at all the gossip magazines about celebrities that are on sale to see how people are taken in by all the fake drama. That's what sells papers and magazines, though, isn't it?

—I've been struggling to find any of Ronan's family or community who might be able to talk to me about what life was like for him and Caris before they came to Stoneminster. There were rumours about a family rift after Caris's mum's death. Do you know anything about that?

—*He didn't talk about that with me, so I don't know what happened before they got here. And I didn't ask him, either. Whatever had happened was his business. But from what he did tell me, his clan weren't a bunch of criminal thugs. They were hardworking, decent, clean people who respected the land and had their own laws and rules that they abided by. I thought Ronan and Caris were lovely people.*

—Do you think Ronan and Caris struggled to adapt to life in Stoneminster?

—*I think it was really hard for them both. The biggest thing was they were both mourning. Ronan said Mary was like their rudder, keeping them afloat in a stormy sea of life. I'll always remember the way he said that. He was actually quite a poetic man. He had an eloquent way of describing things. He was quite deep, quite thoughtful. I bet the Kelly-haters won't expect that now, will they? He was very intelligent too. Very well-read. And he knew more about nature than anyone I've ever met. Living outdoors like that, with knowledge passed down from generation to generation, that kind of thing was more important to them than the latest iPhone or how much money they had in the bank. He had a lot of moral characteristics that were ingrained in their people, their way of life. You see what I mean?*

One day, I went round to see them on a Saturday with a cake or something, and I was limping. Caris asked me what was wrong. One of the dogs had pulled me over when I was walking on the beach, and I'd twisted my ankle. Little monkeys! So while I'm there having a cuppa and a bit of this cake with Ronan, Caris goes into their garden and finds me some comfrey leaves. She soaks them in water then wraps some around my ankle and foot and bandages it all up and tells me to leave it overnight. Then she gives me some more comfrey to do the same with at home. Well, by the next day, it was fine. But that's what she was like. She had a very caring side to her, even though she didn't like to express herself or open up to people. She had trust issues, I think. And I'm not surprised, really, the way they were both treated and what they'd been through.

—Other people have said Caris was into nature, just like it seems Ronan was. Did either of them mention witchcraft to you?

—They didn't specifically say witchcraft, but as well as nature, I got the impression there was some kind of spiritual side that was important to them both. Which, as I see it, is the same kind of thing as white witchcraft or paganism. Ronan was talking about the ancient art of divination once. It was used back in the olden days when they'd have needed that to find water to survive. He told me he used to do it when he was younger. And Caris read my tarot cards a few times, and blimey, I was shocked. She was spot-on! She had a gift for it, that girl, she really did.

—Do you know of anything significant that happened to Caris when she was around fifteen years old?

—I've been listening to this podcast, and I heard what that teacher said about Caris. It all sounds ridiculous to me. Plenty of teenagers write about dark things. I've heard some of the music they listen to about death and destruction. About gangs and gun crime and killing people. It sounds like pretty normal teenage behaviour to me, and I've met quite a few in my job, believe me. It doesn't mean they all turn out to be killers, does it? I think Caris was sad and alienated rather than dangerous or evil.

I don't know if anything happened to her specifically around that time, but then I didn't see her enough to really make a sound judgment on that. I do remember Ronan saying he was more worried about Caris than usual then. They always had a close relationship, but she became a bit more distant from him around that time. Less talkative with him. If he asked her what was going on in her life, she'd clam up. The shutters would come down. So he didn't push her. He put it down to general teenage hormones. When my niece hit *the terrible teens, she could barely grunt a hello to me or her mum for years. She'd hide away in her bedroom for hours and didn't want to socialise with the rest of the family. Again, that's pretty normal behaviour at that age, I think.*

—Did you ever see Flora at the house with Caris?

—No, I never did. Ronan told me how Caris and Flora had become best friends. He was really happy for Caris. He knew it wasn't good for her to be stuck in the house all the time with a semi-invalid, looking after him. He wanted her to go off and have fun, be happy. His illness meant he'd lost his free spirit, and he didn't want Caris to lose hers. So he encouraged their friendship.

Flora was always very sweet when I saw her, but I didn't really know her well. She'd take round food hampers to some of my Helping Hands people at Christmastime and was usually collecting signatures for petitions for various things. I'd see her and Caris both together out and about sometimes. And they both worked in Willow's shop, so I'd see them in there when I'd pop in to get a birthday gift for someone. I loved the candles they had in there. They smelled divine! But with all these animals around, I can never be sure one of the little monkeys won't knock it off a table and the whole place would be up in smoke!

And just then, as if to chime in on the conversation, one of the dogs starts barking. This quickly sets off a cacophony of barks and play fights in the conservatory. The dogs run around, bounding into the glass windows, and the cats scarper out of the cat flap into the garden. The rabbits and ferrets are probably crapping themselves in their cages.

Pam rushes into the conservatory and spends a few minutes calming things down before returning to the lounge. She's tried to tempt me with a slice of carrot cake since I arrived, and I finally succumb. When she comes back with a pot of tea in a knitted tea cosy that's reminiscent of one my gran used to have and a slice of cake, we resume.

—Did you take your dogs to see Ronan on any of your visits?

—*Oh yes. He loved dogs. They always had them on the caravan sites.*

—And what about Caris? Did she ever see your dogs at the house?

—*A few times, yes. She'd always make a fuss of them. She loved animals. They both did. She always put scraps of bread or seed out in the garden for the birds. She loved watching them. She could tell me what every kind of variety was. She'd point them out to me. She could even tell them apart from their song. And it was in those moments, when she was stroking the dogs or looking at the birds, that she seemed to lose all the tension she was holding in tight.*

—That's at real odds from the stories we've been told about Caris killing a bird outside her house, sacrificing animal parts, and being responsible for the animal mutilations in the area. Which side of Caris do you think is true? The crazed bird killer and possible animal mutilator or the bird and animal lover?

—*I don't believe any of those stories at all. It's just more malicious gossip.*

My eyes stray to the conservatory again, where the dogs have resumed a sleepy, head-on-paws position. There's Cookie, Pam's yellow Labrador, and Scooch, her golden retriever.

—There was one more piece of DNA evidence found on Flora's body at the crime scene that hasn't been discussed yet, and that was a golden-coloured dog hair found on the front of her top.

—Yes, that's right. At first, the police thought the hair had been transferred from Caris's clothes onto Flora. And I'm sure their nosy neighbour didn't waste any time telling the police that I brought my dogs round there to see Ronan. The little monkeys' fur moults something awful sometimes, and when I was running a vacuum round Ronan's place, I'd always be finding their hairs.

The police did a DNA test on my pooches. Apparently, they can do DNA testing on animal hairs now and match it to a particular dog. The results proved it wasn't any of my dogs, so then the police changed their theory about the dog hair, believing instead that Flora had picked it up somewhere in Blackleaf Forest as she and Caris walked through it to Witch's Hill.

—From the look on your face, that doesn't sound plausible to you.

—Not when you look at the whole picture. It could've been transferred when Flora and Caris stripped down to their underwear to carry out the bathing part of their ritual and Flora's clothes picked up a stray hair. It could have been blown onto Flora's top, or Flora brushed against it as they journeyed through the forest. But it's also possible it came from somewhere else entirely, isn't it?

—Did you ever see a violent side to Caris?

—Like I said, I didn't know her that well. But in my job, dealing with thousands of people in my career—often people who are at their lowest ebb or are vulnerable because they're ill—you get a good feel for people quickly. You learn to read people. I never saw a violent streak in her. Quite the opposite, in fact.

I think Caris was a very strong girl. She was dealing with the death of her mum, all the rubbish people said about her, a new environment, new way of life, new school, and trying to cope with looking after her dad. Most people at that age would crack under the strain, but she didn't. She just dealt with things. Kept things inside. Carried her head high and got on with the cards she'd been dealt.

—There's another side to that, though. Is it possible Caris was under such emotional and social strain for years, trying to hold things together, trying to be strong, that one day she did snap? Did she suddenly turn on her best friend because everything became too much? All the pressure that must've built up has a release point.

—*I don't believe that at all.*

—What about the report that Caris regularly smoked cannabis? Couldn't a previous heavy use of it in the past have exacerbated a temporary psychosis? Or maybe the ketamine did?

—*Caris didn't smoke cannabis. Ronan did. The disease he suffered from gives people a lot of pain, and he said it really helped. It's not illegal now, is it, if it's for medicinal use? The GP gave him pain meds, which helped at first, but then they didn't touch it anymore, so he got Caris to buy it for him. Ronan would tell me all about the healing properties of plants, the way medicine used to be years ago—just like the homeopathy Willow does. Before there were licensed pharmaceuticals and manufactured drugs, people used plants and herbal medicines. A lot of plants are still the basis for modern-day prescription drugs. And Ronan would always say that's where we've gone wrong. We're messing with nature. Fighting with it instead of preserving it. If you look at most ancient communities, there was always a plant for an ailment. The gypsies were the same. And cannabis and hemp have got some amazing properties. Not just for illnesses, but for manufacturing clothing and all sorts of things. But you can't patent nature, can you? The big pharmaceutical companies can't patent the cannabis plant, so, of course, when people knew way back when that it was a wonder plant, it was outlawed because it would affect their sales of prescription drugs.*

—So the only drugs Caris bought were for Ronan?

—*Yes. It was all for Ronan. And from what I understand, there were no drugs found in either Flora's or Caris's system from that night apart from the ketamine and alcohol.*

—Were you ever aware of any mental health issues Caris might've had?

—Ha! Everyone's got some kind of mental health issues. Whether it's having a low mood for a few days, having OCD, general stress of life, or more serious things. But no, I don't think Caris had any mental health issues. Which is pretty damn amazing when you think about her life, actually. Stronger people would crack under the pressure.

—Do you think it's possible that, whether accidentally or in a ketamine-induced hallucination or with premeditation, Caris strangled Flora?

—No. Absolutely not. I can say that with no hesitation whatsoever. I believe Caris's version of what happened that night. I think someone laced their wine when they weren't looking. I think both girls did their summer solstice blessing—I don't like to call it a ritual, because that's what the gutter press jumped all over, turning it into a satanic murder! And I think the ketamine rendered them incapacitated and unconscious and left Caris with no memory. Someone else was out there that night, I'm sure of it. Someone who ruined both their lives. I also think the dog hair came from the killer.

I just want to add that when I was a nurse, I dealt with a few cases of victims who'd had their drinks spiked and been sexually assaulted. One with ketamine and two with Rohypnol. They came into A&E the next day and none of them could remember a thing about it. Ketamine can actually block memories from forming, which means it's not just a case of a victim suffering from short-term amnesia where a memory might later resurface. It was devastating for those victims, but in some ways, it's probably a blessing that they don't remember. Dreadful, dreadful thing to happen to them. I felt sick for them. I really did. I think Caris is a victim here, just like Flora.

Someone could've been stalking them, like their legal team thought.

—Did Caris ever mention to you that someone was harassing them on their Pretty Little Witch Things Instagram page for a few months when they were fifteen?

—*No, I didn't know that. It's not something Caris would've told me. As I say, she didn't ever truly open up to me. I think Ronan would've told me if he knew, but she probably wouldn't have wanted to worry him with it.*

—Can you think of any particular reason for someone to target Flora and Caris?

—*Gosh, no. I mean, not apart from the obvious prejudice Caris always had to put up with that I've already spoken about—people not liking their gypsy heritage and not trusting them. They called her a witch, when really she was just a spiritual kind of person. And I didn't know Flora well, but maybe someone was jealous of them. They were both stunning girls. Absolutely beautiful. And they were making a real go of their online business with the spell boxes and things. It's really popular now, isn't it? That kind of thing. It was nice Caris and Ronan had some spare cash coming in because they'd been living on Ronan's invalidity benefits before that, trying to make ends meet. And some people just don't like it when others start to do well, let alone someone they feel isn't worthy of it.*

—I have one last question for you. How did Ronan cope with the guilty verdict, and what happened after he found out?

Pam pauses, her eyes glistening with tears. Her lips press together, and she clutches her hands in front of her chest.

—*He couldn't go to the trial. By then it was agony for him to move about, but he still wouldn't admit he needed a wheelchair. At that time, he was sleeping downstairs on the sofa because he couldn't get up the stairs. He needed to be in a care home when Caris was in* prison on remand, waiting for the trial, but he wouldn't leave the house. He was waiting for her to come back. He was pinning all his hopes on her being found not guilty, like any parent would. But he wouldn't get a doctor to reassess him and find a care home placement, no matter how much I nagged at him. He never liked to admit that he couldn't cope, and he knew that if he wasn't there, the council house would go, and Caris wouldn't have a home to come back to.

He couldn't even visit Caris when she was on remand, because he was too poorly. I went a few times. I passed his love onto her. She said to tell Ronan to just forget about her and get the help he needed. She was worried about him, of course. She wanted him somewhere he was going to be looked after full-time, but he wouldn't have it.

I went to Ronan's house, and we watched the verdict together as it was being announced on the news. Naturally, he was devastated. But what with all the tabloids slurring Caris left, right, and centre, it was inevitable she'd be found guilty.

He got really pale, really still. And he just said, 'Well, that's it, then'.

And then... he told me to go. I didn't want to leave him alone, but I had to respect his wishes, so I left there with a lump in my throat. I was due to go round the next morning, which I did. I had a spare key, you see, to let myself in every day.

When I got inside, I... I found him on the sofa. He'd used his strong painkillers and taken an overdose. He was always trying to be strong for Caris, trying to just carry on with what was a daily struggle of pain. When she was convicted, I think he didn't want to struggle anymore.

Whoever killed Flora didn't just kill one person. They killed Ronan too. And they ruined Caris's life and Willow's life, as well. I hope they get what they deserve. I hope you find the man in the woods that night. I hope they finally have to answer for what they've done.

. . .

I leave Pam's house full of tea, cake, and a sense of confusion about Caris's personality. Was she someone who kept things inside until she reached a boiling point, when something triggered her physical anger and she lashed out? Like she lashed out at the bully who'd been tormenting her at school and, possibly, lashed out at Flora because she was keeping a dark secret about Caris that became a simmering catalyst bringing things to a head on that fateful night?

None of us are all just one thing. We're a mixture of good and bad, happy and sad, kind and selfish, and all types of polar-opposite personality traits and emotions. In this episode, I've seen a different side of Caris. The strain she was under in her life is more palpable, but there's a caring side to her nature that was never shown in the media or public eye before. And as Pam seems to be the closest person to the family I've spoken to so far, I think it's perhaps a more genuine version of Caris. But if you believe that version, then it stands to reason you believe the unidentified man from Blackleaf Forest exists. Did he have a motive to kill Flora? Or is there someone else out there who was jealous of Flora? Perhaps jealous of her beauty or her business success? Or a lover or ex-lover of Flora's? Apart from the rumours of Flora and Caris being in a lesbian relationship, there's certainly been no mention of a girlfriend or boyfriend Flora was involved with, no apparent sexual element to the crime, and so far, I haven't found any real motive that, to me, makes sense of Flora's elaborately staged murder.

Some questions are being answered, and some anomalies are clicking into place, but there's still a long way to go. The people you've heard from so far have all really been on the periphery of Flora's and Caris's lives, and in the next episode, you'll hear from someone closer to home.

We've had several leads coming into the research team with tips about the E-FIT picture on the website. Most have been dead ends, but we're still searching for him. Don't forget to check it out, and get in touch if you recognise the man.

Please keep the comments coming on the website. I always love hearing your views.

Thank you for listening to *Anatomy of a Crime*.

Until next time...

123456 • 1 day ago
Leanne was right. Dawn and her family were nasty bullies at school. But no one dared do anything about it. The headmaster was a wimp. He was too scared of their family. They were all thugs!
^ | ˅ • Reply • Share ˃

Currantbun → Reply to 123456 • 1 day ago
I agree. My son was bullied by Joe, one of Dawn's brothers, because he was overweight.
But Dawn used to do it as well. They made his life a misery! And to think Dawn had the cheek to call Caris a dirty gypsy. Dawn's family are scrap-metal dealers and thieves.
They're a bunch of rough, dirty scumbags themselves.
^ | ˅ • Reply • Share ˃

Stormy • 1 day ago
Where did the dog hair come from? I've never heard about that before. Maybe if you find the dog, you'll find the real killer. I've heard too much that makes me think Damian's story is right. I think the hair was transferred from that man on to Flora's top.
^ | ˅ • Reply • Share ˃

LOL369 → Reply to Stormy • 1 day ago
What? It couldve got their any number of wayz. It prob dont mean nothing at all. I rekon Flora got it from walking in the woodz.
^ | ˅ • Reply • Share ˃

666 → Reply Stormy • 1 day ago
The dog hair probably came from one of the animals she murdered!!!!
^ | ˅ • Reply • Share ˃

Whisper11 • 2 days ago
I think we've all been lied to by the police. Who is @InsRule? I bet he was stalking Flora for years. I had a stalker once, and he was crazy. I didn't even know him. He started up some website with these naked photos of me where he'd photoshopped my head onto other bodies, and he made it look like I'd set it up. And he kept leaving presents on my doorstep and following me. It took months and months for the police to do something. Someone had to have followed them into the woods. Then they framed Caris for it.
^ | ˅ • Reply • Share ˃

40Tats → Reply to Whisper11 • 1 day ago
Yeah, right. What's wrong with you? Kelly did it!
^ | ˅ • Reply • Share ˃

AFFFF → Reply to 40Tats • 1 day ago
I'm a local and there is something familiar about that E-FIT, but I don't know what. Why would Kelly kill her friend like that? It would be much easier to drown her in the river and say it was an accident. It all seems too questionable to me. Posing Flora inside the stones and the pentagram all feels wrong. I think Caris's been set up, and I feel sorry for her. She had a really tough life, by the sound of it.

^ | ˅ • Reply • Share ˃

40Tats → Reply to AFFFF • 1 day ago
She was a lesbian drug pusher and a murderer!
^ | ˅ • Reply • Share ˃

FlUff69 → Reply to 40Tats • 1 day ago
Cannabis is a wonder drug that's been suppressed by the
government for years. It should never have been banned in the first
place. And anyway, Caris bought it for her dad's pain. Even if she
was a lesbian, so what? You bigoted bird-brain! If your kind of
person was on the jury, no wonder they found her guilty.
^ | ˅ • Reply • Share ˃

Tuti • 2 days ago
I bet they were lesbians. Then Flora found someone else and Caris
couldn't handle it. That's why she really killed her. Homos are an
unnatural abomination.
^ | ˅ • Reply • Share ˃

Scampi → Reply to Tuti • 1 day ago
Oh, god! Get your head out of your arse and join the 21st Century!
^ | ˅ • Reply • Share ˃

WhitlingSTOCK • 2 days ago
I'm starting to think Caris's innocent. She had a really bad life, and
the one good thing in it was Flora. I don't think she would've killed
her. The stalker angle theory makes more sense. Scary that the
police never tried to trace the man Damian saw. What else did they
miss? How could the jury think there was no reasonable doubt?
There's plenty of doubt here, the more I listen to this.
^ | ˅ • Reply • Share ˃

126

Gooners → Reply to WhitlingSTOCK • 1 day ago
There's NO doubt in my mind Kelly killed her. People have been saying the posed murder scene was too elaborate, but it was all reverse psychology. She MADE it look elaborate so it wouldn't seem like her. The truth is stranger than fiction.
^ | ˅ • Reply • Share ˃

Colonel Mustard → Reply to Gooners • 1 day ago
I agree. Guilty! Guilty! Guilty!
^ | ˅ • Reply • Share ˃

Scampi → Reply to Colonel Mustard • 1 day ago
Wow, such a well-thought-out reasoning. Why is she guilty? I've heard no convincing evidence that she is. The DNA evidence is easily explainable.
It's all circumstantial. There's no proper motive. And a lot of it is based on hearsay and rumours that have turned out to be lies.
^ | ˅ • Reply • Share ˃

Colonel Mustard → Reply to Scampi • 1 day ago
She was keeping a dark lesbian, animal-killing secret and didn't want to be exposed!
^ | ˅ • Reply • Share ˃

CHAPTER EIGHT

FLORA (Aged 15)

The doorbell above the shop door jingled, and I glanced up from the laptop behind the counter, smiling at Andrew Strytch as he came in for his weekly homeopathic appointment.

'Hi. Mum's in her office, so you can go straight in,' I said.

'Thank you.' He walked past me and nodded.

I watched him head towards the back of the shop before looking down at the laptop and grinning. 'Wow! We've had three new orders for spell boxes,' I shouted to Caris, who had her back to me, polishing the candleholders. 'That makes twenty-six this week. I know it sounds small, but once our name gets out there, I'm sure this is going to be huge. Amethyst Witch said when she started—'

A clattering sound broke my gaze away from the screen towards Caris. A brass candleholder lay on its side on the floor where she'd dropped it, and her shoulders were hunched up, her body frozen.

'Are you okay? Caris? Hey, what's wrong?' I jumped off the stool and rounded the counter. She still had her back to me, and her whole body shivered. I stood in front of her, put my hands on her shoulders. Tears streaked down her cheeks, and she wouldn't look at me. 'What's going on? Is it something with your dad?'

Caris took a shuddering breath and squeezed her eyes shut, splashing a dribble of tears onto the floor.

'Hey.' I wrapped my arms around her in a tight hug. Everything about her felt stiff and awkward, like she was a stranger who didn't want me to touch her. 'Whatever's wrong, I can help. I know *something's* going on. It's been going on for weeks, even though you keep denying it. You've been jumpy and nervous, and you keep forgetting things. Are you ill? Has your dad got worse?'

Caris rested her head on my shoulder and sobbed silently, her warm breath on my neck.

'You've *got* to tell me. That's what friends are for. To help. To share things with. *Please.* Just tell me what's going on.' I rubbed her back, the heat from her radiating beneath my palm.

'I can't tell you.' Her fingertips clutched my top as if she didn't want to let go. 'I can't...'

'You *can*. We can sort it out together, whatever the problem is.' I pulled back and looked at her, tears smarting in my own eyes now at the horrified look on her face. 'I'm going to lock the door. Mum'll be in her office for a while. Then you can tell me.' I darted to the door, pulled the catch across, and put the closed sign up. Then I took her hand and led her into the small kitchen, out of sight from the shop floor.

She still wouldn't look at me. Her face was red, her features twisted into a snarl. I knew all her expressions so well, but I'd never seen this one before.

'Why don't we do a spell?' I tried to smile, but I felt nervous suddenly, like something dangerous was about to happen.

'A spell won't work this time!' She glared at me.

I took a step back, the venom hurled at me in her voice taking me by surprise. We didn't fight. We never had done. We were one

129

and the same, Caris and me. I swallowed, the moisture evaporating in my mouth. 'Have I done something to upset you?'

She wrapped her arms around her waist and sank to the floor, her knees up against her chest.

I sat beside her. There was no way I'd give up on her. That would be the same as giving up on myself. I took her hand and squeezed it. 'Just tell me.'

And eventually, she did. Later, after she'd rushed out of the shop. After I'd told Mum she'd had to get back home for an emergency with her dad. After I'd gone through the motions of cashing up the till. I walked home with Mum, trying to pretend everything was normal, then rushed into my bedroom and shut the door.

It couldn't be happening. It could *not* be happening. It was horrific. Insane. And I didn't know what to do about it. I felt so... useless. So angry. So... argh!

I paced the room, chewing madly on my fingernail. Hot pain stabbed at the centre of my chest. My stomach churned. My chakras were blown apart by this. I needed to calm down. *Stop. Take a breath. Think. Get those things out of my head so I can focus on the answer. Work out how to reclaim the power.*

I turned on some solfeggio frequency music to help the ancient, scared chants become stronger. Then I lit an incense stick in the wooden burner on my dresser and sat cross-legged on the floor, watching the scented smoke drifting up, dancing in front of my eyes before I closed them.

I chanted the mantra over and over, visualising an intense powerful light encapsulating me, raining down its special powers. After the meditation, I lit candles and placed them in a circle, sitting down in the middle of them and reciting a spell.

When the ritual was over, I sat cross-legged on the floor with my laptop open, searching for some kind of answer. There *was* something I could do about this.

CHAPTER NINE

HUMILIATION

They laugh at me. They think it's all hilarious. That I'm hilarious. A joke to be ridiculed. They look at me with disgust and contempt, but they need to take a good look at themselves. They're disgusting, shallow, and pathetic.

I've risen above all that now. It used to get to me big time. At first, I'd go into myself. Shrink inside. Scurry away. Hide. Sometimes, though, you can hide in plain sight. Sometimes that's the best place.

I've changed now. I've learned, grown, and found others like me. I've discovered my army, and they understand me completely. They made me realise I'm not the odd one out. I know who I truly am, and I'm fine with it. There's no point trying to stop your inner truth, is there? You can try, for a while, but it never works. It's empowering to know I'm not alone. Makes me bolder. Dream bigger.

I've grown into a chameleon. I can change on the outside, mask the real me when it's necessary. And I don't care what the humiliating dogs think anymore. Because I know now what it takes to fool them. It takes courage. Strength. Intelligence. I'm not being lied to about how things work anymore. I'm making things work how *I* want them to.

I log on to the forum and read through the latest posts, the excitement building, smiling as I digest each one, studying the tips and tricks, looking for new, challenging ways to do things. Sometimes the rage and hatred take over and spew through my fingertips onto the keyboard, and I revel in it. Let it flow.

Eventually, I call up my old posts and look at the one that gives me the most pride. It's had over a million hits now. I'm famous. Not so shabby for someone like me after all.

I think about you again. You laughed, too, once.

But who's laughing now?

CHAPTER TEN

NOW

I finish my current interview and check my phone. I've reached out to a few possible witnesses I'm hoping to speak to and still waiting for their replies. But I've got lots of patience. It's essential in this job. It takes a long time to track down all the threads that tie a crime to its final conclusion.

The only message I've had is a text from my mobile phone provider, telling me I could win a holiday if I send a message to a preset number to enter. I delete it and sip a glass of wine as I sit at the table in the rental cottage's kitchen-diner, editing the latest recording. There have been no more unusual things left for me in the letter box. No sign of anyone following me, although I'm still getting that sixth-sense feeling that someone's watching me. Maybe it's paranoia. Maybe not.

The following morning, my mobile phone rings at 6.16 a.m. I never sleep well, and I've been awake since five anyway, tossing and turning, going over and over in my head everything I've learned so far. I sit up in bed and answer the call, but no one speaks. There's some noise filtering though. It sounds like traffic, like someone's in a car whizzing along the road. I get no response to my helloes, and it could just be innocent—a pocket call or someone dialling a wrong number. That's what I put it down to until the others started.

They're mostly silent, coming in at all times of the day, and always from the same number, which my technical researchers have discovered is an unregistered pay-as-you-go phone—surprise, surprise. I listen carefully, trying to pick up clues as to who might be doing it, but all I hear is background noise, sometimes people's voices, and occasionally the sound of music or a TV in the background. Usually, I stay on the line for a minute or so, picturing the person on the other end laughing to themselves. It seems I have my own troll right now. I could block the number, but I don't. I want them to keep calling. I want them to slip up and show themselves.

Two days later, my phone rings again. I glance at the screen before I answer, but it's a different phone number to whoever's trying to harass me.

'You're the person doing the podcast about the witch killing, yeah?' a woman's voice asks.

'I am indeed. How can I help you?'

'Um... I know something. I've got some information about Caris and Flora you need to know.'

'Can you give me an indication about what kind of information?'

She hesitates for a moment, and I imagine her on the other end. I listen to people all day long, and I'm usually good with voices. She sounds in her early twenties.

'I'd rather not say yet. Can we meet up?'

'Of course. Where and when were you thinking of?'

'What about today? This afternoon? Maybe oneish? I could meet you at the café at Lulworth Cove.'

I grab a pen from the kitchen table and scribble that down on my pad. 'I can do that. Can you give me your name?'

'I want to be anonymous. Like that teacher.'

'Okay. How will I recognise you?'

'I've got long dark hair and brown eyes. I'm twenty-three. I'll be wearing black leggings and a pink T-shirt that says Drama Queen on it. I'll wait for you at the entrance to the café's terrace, where there's a picket fence.'

I'm about to tell her what I look like, but she says in a hushed voice that she has to go and hangs up abruptly.

It's a twenty-mile trip from Stoneminster to the cove that's a World Heritage site near the village of West Lulworth. I pull into the huge gravel-lined car park that can house thousands of vehicles with ten minutes to spare. The place is almost full already, and I park in a spot next to the hedgerow at the back. Hundreds of thousands of tourists visit here every year, and it's already littered with swarms of them. Some walking up the steep incline of the coastal path leading to the rock arch of Durdle Door. Some eating on the terraced area of the café, making the most of the summer's day. Thick clusters of them heading down the narrow path to the cove. Families pushing buggies or holding onto toddlers' hands. Couples. People in hiking gear. An elderly tour group disembarking from a bus.

I watch the entrance to the café for a few minutes but can't see Miss Anonymous waiting yet. With five minutes to spare, I get out of the car and slip into the crowd. I wait next to the picket-fenced entrance to the café, where two blackboards proudly display the menu and daily specials. I scan the people filtering past me. A child bursts into tears when the ice cream he's holding slips from his hand and onto the path. A group of teenagers laughs loudly on the terrace as they share one chocolate Sunday with four spoons. A couple pause in front of the blackboard, deciding what toasted sandwich to have. No one pays me much attention.

I glance at my watch again. *1.16 p.m. Is she going to be a no-show?*

At 1.20 p.m., I call her number, but it's doesn't ring. The number's dead. Either switched off or now out of service. It's not unusual for a witness to get cold feet or have second thoughts. I give it another ten minutes and head back through the throngs to my car.

I press the remote control to open it, but the flat sound I hear tells me it's already unlocked. I glance swiftly around the car, checking for a broken window or a missing stereo, but there's no damage. Although I don't remember locking it, it's an automatic action, like putting on my seat belt. Just one of the thousands of subconscious habits we do every day. It was definitely secure when I left, which means someone's overridden the central locking somehow, which isn't difficult if you know what you're doing.

I look around the crowd, searching for someone paying me too much attention, anyone who looks suspicious. There's no one obvious. No one watching me. They're minding their own business. Lost in their own worlds. As I clutch the door handle and pull it open, I stare at the message sitting on the driver's seat.

It's a wicker doll, crudely made, with dobs of black pen for eyes and out-of-proportion lips drawn in red. Black plaited string covers the head as makeshift long hair. A pin sticks out of the area where the heart would be. A poor attempt at a voodoo doll.

Somehow, the threat feels more sinister because it's subtle, psychological. If an assailant came at me full-on, showing themselves, I'd know who the enemy was. So, yes, I'm unnerved. Scared. I'd be stupid not to be. The knife I've been keeping close at hand in the cottage is for protection. I know they want to get to me, stress me out, and make me stop what I'm doing. Are they listening to the podcast? Most definitely. I know they want me to speak about what they're doing on air, and I won't give them the satisfaction.

But I'm not the only one who's scared. My stalker is too. Otherwise, they wouldn't be going to all this trouble.

CHAPTER ELEVEN

EPISODE 4
HEARTBREAK

—I don't think I can ever forgive her. I let her into our lives, and she betrayed us. I know other people, other parents, often publicly declare their forgiveness to their child's murderer, and when I hear them say it, I always think, How can you do that? How can you forgive someone for ripping your heart out? For taking away the child you nurtured and watched grow into an amazing person. I can't. I just can't do that.

Welcome back to *Anatomy of a Crime*. In this series, we're exploring the tragic murder of Flora Morgan in June 2017. Her best friend, Caris Kelly, was convicted of the crime and is now serving a life sentence.

The voice you've just heard belongs to Willow Morgan, Flora's mum. She's agreed to break her three-year media silence and speak to me.

In previous episodes, you heard how she ran a New Age shop and homeopathy practice from a premises in Stoneminster's high street, but in late 2017, she closed the shop and moved to a village on the outskirts of Bath, where she now runs her homeopathy business from her home. This is where I meet her.

There are essences of that old shop dotted around her small cottage. Buddhas, candles, incense burners, colourful Indian prints on the walls, wooden elephants. It feels cosy and homely, but there's a gaping, empty chasm where Flora should be.

—You've never spoken to the press before about Flora. Can you explain to our listeners why you kindly agreed to speak to me now?

—*When you contacted me at first and said you were going to do a podcast about Flora's murder, I was devastated. I didn't want everything being raked up again. It was painful enough the first time. The press just wouldn't leave me alone. They were camped outside the shop. Outside my house. And they were making up all kinds of stories to sell their papers. Not just stories. Lies. Blatant lies. They printed absolutely ridiculous things, like Flora and Caris used to drink blood. That they worshipped the devil. That they did animal sacrifices. At one point, they were saying my daughter was having a lesbian love affair with Caris involving sadomasochism fetishes, and that Caris was jealous of Flora seeing someone else and killed her. You saw what they've written over the years. They didn't care about Flora. They didn't respect my privacy. I know you're playing devil's advocate sometimes, and you have to try to be impartial, but you're still giving people a fair hearing.*

—Thank you for telling your story now. My aim is always to get to the root of the crime, and I'm glad you approve of the podcast so far. As you said, the press didn't care about Flora or what she was like. How would you describe your daughter?

—*Flora was... different from most of her peers. She was a real* individual. I suppose that was partly my influence. I've always been an old hippie at heart. My parents were the same. I suppose with a name like Willow, that's a bit of a giveaway.

When other kids her own age were playing their computer games or on their social media accounts or glued to a TV, I was teaching Flora about nature and the outdoors. Being a homeopath, it was my business and my passion. I'd teach her about plants, and she loved it—she really did. She always hated being cooped up inside.

She dressed differently to her friends too. She didn't follow the latest name-brand fashions these young girls do these days. She liked getting vintage clothes from charity shops. And she was New Agey, as well. Again, that's probably my influence, but I never forced her. I always let her choose her clothes and the hairstyles she liked, even when she was young. I always let her express herself how she wanted to.

I think she was self-aware, self-confident. She knew who she was from an early age. She was also very principled. She hated injustice. She cared about the environment and people and the world in general. She was always doing some sort of activism, either getting people to sign petitions or donate to various causes. She'd make things to sell in the shop to save the badgers or save the hedgehogs or bee boxes for people to use in their gardens, and she'd donate some of her profits to various charities. Or she'd be rallying up people she met into donating to various causes. We used to go on some social and ethical demonstrations together, as well. I couldn't keep up with her, though. One minute, she was trying to raise awareness to famine and drought in various places in the world, and the next, she was organising collections of food and clothing donations for the homeless shelters. Again, most kids are too distracted with things to really take on board the world they're living in at that age. But Flora was... if she'd... if she hadn't have been killed, I could see her becoming full-time activist or something like that.

She could be stubborn. When she'd made her mind up about

something, that was it. And she was loyal, caring, loving. She was someone who followed her passions.

—Flora and Caris became friends soon after Caris moved to Stoneminster, didn't they?

—Yes. When they were both thirteen. So it would've been 2012. As other people have told you, they went to the same school. Flora didn't have many friends. She hung around with Leanne a bit, but most of Flora's social causes kept her pretty busy. She had I suppose what you or I would call acquaintances. She liked a few people at school, but she didn't like them enough to make them her friends, if that makes sense. She was an all or nothing kind of girl. She was happy in her own skin and didn't really need any friends to hang around with. Didn't need others to validate her. Maybe it's because she was an only child, so she was used to it. Her dad, my husband, died when Flora was two. He was a fitness fanatic. He'd run ten miles before breakfast. He watched what he ate and drank. And then suddenly, he had a heart attack and died. We found out later that he had a congenital heart condition that no one ever knew about. So from a young age, it was just me and Flora.

I think people at school liked Flora, too, but they didn't really get her. Until Caris came along. Flora came home one day and said she'd been talking to this girl who'd just moved to the school and that they'd really hit it off. She said Caris was into the same kinds of things—nature, alternative medicine, and witchcraft. Not, I hasten to add, all the rubbish the tabloids talked about. Flora had a passion for Wicca and pagan-style spiritualism. Flora would have her book of modern spells and read angel cards for me or herself. I'd come home and find crystals or coins and other charms hidden under furniture in the four corners of the house, and it was one of Flora's spells.

—How did you feel about these spells?

—A spell is just a series of words with magical belief in them. It's about putting out an intention to the universe or earthly *goddesses or archangels or whoever you believe in, usually either asking them for something you want or thanking them for something in your life. It's no different to praying to God or Allah or Buddha. It's not all this rubbish about using bits of animals or voodoo dolls or a coven of witches plotting evil things around a cauldron. Flora's spells used incantations to manifest what she wanted in life. Or to help people. Or for the healing of the earth. And the charms she used in the spells were things like candles, feathers she found, stones, crystals, earth, leaves, essential oils. They were prayers. Just prayers.*

—Do you think Caris's gypsy heritage, which encompassed those kinds of old elements, helped forge the friendship?

—I'm sure it did. Caris and Flora just connected in a way that had never happened with Flora before. And I encouraged it because both girls seemed to love each other. Again, there were a lot of rumours about Caris and Ronan going round the town. Spiteful rumours. I didn't believe them at the time. I always took people on their face value, and it was something Flora always did too. Maybe that's a mistake now, looking back on things. Maybe I should've listened to some of the things people had been saying. I think there were warning signs already there, but I just didn't listen or see them. I was...

Willow fiddles with the ends of the sequinned scarf tied around her hair and chews on her lower lip for a moment before looking towards a photo of herself and Flora on top of an ethnic wooden sideboard. Their heads are pressed together, smiling for the camera, and the similarity between them is very striking. I find myself imagining Flora and Caris together. Flora with her peaches-and-cream complexion, pale blue-grey eyes, freckles, and rich auburn hair, and Caris, with her olive skin, jet-black hair, and jade-green eyes with lashes so thick they look almost doll-like. Total opposites on the outside, but with personalities and interests that were so firmly interlinked.

It's obvious to me Willow is trying to remain stoic, and it's only the wobble in her voice and the pain behind her eyes that tells me this is still as raw for her now, three years on, as it was then.

—*I guess I was partly to blame for letting Caris in, but I never saw that side to her. The side that made her kill Flora. I just… It all came as a complete shock. Caris ended up being like a surrogate daughter to me. She spent a lot of time at our house with Flora and also in my shop. Caris helped Flora make craft items to sell, and Flora and Caris both worked at the shop at weekends and in the school holidays. It was a bit of pocket money for Caris, because Ronan had his health problems and was on disability benefits. It was tough for them. And before they'd even left school, when they were fifteen, Caris came up with the idea of running an online business together. Flora designed the website, and they made up these spell boxes. They had things like individualised spells written in them, a tarot card, candles, dreamcatchers, crystals, little knick-knacks like that. It was going really well. And Caris also did online tarot card readings from the website. Caris's mum taught Caris how to read them, and she was spookily accurate.*

—How would you describe Caris?

—*Back then, you mean? Or how I see her now?*

—Back then. When she was friends with Flora.

—*When I observed Caris and Flora together, it was like Caris was a different person. But when she wasn't with Flora, she was very introverted. I'd see snatches of… I don't know. At the time, I thought it was sadness, but now I think it was just an emptiness inside her. Something was missing in her that makes people human. She was polite and friendly to me, but there was always something about her… something closed off… on guard, as if she never really wanted to* let herself go. Whenever I'd ask her something personal, she'd just clam up. Shut down. She never confided in me about anything.

—As if she was playing a part when she was with Flora? Do you think it was an act?

—I didn't at the time, but I suppose I must've been blind and stupid. Now I think it must've been an act. I knew her for five years, but I didn't really know her. It was as if she had this shield around her. And back then, I could kind of understand why. The difficulties she went through when she was young, losing her mum like that, her family, her whole lifestyle and sense of identity, really. And then there was the other side of it. She was caring for Ronan a lot of the time. She was doing all the adulting—food shopping, cooking, cleaning, plus her studies. And there was a lot of prejudice and racism against Caris and Ronan, too, as you know. I just felt really sorry for her. I don't think she let people get close to her. She didn't want to let people in. Except Flora, of course. And Flora was totally under her spell.

But now I see it wasn't a difficult life she was trying to hide from people. It was her evil darkness.

—Did you ever see any cause for concern with Caris's behaviour?

—No. That's the thing. I didn't see any of this coming. I look back and go over and over things, and I just can't... I couldn't predict what would happen.

—Did you ever witness any arguments or tension or jealousies between Caris and Flora?

—No. Never.

—Were you aware of the troll hassling Flora and Caris on their Pretty Little Witch Things Instagram page when they were fifteen?

—Flora didn't call them a troll. She just said someone was putting messages on their posts that weren't very nice. Attacking them personally. Just saying really horrible things. I'm sure if it wasn't Flora and Caris they were harassing, it would've been

144

someone else. Those kinds of people just like to cause upset, don't they? There are always plenty of nasty people out there who want to hurt others. I told them to delete the comments and ignore it all. I know you interviewed the Amethyst Witch, and she told them the same thing when they asked her for advice.

—Do you remember some of the things he wrote?

—Not specifically. But they were saying things like, 'You think you're pretty, but you're nothing', and they said something like, 'You don't deserve anything good to happen to you'. There were swear words too. It was abusive, and I just thought someone was jealous of their business. Maybe someone who was in competition with them. It only lasted a few months, and that was the end of it.

—Do you know of anyone who might've been jealous of the girls' success with their business?

—No. Not at all. But it doesn't take much for some people to be jealous, does it?

—Did you ever think the problem could be something more serious than that? That it was more than trolling? It was harassment?

—I thought if the person didn't get a response, they'd get bored and stop. And that's what happened in the end. All of us just forgot about it after that. It was just some jealous person who wanted to hurt someone else. I don't think it's relevant in any way to what happened when Caris killed Flora. It was Caris who did this. She's responsible for everything that happened to my daughter.

When the police did their investigation and they told me Caris had murdered Flora in some kind of ritualistic thrill kill, I thought they were telling me some kind of sick joke, but they were adamant that's what had happened. I couldn't believe it at first. But the more I did research on that kind of murder, the more I thought they were right. Police think thrill kills are on the increase. And the evidence all fitted. Flora had Caris's skin under her nails. Caris had corresponding scratch marks on her arm from when she strangled *her. Defensive scratch marks as Flora fought her through the drugged haze Caris had put her in. And Caris's hair caught on Flora's bracelet.*

—Caris's defence team has given an explanation for how that evidence got there. Do you think their version sounds implausible?

—*I think Caris lied about that. I think she lied about a lot of things. Afterwards... when I thought about it, all the dangerous elements in Caris's life were there already, staring me in the face. And I'd missed them. That's when I thought that a lot of the rumours about her must've been true all along. They had to be in the end. And I'd trusted her with my daughter. My...*

Willow breaks down then, and the tears she's been trying to hold inside have free reign to release. I find myself tearing up, too, and I take Willow's hand and sit in silence with her as she lets everything out. Sometimes words aren't needed. Sometimes words aren't good enough.

As I wait for Willow to compose herself, I think she's on the verge of telling me to leave. To end the interview there. After a few minutes, she walks out of the room. I hear the tap in the kitchen going and imagine her splashing water on her face. When she re-enters the room, she sits beside me and tells me she's ready to continue.

—*I feel guilty. As if I should've spotted something really wrong with Caris. I thought I was quite an intuitous person, but I didn't realise. I just didn't know what she was capable of.*

—I can understand that completely. None of this is your fault.

—*I think what hurt a lot at the time was that some people in Stoneminster were saying that it was my fault for encouraging their friendship. That I should've known better than to allow Caris into our lives. I felt the same, but I didn't want it shoved in my face. That was one of the reasons I closed the shop and moved away. That, and because there were too many memories of Flora around. My heart was broken. No, not just broken. Splintered into a million pieces.*

Willow falls silent again. I take a moment before changing direction.

—Did Flora or Caris have a boyfriend?

—*No. At least, not that I knew of anyway. They were always in each other's pockets.*

There was a boy who liked Flora at one point. It was before they'd left school and were working in the shop part-time. She was probably fifteen at the time.

He used to come in a lot at weekends and browse. Except he wasn't browsing. He'd be picking things up and pretending to look at them, but really, he was watching Flora in this kind of love-struck way boys do at that age.

I asked Flora about him one day, and she said he was in the same class as her at school. She said he was okay, but she didn't... How can I put this without sounding rude? She said the boys around Stoneminster weren't on the same level as her. She didn't mean that she thought she was up on this pedestal and they were down there. She just meant that they weren't interested in the same kind of things. They wanted to mess around, not bothering to get jobs, or taking the easiest route possible. Or they were only interested in cars or video games or things Flora didn't care about. That was the other thing about Flora; she was quite a deep person. She didn't care much about small talk or petty things. Maybe some people saw her as aloof or hoity-toity or something. But that wasn't it. She was just different. She wanted to connect with someone deeply. And the person she did connect with on those levels was Caris. Unfortunately.

—What happened with the boy?

—*She said he did ask her out on a date. She told me his name was Lucas. Again, I don't want to sound rude, like he wasn't good enough for my daughter or anything. Who she dated would always have been her choice. But he was an odd sort of boy. For weeks, he'd sit on one of the benches on the village green opposite the shop and just watch the place. That was before he started coming inside and pretending to look at things. You could tell he was totally smitten with Flora, plucking up the courage to speak to her. Apparently, he lived just outside Stoneminster, nearer to Weymouth, and he used to get the bus over just to catch a glimpse of Flora.*

She told me he came into the shop one Saturday and asked her if she wanted to go to a rock concert that was on in Dorchester. Flora told him she wasn't interested. I think she was polite about it. I know she would've been; she was that kind of girl. She wouldn't want to hurt anyone's feelings. She told him no, and he left. And he never came back after that.

—So this would've been in 2014?

—*Yes, sometime then. In the summer.*

—And Flora never heard from Lucas again?

—*Not that I know of. I never saw him again near the shop. Flora never mentioned him again. I think she was relieved he'd stopped hanging around. But she just forgot about it. It wasn't a big deal.*

—Did you ever consider his behaviour to be stalking?

—*What? No! You know what teenage boys are like. He was harmless. When she said no, he disappeared.*

—The troll was at work in the summer of 2014 for a few months around the same time as when Lucas wanted to date Flora. If he'd fixated on Flora for a while, do you think Lucas could've been the troll? That maybe his fixation had become an obsession, and when she turned him down, he fought back online to humiliate or upset her? Teenage boys can be awkward and shy, but they can also be fuelled by anger and raging hormones, especially when they've been rebuffed or feel slighted.

—No. I don't think it was him. He seemed harmless. I heard on one of your earlier episodes with Caris's solicitor that even they didn't think the trolling was relevant to anything. And the idea that there's an imaginary stalker out there is just trying to pin this on someone else so Caris can appeal her conviction. It's completely inconsequential because it happened three years before Flora was killed. It's not important, is it? The police certainly didn't think so. This was all Caris's fault.

—Do you know of anyone else who seemed to pay too much attention to Flora? Or whether she had any enemies?

—No. She didn't have many friends, but there were no enemies that I knew of. Unless you count Caris—the cold and calculating enemy hiding in plain sight.

—I know this next question might sound insensitive, but there have been all sorts of rumours about this case.

—Don't I just know it!

—Apart from the witchcraft-devil-worship angles, the press said Flora and Caris were in a sexual relationship with each other, which you mentioned earlier. Is that another fabrication?

—I want to make this absolutely clear, because the press had a field day with that ridiculous claim. If Flora had been a lesbian, I'd have been the first one telling her to be proud of who she was. It wouldn't have mattered to me what sexual orientation she was, and Flora knew that. As I said, I always gave her the freedom to express herself, and she felt comfortable enough to talk to me about a lot of things. So, no. I don't think they were in any kind of sexual relationship. They were friends. Flora loved her as a friend. I thought Caris loved her the same way—as friends. But she wasn't capable of love, was she? She had a dark void where her heart should've been.

. . .

I think, understandably, Willow could be looking at Flora through rose-tinted glasses. Did you tell your parents all your secrets at that age? I certainly didn't. And even in the most open, progressive parental relationships, the son or daughter might be struggling with ways to express their sexuality or finding it hard to tell their parents. And while I think it's highly likely this was yet another unfounded rumour surrounding the case, and no one has come forward yet to prove the girls were anything more than just friends, if it *is* true, it could be an important part of this case. Love and jealousy are a big motive in many crimes. They're called crimes of passion for a reason. And even if they were just friends, plenty of people have described their relationship as very close. That they loved each other. That they were soul mates. Two halves of a whole. That they connected deeply. Even that kind of platonic love is capable of inciting murder.

—Can you go back to that day? The twenty-first of June 2017. When was the last time you saw Flora, and what did you know about what she and Caris were going to do that night to celebrate the summer solstice?

—*They'd been working in the shop that afternoon. Then she and Caris left at five and said they were going to get some wine before heading to Witch's Hill.*

—Did anyone else know they were going to be at that location that evening?

—*I don't think Caris and Flora really talked to other people around here about the spells they did and the little healing rituals and things like that. People thought they were weird enough as it was. So I doubt they would've told anyone their plans. I didn't even know their plans, actually, until they left. I mean, I knew they were going to celebrate the summer solstice, but I didn't know where they were going or what they were doing specifically.*

When they were leaving, I was a bit distracted because someone had been in the shop and pulled out all of the fabric wall prints to look at and left them in a pile on the table. So I was trying to put them back in some kind of neat order before another customer came in.

They... I'm trying to think now... Flora took some candles from the shelf that she said they needed and put them in her bag, and they walked to the door and opened it. And just as they were leaving, I called out and asked where they were going and when Flora would be home. Flora told me they were going to Witch's Hill to do a spell and ritual and that she probably wouldn't be back until after midnight.

—So the door to the shop was open. Is it possible someone outside on the street could've heard what Flora said?

—*It's possible, I suppose, but what does it matter? It was Caris who did it.*

—You've heard Damian's version of what he saw that night— the man running away from Witch's Hill with Flora's bag. If what he says is true, then Caris might've been telling the truth all along about her innocence. And if that man knew in advance where the girls would be, isn't it possible he followed them and spiked the wine? Then killed Flora?

Willow's face flushes with anger here, and I don't blame her. From the comments coming into the *Anatomy of a Crime* website, there are plenty of people out there who still believe the official police theory. The vast majority think Caris is exactly where she deserves to be. That she's evil, a monster, a psychopath, a witch. But I have to ask the question. There's something deeper going on in this case; I'm sure of it.

Although Willow's been obviously distressed recounting this, she's still been poised. But now her mouth flattens into an angry line as she looks at me with intense dislike. Again, I think she's about to ask me to leave. But she doesn't.

—I don't think Damian is... let's just say reliable. The police didn't think he was a credible witness. I mean, look how he described the man! With a bat face! I understand he's autistic and his linguistics are different to what ours might be, but I never believed what he says he saw.

—Do you think he was lying?

—Maybe that's too strong a word. I can't see why he would lie. But I think he's mistaken. Either he imagined it, or it was some other event that happened in the woods at another time and he mixed it up.

The jury didn't believe him. No one did. There was no one else there that night! Caris killed my daughter, and that's all there is to it.

—Have you looked at the E-FIT picture on our website that Damian helped us to compile?

—Yes. And it doesn't look like anyone I know. I'm not saying Damian did this to hurt me or anything. I'm just saying he's... he's confused.

—But isn't there an anomaly in this case? Damian reported the sighting to the police on the morning after the murder. At that stage, Flora's very distinctive bag hadn't been mentioned in the press or on the internet. So how could he have described it so well?

—He... He must've seen Flora with it before. Before that day. He could quite easily have seen her around the area. He lived in Dorchester, and Flora and Caris sometimes went there to look around the shops. Or he could've seen Flora collecting signatures for some of her petitions in any number of places.

—Do you know when Flora got that particular bag?

—I don't know! She had lots of bags. She used to pick them out from the shop. Why are you asking me about all of this? It's Caris

152

who did it, not some made-up man. That's just a smoke screen. Caris's solicitors probably put Damian up to saying it.

I can't... I can't talk to you anymore. This was a mistake. You say you want the untold story, but there is no untold story. There's only the truth. And the truth is that girl—that evil girl—murdered my daughter in cold blood!

And that's when Willow does ask me to leave. My intention was never to upset her, and I drive away from her house with a heavy heart. But there are two loose threads for me, and I can't leave them dangling. The first comes back again to the tenuous motive and evidence against Caris. I think there could be another possible rationale for Flora's murder that makes more sense.

There's a dark side to free speech, and it seems like online abuse is now so common that any harmful or offensive comment posted on social media is called trolling. But it can go deeper than that. The cyber abuse can range from a single sexist, racist, or hateful comment to threats of rape, violence, and death or sustained vicious campaigns against people that can last for years. So is there a difference between trolling, cyberbullying, and cyberstalking? I think so. And research suggests that there's a high degree of overlap between online and offline stalkers. Although the troll was targeting the business Instagram page belonging to Flora and Caris three years before the murder, do trolls simply disappear? Or is there a possibility of them going further than just cyber hatred?

Two years ago, American author Christa Bell wrote a book about an investigation into predator trolling that went viral. Today, I speak to her via Skype to get her take on all things troll-like.

—How would you describe trolling?
—*It's a type of behaviour where the troll wants to upset, inflame,*

or disrupt the online communication of others, using vile insults and verbal argument or havoc to unleash their maliciousness from behind a computer screen. It makes them feel powerful.

A lot of the time, it's misogynistic, racist, anti-gay, or attacking certain religions. And the majority of trolls don't act alone. They operate in organised, international syndicates. Sometimes these syndicates work together to target one specific victim.

—Like a troll mafia?

—Exactly that. No target is off-limits to them, and they like to scour the internet for bait. Statistically, they're a group of angry white men, aged between eighteen to thirty-five.

There's a misconception that these people are uneducated or ignorant, but on the contrary, the many I've investigated are quite the opposite. Unfortunately, you can be very well educated and still believe terrible things. Sitting behind a keyboard anonymously removes a lot of inhibitions a person might usually have and can lead to some very damaging abuse.

—What's the difference between trolling and cyberbullying?

—Most of us probably think bullying is only reserved for our school days, but that's far from the end of the story. As a society, I think we often reward adult bullies. We have aggressive managers in the workplace; our politicians are usually bullying in nature. We celebrate bullies in entertainment as winners and sports personalities as champions and warriors. It's all around us in real life, but cyberbullying ratchets it up a step further. It involves using the internet or any other electronic technology to post messages, emails, embarrassing photos or videos or to make threats, sometimes serious threats.

Some are one-off events, but some are sustained campaigns of harassment organised to effect as much distress and harm as possible. Cyberbullies feel empowered by what they're doing. They like to humiliate, intimidate, and be offensive.

Any kind of cyber attack like this wreaks havoc to victims, and the anonymity means there's no one to fight back against. The cyberbully is emboldened to carry on because they don't have to answer for their actions. Sometimes these incidents take on a life of their own and go viral. One example of that is posting revenge porn. Even after the attack by the initial cyberbully, other people take pleasure in sharing or reposting such incidents with a kind of pile-on effect, often adding their own vile insults and multiplying the damage done. Some people delight in this.

Unsurprisingly, victims of cyberbullying suffer a lot of harm. Their self-esteem and self-confidence are devastated. They feel 'cyber raped'. Some have been driven to take their own lives.

A recent study by Amnesty International told us what any woman with a social media profile already knows: that online abuse is a daily part of their lives, with one in five being subjected to some kind of harassment, particularly sexual, or threats of physical violence. Their study also counted over a million abusive tweets to women in 2017. Which equates to one every thirty seconds.

—And how would you define cyberstalking?

—It's a more specific type of cyberbullying, using technology to harass or target a particular person in a way that causes distress and fear. A victim might not even know they're being cyberstalked or spied on at first, as the perpetrator keeps an eye on their targets electronically, sometimes by using fake identities.

With the prevalence of social media, a lot of people put their lives out on full display. Posting their location. Their photos and videos. Their families. Their jobs. Which makes things for the cyberstalker that much easier. If they research their victim enough, they can guess their victim's passwords to emails or social media, thus finding out even more. Sometimes they hack into emails and impersonate their victim when sending out embarrassing information that seemingly came from the victim themselves. Cyberstalkers can infiltrate every aspect of their victim's lives if *they're clever enough—financial, social, work, and family life—and take great pleasure in trying to damage the victim's reputation.*

Trolling, cyberbullying, and cyberstalking are sometimes used interchangeably, and they do overlap, but there are some differences between those who carry out each type of behaviour.

—What kind of differences?

—*Studies suggest that the personality characteristics of trolls are a willingness to deceive and manipulate others. They're narcissistic, with a sense of entitlement and grandiosity. They have psychopathic traits, lacking in remorse and empathy, and they are sadists, taking pleasure in the suffering of other people.*

Cyberstalkers, on the other hand, often stalk a person offline and online, with around eighty per cent of cyberstalkers carrying out both types of behaviour. And when their actions go from taking place behind a keyboard into the real world, they've been responsible for many real-life horrors.

—What kinds of horrors are we talking about?

—*Historically, these acts have included dire threats to people—child abuse, identity theft, violence, sexual assaults, and even homicide. Predatory stalking is often a precursor to violent or sexual assault. They get a sense of excitement and anticipation from covertly watching an unsuspecting victim, and for them, the watching can be as gratifying as the actual attack. Recent studies carried out by criminologists found that stalking behaviour was present in ninety-four per cent of murders, with covert watching and surveillance activity present in sixty-three per cent.*

These offenders have low emotional control and commonly have antisocial attitudes. And instead of primarily taking pleasure in what they do, they're more likely to have an emotional attachment to their victim, be it hatred, anger, jealousy, or, even, perceived romantic attachment or love.

—In your experience, do the police take incidents of cyberstalking seriously?

—While it's illegal in many parts of the world, often cyberstalking doesn't reach the level where law enforcement will take it seriously enough or investigate. Unless there are dead bodies, it seems a lot of victims are unable to get help and are expected to put up and shut up or try to fight back themselves.

The general public needs to be very thorough with their online security. And the police need to do more to protect victims.

—Often the advice is just to ignore trolls or bullies, but will that make them stop?

—There are no hard-and-fast rules because they're all different. Sometimes, when a troll doesn't get the response they want to provoke, they'll look elsewhere for their fun, just like bullies in person. If their motivation is sadistic, they'll keep doing it, but maybe they'll move on to another person.

But with cyberstalkers, ignoring them can have the opposite effect. With the stalker, it's more personal, more victim-specific. They need a response to satisfy themselves.

Interesting and scary stuff. Is it possible the troll or cyberbully targeting the Pretty Little Witch Things Instagram page turned into a cyberstalker? Did he step out from his virtual world into real life? If some victims don't even realise they're being cyberstalked, it's possible he was stalking Flora for years without anyone knowing about it.

With that in mind, I try to track down Lucas, the teenage boy who was watching Flora before he asked her on a date. I want to find out if a teenage crush could've led to something darker. Maybe, like Willow says, something that happened three years before the murder isn't relevant. But what if it is?

It takes a while to find him. These days, the twenty-one-year-old is living in America, so I talk to him by phone.

. . .

—Yeah, I remember that summer. I'd always liked Flora, but I don't think she ever really noticed me at school. I was one of the geeky guys. Mind you, I don't think she noticed a lot of people. I only ever remember seeing her with Caris.

Oh, man, I do remember asking her out. How embarrassing! She turned me down flat. She was nice about it and all. I was like a lovesick puppy. I used to go in her mum's shop all the time and pretend to look at things, but really, I just wanted to ask her on a date. Then every time she looked at me, I lost my nerve.

But the weird thing is, it wouldn't have worked out with Flora even if she'd said yes. About a week after I asked her out, my dad got this amazing job offer in the States, and we moved here about a month afterwards. I've been here ever since. Bit of a difference from sleepy old Dorset, but there you go. Funny how things turn out, isn't it?

—You've been in the States since the latter part of 2014, then?

—Yeah, that's right.

—Do you know anything about the troll who was harassing Flora and Caris on their Instagram page back in 2014?

—Huh? Sorry, no. I don't know anything about that. I haven't been listening to your podcast, so I don't know what's been said by people. But surely they didn't think it was me? This is going to sound a bit shallow, but to be honest, there was so much going on when we moved to America that I actually didn't think about her after she said no. You know what teenage guys are like—one minute, they're infatuated with something, and the next minute, they're on to something else. There were way too many exciting things going on in my life after that to give Flora a second thought. It was just a mad crush for me. And then it was over.

After what happened, after she was murdered, I heard about it then, and yeah, that was horrendous. I was totally whacked out over it. Couldn't believe it. And that was the first time I really thought about her again.

It's really sad what happened to her. But I can assure you I'm definitely not a troll, and I never have been. And even if I was, and you think it might be connected to her homicide, I was on an outward-bound trip with some mates the weekend it happened.

We were over in Carolina then, at a wilderness camp called Camp Blue Ridge. We did all this canoeing and whitewater rafting and hiking-expedition stuff. There were ten of us. I remember because when I got back, my mum had been looking on the internet and found the news stories about her being killed, and it obviously said Flora went to the same high school as I had. Mum asked if I knew her, and that's when I found out about it.

I have no reason to doubt Lucas, but to be thorough, I did some further digging and found a photo gallery on the Camp Blue Ridge website of previous guests. On the twenty-first of June 2017, Lucas and his team of six were being handed a prize for beating another team in a whitewater rafting challenge. The camp has confirmed his attendance at that time.

Maybe I'm clutching at straws. Maybe the troll really has nothing to do with any of what happened three years later and is yet another anomaly that I'll never find the answer to. So I turn my attention to the second loose thread brought up from Willow's interview. And for that, I go back to Damian and ask him the question I should've asked before.

I find him at Wentworth Hall again, bent over a sage plant in the herb garden. He's surprised to see me, and because he likes routine and pre-planning, he doesn't want to speak to me at first until he's processed my arrival. I agree to meet him back on the grassy area where we first spoke half an hour later.

Eventually, Damian approaches, head down, eyes on the ground, and I ask him the question that might blow the police's theory that he's not a credible witness out of the water.

· · ·

—Did you ever see Flora or Caris before the night of the twenty-first of June 2017, when you were in Blackleaf Forest?

—No. I don't really notice people. Especially girls. I kind of... They're a bit scary, like. I mean, not really scary, not as in they'd hurt me or anything. I just don't like looking at people. I don't like eye contact. Makes me feel weird. I don't like it.

I can vouch for that. As I speak to Damian now, and when we chatted before, he wouldn't look me directly in the eyes. This is common with people on the autism spectrum and also another reason why the jury might not have found Damian trustworthy, even though it implies no such thing. We have this ingrained idea that if people are telling the truth, if they're being sincere, they look at you when speaking. But for people like Damian, that's not always a comfortable option.

I also think the prosecution barrister would've had an easy time in discrediting Damian. Our adversarial criminal justice system is based on the power of persuasion and storytelling. It's not about getting to the truth in court. It's about manipulating the witness into giving you the answer you want them to in front of a jury or undermining their credibility. It can, and does, distort the truth.

—They know about it here. You know, the not-looking thing. They don't mind. My boss is really nice. He doesn't make me look at him. Sometimes I hear some of the other staff talking about me, but I don't care. Because my boss says I do a good job. He says I talk to the plants. I'm a plant whisperer—that's what he says.

—Are you sure you didn't see either girl before? You live just outside Dorchester, which is only fifteen miles from Stoneminster.

And you go to Blackleaf Forest a lot, which is only two miles from the town. Here, where you work, is only eighteen miles from Stoneminster. It's possible you might've seen them before that night, isn't it?

—*No. I didn't see them before. I didn't. I mean, I might've walked past them or driven past them but not seen them. I didn't see them see them.*

—Had you ever seen Flora's bag before that night?

—*No. I definitely didn't see the rainbow bag. I've never seen one like that before. 'Cause I remember thinking, the first thing that I thought of, before I thought seeing that man there was a bit strange, the first thing I thought was that my mum likes rainbows. Every time she sees one, she tries to take a picture. Did you know that no two people see the same rainbow? See, the light bouncing off certain raindrops on your rainbow is bouncing off other raindrops at a completely different angle for someone else. It makes a different image. Even if you stand in the same spot at the same time, you can't see the same rainbow. You might think it's the same, but it's not. I mean, that's pretty amazing, right? Nature makes all these unique things. Like snowflakes. No two are the same. And fingerprints. They're not the same. And DNA, unless you're twins. So I remember thinking, Mum would like a bag like that. She'd like a rainbow she can carry round with her all the time.*

—Is it possible that when you saw the man in Blackleaf Forest, it was on another date?

—*No. No, no, no. It was the evening of the murder. Because I told my mum the morning after when she said it had happened.*

I press Damian some more, and he's still adamant about not seeing the bag or Flora or Caris before that night in 2017. But has he given proof beyond a reasonable doubt? That's always going to be a sore, subjective point with Damian, I think.

As I leave, Damian's words about rainbows stay with me. There's a lot about this case synonymous with what he's said. Because, like rainbows, maybe no two people see the same things, either. It's common for multiple witnesses to see different things from the same crime because their perspective, recollection, or memory reconstruction is unique to them. People might not intend to distort facts. And they might be susceptible to suggestion. But what's been obvious in this case is all the opposing versions of the same event coming through different eyes. So do I believe Damian, or is he, like other witnesses I've spoken to, seeing what he wants to? Or describing what he *thinks* happened? Is there just one truth or only different perspectives of it?

Yes, I do believe him, but I don't know where to go next. Maybe I'm looking for answers in the wrong places. And just as I think the whole podcast is floundering, I find someone who can shed an explosive light or, in fact, darkness on Caris's life and on this case. We'll be talking to them in the next episode.

Don't forget to check out the E-FIT picture on the website and see if you recognise the man from Blackleaf Forest. And please keep your comments coming. What do you think so far?

Thank you listening to *Anatomy of a Crime*.

Until next time...

Ruffles66 • 2 days ago

Will you stop going on about that man in the woods! He doesn't exist! Damian made him up. He doesn't know what he's talking about.

^ | ˅ • Reply • Share ˃

SimonSays → Reply to Ruffles66 • 1 day ago
I agree. The troll thing is getting boring now too. Something that happened 3 years before the murder is irrelevant. It was Caris who did it.
^ | ˅ • Reply • Share ˃

HXHOP → Reply to Ruffles66 • 1 day ago
I disagree completely. It's obvious Damian never saw Kelly or Morgan before that night. And he didn't see the bag, either. The real killer took that bag.
^ | ˅ • Reply • Share ˃

Harmony → Reply to SimonSays • 1 day ago
You have no idea what it's like to be subjected to vicious bullying and misogynistic degradation. That author was right. We have to suffer vile comments every day! It's scary! When you're being threatened with rape and violence, no wonder some of these poor women kill themselves or even BE killed!
^ | ˅ • Reply • Share ˃

Betsy → Reply to Harmony • 1 day ago
I agree with you. I was trolled for months by some madman who kept posting death threats! I was so scared I couldn't leave the house and developed agoraphobia! No one knows the depths of how it affects you until it happens to them.
^ | ˅ • Reply • Share ˃

SimonSays → Reply to Harmony • 1 day ago
Oh boo-hoo!
^ | ˅ • Reply • Share ˃

TrippyH • 2 days ago
I feel really sorry for Willow Morgan. You have no right to upset

163

her. Why are you raking up all these old memories? It's really nasty.
^ | ˅ • Reply • Share ˃

Jester → Reply to TrippyH • 1 day ago
You do realise you're listening to a true crime podcast? And that's the whole point of a TRUE. CRIME. PODCAST! If you don't like it, don't listen.
^ | ˅ • Reply • Share ˃

110011 → Reply to TrippH • 1 day ago
I feel sorry for Willow Morgan too. But something's not right about this. How would you feel if you were put in prison for a crime you didn't commit?
^ | ˅ • Reply • Share ˃

Stationmaster • 2 days ago
I don't think the 'thrill kill' makes sense. But I think they were lesbians and they had a domestic dispute that ended up with one of them dead.
^ | ˅ • Reply • Share ˃

Colonel Mustard → Reply to Stationmaster • 2 days ago
Lesbian witches. The world is better off without them.
^ | ˅ • Reply • Share ˃

Scampi → Reply to Colonel Mustard • 1 day ago
Oh, god, not you again! You misogynist, ignorant, gay-basher.
^ | ˅ • Reply • Share ˃

TrT3 • 2 days ago
Someone could've overheard where they were going to be that

night when the door to Willow's shop was open. What if there really was a stalker who followed them there?

^ | ˅ • Reply • Share ˃

.

Dreamscape → Reply to TrT3 • 2 days ago
That's pushing things. They'd have to have the ketamine on them, waiting for the right opportunity. Seems like a once-in-a-million lifetime chance, doesn't it?

^ | ˅ • Reply • Share ˃

Bebe → Reply to TrT3 • 1 day ago
There's no proof of a stalker. And no proof the troll ever stalked them. Anyway, if there was a stalker, why kill one girl and not the other?

^ | ˅ • Reply • Share ˃

TrT3 → Reply to Bebe • 1 day ago
Maybe they were only stalking one of them.

^ | ˅ • Reply • Share ˃

AmericanDream • 3 days ago
Wow, this is like Serial! It's absolutely awesome. Can't wait to see what you find out next. A fan from the USA.

^ | ˅ • Reply • Share ˃

CHAPTER TWELVE

CARIS (Aged 15)

I sat in the circle and glanced around. So many pairs of eyes on me made my skin crawl. I attempted a smile, but it fractured on my face. I was a few seconds away from throwing up.

I'd thought about nothing else for months. It was like a constant pressure squeezing my skull, and I wanted to get it out of my head. I *needed* to. If only it were that easy, though. There would never be a magic wand to wave that made things right. No spell that worked to make it go away. I'd tried. Now I needed to try the opposite.

Anger swirled in my stomach as their words washed over me. I glanced down at my lap to avoid looking at their faces, listening and trying not to listen at the same time. I clenched my fists, trying to hold it all together.

I can't do this. I can't do it.

I braced my feet on the floor, ready to stand up and leave. I imagined myself running away. Crashing through the forest, the sweat streaking down my forehead and between my shoulder blades. My heavy breath filling the air. My muscles tight and heavy, like blocks of concrete dragging me down. My tired limbs trembling as pain squeezed my chest and my vision blurred.

Flora's words echoed in my head, jerking me back to reality, telling me I could never outrun myself. I was glad she wasn't with me. I couldn't stand the thought of that. I loved her too much to let her see this. I didn't want us tainted by this darkness. I didn't know who was going to survive in the end.

I refocused on the circle as I clenched my fists again. And then it was my turn. I could've said no. I could've still bolted. But I didn't.

I opened my mouth to take the plunge, not knowing if it was going to hurl me deeper into the abyss or drag me out of it.

CHAPTER THIRTEEN

EPISODE 5
DARKNESS

I've agonised over whether to share this next story. It's something very personal to Caris and my next guest, who, for reasons that will become apparent, wishes to remain anonymous. But I think it's very relevant to the backstory of this case. A vital part of this tragedy that needs to be told, because it lays the foundation for a bigger element in this crime.

Before we start, I can assure you now that it won't make for easy listening. It's kept me awake, believe me. This, ladies and gentlemen, is a trigger warning. But I promise you this is not just something gratuitous I've thrown in here, either in description or necessity. The reason for hearing this story will become clear.

For the purpose of this conversation, I'm going to call the witness 'Jenny'. Between 2013 and late 2014, she was a student at Bournemouth University, which is a popular seaside town thirty-five miles from Stoneminster. I speak to her by video call on WhatsApp, and like the teacher from Stoneminster High School,

Jenny's voice has been digitally altered to protect her identity. She takes a few deep breaths, and there are few false starts as she fiddles repeatedly with an elastic band on her wrist, pulling it back and letting it hit her skin again and again.

—*I don't really know where to start. I don't... it's hard. This is really hard. It's the first time I've told it to anyone outside of the... er... sorry. Sorry.*

—Clearly, none of this is comfortable for you, so I'm not going to rush you. Just start in your own time.

—*Yes. Um... well... it was 2013. In October. I was eighteen at the time, studying at Bournemouth Uni. I'd been out with a group of friends in the town centre. We were doing a pub crawl, and we were all pretty pissed. I got talking to this guy at the bar, and then when I looked around, my mates had gone.*

I had a vague recollection of them telling me they were going to get some food somewhere—a kebab or something—but I was having a good time, and I just kind of said, 'Yeah, I'll see you there', and then before I knew it, probably half an hour had gone past.

I left the pub. Left the guy there. Walked up to the chippy and kebab shop but couldn't see my mates. There were still plenty of people about. It was about half ten in the evening, but we'd been drinking since the afternoon. And... stupidly, I decided to walk home on my own back to the house I was student-sharing. But...

Jenny shakes her head, her eyes wet with tears. The elastic band starts up again. The silence hangs between us, and just as I'm about to ask her if she wants to stop now, she continues.

—*You think you're invincible, don't you? When you're that age, you*

169

think nothing bad will ever happen to you. When you're drunk, you think you've got superpowers or something. Your inhibitions go right out of the window. So I walked, and I didn't think anything of it.

I was getting further away from the town. It was dark by then. People I passed got sparser. And I cut across a children's play area. A shortcut back to the house. It was well lit. I'd walked across there hundreds of times. I was on the path, halfway through it. Past the seesaw and slides and... and I heard something. A scuffing sound. It didn't sound like footsteps. It was softer.

I turned around, expecting someone to be behind me. Fearing someone was behind me. But they weren't. They were to the side of me.

He'd... um... um... He'd been following me, but he came at me from the side. He must've been walking on the grassy area, which was why I didn't hear him until it was too late. And then he was just this big... this big shadow. This shape, looming up at me.

He punched me in the face. It felt like I'd been knocked over by a wrecking ball. I landed on the floor, and he dragged me by my hair to the edge of the grass, where it was lined with trees. There was no lighting there; it was in shadows. I was just so shocked and terrified, I couldn't even scream. It was like my throat had closed up. It wouldn't work. Nothing would work.

Jenny's hand goes to her throat, and the other massages her stomach, as if this still makes her feel physically sick. I'm not surprised. A chill ripples over my skin as I listen. She inhales and exhales short, sharp breaths in a staccato rhythm.

—We can stop now if you prefer.

   —*Sorry. Sorry. I want to go on. It's just... Sorry.*

—You have absolutely nothing to be sorry for. Take your time. You're being really brave here.

—So... uh... *I was wearing a dress with a thin cardigan over it. It was quite a warm night for that time of year. I had boots on. Flat ankle boots. I wasn't dressed provocatively. My dress came to my knees. I looked like a normal young woman. And I remember thinking afterwards, what if I'd chosen something else to wear that day? Would he have still picked me? What if I'd chosen black trousers or jeans? What if I'd worn a jacket over my clothes? What if I'd put my hair up in a ponytail instead of leaving it down? What if I'd worn less makeup?*

I still live with these what-ifs every single day. Do you know how long it takes me to get ready every time I leave the house? Hours. It's ridiculous. Most people can choose an outfit and go. I stare at my wardrobe. Try things on. Try to see how other people would see me. Other men. And I try things on and take things off again. Just something simple like deciding what to wear has been taken away from me now.

—I think that's very understandable. Have you been speaking to someone? A counsellor or therapist?

—*Yes. I'll get to that later. But... I'm sorry... I just got sidetracked.*

—I don't think it's a sidetrack at all. It's a symptom of trauma you were explaining. It's very common. It's PTSD.

—*I know. I know. I don't want to sound like a victim here. I want to be better than that. Stronger than that.*

—It already shows you've got immense strength and courage to talk on air about this.

—*Thanks. So, um, we were in the shadows. He was astride me, sitting on my chest. One hand had hold of my wrists. With the other he was... He was... pulling up my dress and pulling down my underwear. I think I passed out then. I don't know if it was because he'd punched me in the head or because it was so scary. I don't know how long I was out for, but when I woke up, he was... He was raping me.*

I could hear ringing in my ears. Really loud. And his breath. And this... pain. He had his forearm pressing over my mouth so hard, I thought my teeth would break. His other hand was forcing my arms over my head, pressing down on them. His weight on top of me. And I remember thinking, Just do something! Try to move. *And I couldn't. I couldn't do anything. I could barely even breathe.*

—People often think there are two automatic reactions to danger—fight or flight. But there's another one. Freeze. Research suggests that at least seventy per cent of rape victims freeze like you did. It was a natural reaction of your limbic nervous system. One that might even have kept you alive that night.

—*I know that now. But, again, it's kind of hard to cope with. The what-ifs come back. What if I'd done something? What if I'd tried to fight back? I don't think that will ever go away.*

He kept saying something as he was raping me. He kept calling me a slag and saying, 'Fucking void. Fucking void'. I don't know what he meant. And he kept saying he had power. He was powerful. And even though we were in the shadows, I saw his face. He didn't try to hide it.

—Can you describe him?

—*His hair was scruffy and dark. He had thick eyebrows. In the shadows, I couldn't see his eye colour, but he was thin build. I think it was him... the man... in the E-FIT picture you put on your website. The face doesn't look the same as him, but there's something about him, something that makes me think it was him. The shape of his eyes are the same. I'm sure of it. I'm... sorry. Sorry, I can't do this anymore at the moment. I just...*

The strain of telling this part of Jenny's trauma has obviously taken

172

its toll, and her final words trail into a guttural sob. Even though we're miles apart, I feel her agony and pain.

It takes a few days for Jenny to regain her courage and speak to me for a second time on WhatsApp. And in that time, her revelation cements some pieces of this case into place. Jenny has taken a huge step coming forward. She has no reason to lie and every reason to keep quiet to protect her privacy. It's a step that I think confirms Damian was telling the truth about the man he saw that night at Witch's Hill. The man who ran away from the scene of Flora's murder. The man who took Flora's bag. But what else did that man take? Flora's life? Caris's freedom? And who is he? The other leads that have come into our researchers from people who've seen the E-FIT, trying to trace him, have led nowhere. Maybe the rest of Jenny's information might help to find him.

—*I'm sorry I couldn't carry on. I'm okay now. I'm ready to tell you the rest.*

—Thank you for taking the time to speak to me again, Jenny. As before, we can stop any time you want to. Please start wherever you feel comfortable.

—*Okay. Afterwards. After the rape... You don't know how long it took me to even give it a name. But... yes... I... um... Afterwards, when he'd finished, he got up and ran away. It's a bit of a blur, but I sort of remember somehow pulling up my knickers. My legs wouldn't work. They were shaking so much.*

I rolled over onto my hands and knees and was sick. My head was pounding. My eyes felt a bit blurry. I don't know if that was from the tears or because of the hit to the head.

I was looking for my bag, and I couldn't find it. I started panicking. It was a small clutch bag, but it wasn't there on the ground. He must've taken it. It had my purse in there, but it wasn't the money I was worried about. It was my ID and my phone. It had

173

my name and address in that stuff. My phone was locked, but people can still find ways to unlock it. He knew who I was. That was really scary. Terrifying.

Jenny cups her hands to her mouth, her eyes wide and tearful, as if reliving that moment again. The minutes tick by as she takes deep breaths and flicks at the rubber band on her wrist repeatedly, no doubt trying to push down the anxiety, the horror. I feel like a sick voyeur in those moments and tell her we can speak again later, when she feels more comfortable, but she wants to carry on.

—*Now I've found the courage to say all this aloud, I want to get it out there. I think I need to. Thank you for being patient.*

Luckily, my bag didn't have my front-door key in it. That was in my cardigan zip pocket. I always had a habit of putting it in a pocket rather than my bag. And even more luckily, it hadn't fallen out when he'd... um... when he'd done it.

I hurt everywhere. The physical pain was immense, but it was the fear that he knew my name, where I lived, that weirdly seemed worse at that point. I was in shock, but eventually, I staggered to my feet and dragged myself home.

One of my friends who I shared the house with was in their bedroom with the TV on. The others were all still out. So I didn't see any of them.

Part of my brain knew I had a decision to make about what to do. Part of me just wanted to get clean. I felt soiled, dirty. Disgusted with myself. I wanted him off me. Out of me. It felt like I had insects crawling over me. Inside me.

Part of me thought about calling the police and reporting it. And although I was stupid that night, I wasn't stupid about knowing what would happen if I reported it. I knew it was likely—very likely —I wouldn't be seen as a victim. I'd have my private life on show. My intimate details talked about and talked about as if people were just talking about something casual, like what they had for tea. I'd have to tell it over and over again. And if they found him, I'd have to tell it in court, with more strangers staring at me. Some of them, probably a lot of them, judging me. I'd walked home alone. I'd been drunk. I must've been asking for it. My actions had consequences out of my control. But it would be my actions that would be called into question. Not his. Every piece of my life would be picked apart. If I'd had a one-night stand in the past, I'd be a slut. If I liked something kinky when I was being intimate by choice with a partner, then I'd have some kind of rape fantasy. If I was fatter, uglier, quieter, I wouldn't have tempted him. It goes on and on, doesn't it? Nothing about women is ever good enough for some people.

I couldn't go through that. I couldn't report it to the police. It would be like being violated all over again. I was ashamed. I thought it was my fault.

—It's not your shame to carry. All rapes are caused by rapists. You weren't to blame for the vile thing he did to you.

—I know that's what people say. It doesn't make it easier to believe. Not then and not now.

So... anyway... I had a shower. I was... scrubbing and rinsing and washing until my skin was raw. I even pulled some of my hair out because I was tugging on it that hard, trying to get the shampoo through it.

And I thought I could forget about it. I covered the bruises on my face with foundation. Those bruises faded over time. But the internal bruise... the giant, internal bruise that scars you deep inside and sucks out your soul... I don't know if that will ever go. You can try to disguise that, as well. Put one foot in front of another. Try to forget. But it's hard. It's so fucking hard to get rid of that cancerous

175

bruise that affects every single part of your life. Of who you are. Or of who you used to be.

So I was really struggling with it. I couldn't concentrate on my coursework. I didn't want to go out and socialise. Couldn't cope with being out on my own. I wanted to be in crowds. And if I found myself on my own, I'd panic. I'd get these anxiety attacks that felt like my heart was burning a hole through my chest. My work started slipping. Everything was just falling apart. I was falling apart.

—Did you find someone you trusted who you could talk to about the rape?

—*Yeah. But not until seven months later. One of the girls I house-shared with. She noticed something was going on with me. I was losing weight. I cut my hair off because I didn't want to be attractive or be noticed by men. And because I thought if I had short hair, no one would be able to drag me into the bushes again. You never realise how vulnerable having long hair makes you.*

I thought I'd been trying to hide it, but she knew what had happened to me. She just knew. The same way other women know from an early age there's a danger out there every time they breathe— just for being a woman, there are some people who want to hurt them. They can also spot the reactions to that danger, a lot of the time. My reactions were classic responses, so I've discovered now.

She waited until we were the only ones in the house one morning. And she told me a story about herself. How when she was fourteen she'd been sexually assaulted by her uncle. About how she'd told her parents, who thought she was making it all up, because she was a feisty teenager who wanted attention. It couldn't possibly happen to her. It couldn't possibly be a family member they'd known all their lives. She still had nightmares about it. She had low self-esteem. She ate to cope with things. She wasn't raped, but she knew enough about what I was going through. And she talked me into going to a support group for survivors of sexual abuse.

She came with me. I don't think I could've done it if she hadn't been there. I would've just walked out. But she'd worked out by then that she also needed to talk about what had happened to her. It was consuming her. She was really overweight by then. Overeating was a coping mechanism to the self-hatred she felt and also, again, to make herself as unattractive as possible so she didn't attract the wrong kind of attention.

—Where was the support group?

—In Dorchester. It was called RASAS. The Rape and Sexual Assault Support group. We went there, and my friend shared her story with the group. Everyone was really supportive, but I still couldn't bring myself to talk about it yet. But I saw Caris there. This was 2014, in May, so she would've been fifteen, but she looked older. She looked about the same age as me. She came on her own and left on her own after the session. And she didn't speak.

I didn't think much about it then. I didn't know who she was. But she had the same look I saw in the mirror every day.

—Did you ever see Caris again at a RASAS meeting?

—Yes. I went the following week. Even though I hadn't told my story the week before, it felt helpful. We knew what each other was going through. I thought if I could get it out there in that environment, it might be good for me. My friend went with me again, and I was all set to talk, but I bottled it. I just couldn't. But Caris did. She told her story to us all.

I'm not going to tell you exactly what she said. That's her story to tell. And I feel really bad about even telling you she was there. I'm betraying some kind of unspoken confidence. But with all the things they said about her in the papers and stuff, her life has already been plastered out in the open, and not in a good way. But you'll see why I have to tell you in a minute, because I think everyone's been looking at the Flora tragedy from the wrong angle until now. I don't think it was ever about Flora. I think it was really all about Caris.

She didn't go into a lot of details about what had happened to her. Just that it had happened. So I didn't know specifics. I didn't *know if it sounded like the same man who raped me too. I didn't know then there were similarities.*

—Do you know if Caris reported the incident to the police?

—*Not as far as I know. She said her friend was pressuring her to go and report it, but she was struggling with that idea. First of all, because of the same reasons I told you why I didn't report it. And also because she didn't think anyone would believe her. She said she had a bad reputation. She said people had spread rumours about her before. She said she couldn't cope with all the negative and nasty attention it would bring her.*

I was all set to tell my story that night. But again, when I got there, I just couldn't find the words. If I had, if she'd heard my story, and maybe the same horrible words he said to me that were pretty specific, pretty unique, then maybe she, or both of us, would've gathered strength from each other to report it to the police.

—It wasn't your fault. It was the rapist's fault. He's one hundred per cent to blame for all of the agony he's caused.

—*You don't get it, though. That's what everyone says. All the counsellors I've seen have told me it's not my fault. But that doesn't make it easier for me; it makes it worse. Because if it wasn't* my *fault, if it wasn't something I did that I can change in the future that made him pick me, then it actually makes me feel even less in control, because it could happen again. And I'd never see it coming.*

I still couldn't tell the police, either. I tried so many times. I thought of nothing else for months. I even got as far as walking up the steps to the police station. But every time I got close to it, I'd get physically sick. I'd shake. I'd have pain in my chest. Panic attacks that felt like I was dying. I just couldn't go through with it.

So I didn't say anything that night. Because... Because I was weak. Because all the reasons I told you about before, about why I couldn't do it, were exactly the same. And I know you're telling me I'm not weak. And it's kind of you to say that. But you're wrong.

I also didn't say anything until now because I didn't know it had anything to do with what happened to her later. I had absolutely no idea. How could I? And she probably didn't know, either. All this stuff that's come out in your podcast has made me realise that... well, I think this is all connected because... That wasn't the end of it all.

—What happened afterwards?

—I saw him in my nightmares. I saw him at the edge of my vision, and when I turned my head, he wasn't there. I saw his face in crowds, but when I froze again and blinked, it wasn't him. It was someone else.

—Just to make it clear to listeners, were you imagining seeing him because of the trauma you'd suffered?

—I don't know. There were a few times when I really thought it was him. But I'd just get a glimpse of him, and then there was no one there. I think it was my mind playing tricks on me. But the other stuff he did, that wasn't a mind trick. It was real.

—What else happened?

—He knew who I was. And when he took my bag with my phone in it, it had my email account and Instagram page logged in. So if he managed to get my phone unlocked, which he must've done, he knew what my profile names were.

About two months after the rape, he started posting things on my Instagram page. After the rape, I didn't post anything new on there, but he started putting comments on old posts of mine. His profile name was @InsRule. I took screenshots of them. These are some of the things he said...

Jenny turns her phone round to a laptop in front of her and shows me the screenshots she saved, reading them aloud as she goes through them.

—@InsRule you ugly bitch. Don't forget I have the power.

—@InsRule I can see you even when you think I'm not looking.
—@InsRule you're nothing but a dirty slag.
—@InsRule think you're something special? You're not!

Jenny turns the phone back to herself, her face scrunched up with anguish, her eyes glistening with tears.

—He was taunting me. Harassing me. It wasn't enough for him to steal from me what he already had. My happiness and my freedom and my whole life. He wanted more. He wanted to drive me mad.

I knew then that I couldn't stay in Bournemouth anymore. I shut my Instagram account down, left uni, and moved somewhere else. Somewhere he wouldn't be able to find me. And when I heard on this podcast about the messages left on Caris's Instagram page, I thought—no, I knew... It was him. It was the same kind of things. The same profile name. It couldn't be coincidence that Caris had suffered the same as me, and then she was being trolled online by him. It was the same man. Definitely.

This totally flips things on its head for me.

While Jenny can't identify the E-FIT picture of the man with absolute certainty, it still sounds likely that the man who attacked both Jenny and Caris was the same person because of the trolling by @InsRule. But it wasn't just the horrific assault for Jenny. She was mentally assaulted over and over as he harassed her, never knowing if he was going to strike again. Caris didn't have a personal Instagram page, so instead, I think he targeted her business page in the same way. It seems he developed a pattern. An MO. And like Jenny, Caris never reported any of this to the police.

I completely understand why Caris and Jenny wouldn't have

reported the rapes. I totally get why Jenny didn't report the harassment afterwards. It's very possible Caris didn't know the trolling she was getting on the joint Pretty Little Witch Things Instagram account was directed at her or related to what she'd suffered. And as the Amethyst Witch told us previously, she'd been trolled on her account before and advised Flora and Caris to ignore it. Sadly, it's nothing new. These keyboard warriors are nothing more than bullies, hiding behind an anonymous VPN or internet account and a screen.

The police didn't consider the troll to be connected, either, when they investigated Flora's murder. And although Caris's defence team did make some enquiries in this area, the @InsRule account had been deleted by then. It was a dead end. Or maybe they didn't look hard enough. Maybe Caris didn't tell her solicitor or barrister about a rape that happened in 2014. How could she have known it was connected to the troll, who was really a rapist? What everyone seemed to think was an insignificant annoyance of a jealous person leaving nasty comments on social media could've been, in fact, a prelude to something far more sinister.

To recap, the man running away from the murder scene in 2017 at Witch's Hill was also carrying Flora's bag. Was he the rapist, who also liked taking trophies from his victims, like Jenny's bag, which he stole? There are too many similarities to ignore.

I understand what-ifs, and I have several of my own now. What if Caris really *was* telling the truth about that night on the twenty-first of June 2017? What if she's a victim in this horror story too? What if this man didn't just stop the trolling and forget about Caris? What if he turned into a stalker? Did he follow Caris and Flora to the woods that night? Did *he* murder Flora?

More pieces click into place here. The description given by the anonymous teacher from Stoneminster High School about Caris's dark medical artwork theme and the poem Caris wrote. If we read it again, with this new information in mind, it takes on a whole different meaning...

'In darkness shines the fires of hell; the devil's calling me to sleep. To take the soul from where it fell and drift down to the chasmic deep. I try to stop; I try to leave. But there is no more last reprieve. With the hands around its throat, it dies inside. It dies. It chokes. Taking life without within; there's nothing left from where it's been. Nothing is what nothing wants. It hurts forever. It will always hunt'.

I don't think that was a form of prophecy at all. It seems to me, Caris could well be referring to someone who'd hunted her, hurt her, stolen a part of her, and she felt suffocated by it. As if a part of her had died.

But two things puzzle me. If it *is* the same man, why was Flora murdered instead of Caris? There appeared to be no sexual motive for Flora's death—she wasn't sexually assaulted, so was he getting his sexual gratification this time in an escalation of violence that ended in murder? Or was he disturbed by Liz and Bill before he'd finished the full horrors of what he'd planned?

As you know, I've been trying to get Caris to agree to talk to me. Finally, she's consented. In the next episode, I'll be speaking to her from HMP Ashmount, an all-female prison in Dorset. I've had enough of rumours and whispers and supposition. I want to hear about the real Caris Kelly from the horse's mouth.

Again, if you recognise the E-FIT picture on the website, or you have any more information about who this man is, please get in touch.

Thank you for listening to *Anatomy of a Crime.*

Until next time...

DeeDee9 • 2 days ago

OMG! I feel so sorry for Jenny and Caris. This is horrendous. This evil man has to be the same one in the woods that night.

^ | ˅ • Reply • Share ˃

TweedleDum → Reply to DeeDee9 • 2 days ago

You don't know that. Jenny couldn't positively identify him anyway. I think it's all set up by Caris's defence lawyers to get her an appeal. I still think she's guilty!

^ | ˅ • Reply • Share ˃

YoYo4 → Reply to TweedleDum • 1 day ago

I bet you're a man! Everything I've heard about Caris's life on this podcast is the complete opposite to what I heard in the press. I wonder if the jury would be so quick to convict her again after listening to this? I doubt it. There's too much reasonable doubt here. Dum by name, dumb by nature!

^ | ˅ • Reply • Share ˃

77777 → Reply to TweedleDum • 1 day ago

Loads of women have been murdered by stalkers. Statistics say 1 in 5 women may be victims. If it was happening to men, then people would do more to stop it happening, but as always, the MEN making the rules aren't interested. Jenny's rape happened six years ago now, and it was a traumatic event, so no wonder she couldn't positively ID him. But the telling thing is she recognised his eyes.

^ | ˅ • Reply • Share ˃

Tweedledum → Reply to 77777 • 2 days ago

If you want equal rights you need to be a bit tougher, don't you?

You need to stand up to a stalker instead of letting them get away with it.

There's no way he stalked Caris for THREE years without her knowing!

^ | ˅ • Reply • Share ˒

BHK → Reply to Tweedledum • 1 day ago

Wow, that's so ignorant it's scary.

^ | ˅ • Reply • Share ˒

8B*B • 2 days ago

If this man was stalking Caris, why did he kill Flora instead of Caris? I don't get it. Doesn't make sense to me.

^ | ˅ • Reply • Share ˒

ProCycle → Reply to 8B*B • 1 day ago

I think he killed Flora first and then heard Liz and Bill coming so he ran off before he could kill Caris too.

^ | ˅ • Reply • Share ˒

Satyy → Reply to ProCycle • 1 day ago

They were way over the other side of the woods then, according to Damian's sighting. But he might have been disturbed by someone else. Was someone else there who hasn't come forward?

^ | ˅ • Reply • Share ˒

C))P→ 8B*B • 1 day ago

Or maybe he's just a fucking psycho with no rhyme or reason!

^ | ˅ • Reply • Share ˒

Dru → Reply to C))P • 1 day ago

1000% agree.

^ | ˅ • Reply • Share ˒

Tuti • 3 days ago
Oh, come on! This is just a sympathy story to get Kelly an appeal. I reckon it's all a set-up.
^ | ˅ • Reply • Share ˃

.

ToppEr → Reply to Tuti • 2 days ago
The only set-up has already happened! I don't believe Caris's guilty.
^ | ˅ • Reply • Share ˃

GhGF55 • 3 days ago
I don't know what to think anymore. But that was hard listening.
^ | ˅ • Reply • Share ˃

DownUnder • 3 days ago
I've been telling my friends about this podcast. It's weird because one of them was in Dorset at that time. Spooky coincidence!
^ | ˅ • Reply • Share ˃

CHAPTER FOURTEEN

NOW

I head back from Liz's supermarket with a few provisions in my bag-for-life. I pull up outside the rental cottage and parallel park in between the neighbours' cars. At least they're in, which could mean witnesses in case something else has been left for me. But there are no special-delivery photos again, and I open the front door and head into the kitchen to cook a quick dinner of cheese on toast while I work on some more research. I eat with my eyes glued to my laptop, barely tasting it as I swallow small bites. It's not really food. It's just sustenance to keep me going.

It's not until later that I notice it. I've been immersed in interviewing and tracking down witnesses, in editing the recordings, and it's just gone 9.30 p.m. when I go upstairs to take a bath.

I see it when I go into the bedroom to strip off my clothes. The white duvet has been turned down at the corner and a chocolate heart wrapped in red foil placed on the pillow, like the turn-down service in a hotel with a complimentary evening treat. But this isn't a hotel. And I've stayed in a lot of rental places over the years during the course of my work to know this isn't the kind of extra that's ever included.

I stare at it for a moment, unease gnawing inside my gut, before calling the contact number I have for the owners of the cottage to double-check my suspicions. I don't tell her what's happened but enquire in a roundabout way. And it seems there are no extras included like complimentary chocolates and a turn-down service. No one other than the cleaner and the owner have keys.

I don't tell her what's happened as I glance around the room. Instead, I thank her and end the call to search my suitcase, still overflowing with clothes that I've been too busy to unpack. I go downstairs and search the rest of the cottage and check my laptop, notes, and work equipment. I check the security.

The cottage is seventeenth century, with the original studded wooden front door that's sturdy, but the lock is a modern edition. A simple Yale that could be easy to pick. The front windows are old wood in good condition with window locks that don't look tampered with. The back door leading from the kitchen to the tiny box garden is modern double glazing. Locked. Nothing else has been obviously disturbed.

But I can't ignore it anymore. This isn't the work of a bored troll. Someone far more dangerous and evil is out there, taunting me, stalking me.

I fumble with my clothes, shoving everything into my case, my fingers still shaking, even though I'm trying to override the fear that's crept up on me more every day. Within twenty minutes, I'm packed and loading my belongings into the boot of my car and heading back home. I might be leaving Stoneminster, but the podcast isn't going anywhere.

CHAPTER FIFTEEN

EPISODE 6
JAILBIRD

I—*did kill the bird. The one Bea told you about. It wasn't a blackbird, though. It was a thrush. It was beautiful. I could feel its heart beating against my hand. And then I hit it with a rock.*

Welcome back to *Anatomy of a Crime*. That is the voice of the now infamous Caris Kelly, better known by some as the Sleeping Beauty Killer.

I sit with her in a visiting room at HMP Ashmount that's been provided for our interview. It has harsh strip lighting, lino that goes halfway up the walls, and moulded plastic furniture. The table is fixed to the wall—all the better for not throwing it—and the colour scheme painted an institutional bland green is supposed to be calming but, instead, conjures up a feeling of hopelessness and malaise. The prison governor is a fan of the podcast, he tells me, and he's been very helpful in arranging for me to speak with Caris.

This is a top-security, purpose-built private prison run by Safe Corp. It's been the subject of constant media attention since its opening. Notably, in recent years, it's been criticised in an official report for subjecting female prisoners to 'inhumane, cruel, and degrading treatment, and systemic breaches of human rights,' which 'appears to amount to torture'. Amongst the serious concerns raised in the report were women being kept in squalid cells, widespread substance abuse and violence, and several neglect-related deaths at the prison. From what I've heard, things haven't improved much since.

Caris's prison uniform is a black T-shirt and grey jogging bottoms. Her skin is still olive, although I doubt she spends too much time outdoors in the sun. Due to cutbacks in staff, inmates are locked in the cells for much of the time and only allowed outside in the open-air recreation area for an hour a day. There are few photos of Caris that I've been able to get hold of. The Pretty Little Witch Things Instagram page was always professional and never contained personal photos. Flora and Caris didn't have any personal social media pages, and neither of the girls I feel I've come to know seem the type to plaster selfies anywhere. So I can't really say with certainty if she seems outwardly changed by prison, apart from the fact her long raven-black hair, now scraped back in a harsh ponytail, has a thick white streak at the front, a condition called poliosis, that's happened since she's been in prison, which, unsurprisingly, can be caused by extreme psychological stress.

—Why did you kill the bird?

—*What Bea said was only partly true. She didn't see the whole thing. She just saw the aftermath. And like most people, she saw what she wanted to. What already fitted her opinion of me. Back then, I didn't even know she'd seen what I did.*

I was coming out of the house, and I saw the thrush fly into the path of an oncoming car. The car hit it and drove off. I rushed over, and it was lying on the verge. Its legs were broken. One of its wings was badly broken. I could tell. Part of its guts were seeping through its stomach, and its beak was broken off. It was twitching and in immense pain, and it was never going to survive. It could never be rehabilitated. And I didn't want to see it suffer, so I hit it with the rock. Once. That was all it took. I did crush its poor little head, but it was quick. And then it was over. It was at peace, not in excruciating agony. Maybe that sounds cold and callous, but I didn't enjoy it. I did it because it was necessary to end its suffering. What would you have done?

—I'm not sure I could've killed it myself. Maybe I would've taken it to the vet. But I can understand why you did it.

—*People put you in some kind of box. Think you're this or that. Label you. Lie about you. They don't care about the truth. They twisted things out of all proportion. They thought I was all these terrible things, and that example with the thrush is just one of them. They thought if I'd killed a bird, I was practicing killing animals, and so it stood to reason I then killed Flora. But from what I've been told about these episodes from my solicitor, I can see you're not like that. You're not putting words in people's mouths, like the press, or even worse, making them up. It's why I decided to use this platform to finally set a few things straight.*

—And I'm honoured you've agreed to choose this podcast as the first interview you've ever given.

—*Maybe I didn't choose you. Maybe fate chose you. There's a psychoanalyst and author called Stephen Grosz, and he said, 'When we cannot find a way of telling our story, our story tells us'.*

I can already feel an intensity about Caris. Not just because of her choice of words or the still serenity about her, the way she sits ramrod straight, her striking beauty at odds with the drab surroundings. She's hard to read, but at the same time, there's also a depth to her startling green eyes that seem to see right through you and an energy about her. Something hypnotising. Something that's hard to put into words.

—And you believe in fate?

—*Fate. Karma. The will of the Universe. I believe in all those things. I believe the Great Goddess is guiding us on our pathway.*

—But if you're innocent, as you've always maintained, why would fate put you here? Why would you be found guilty?

—*People who believe in God still believe in him when things go wrong. Sometimes there are no answers for things. At least, no answers that you can see at the time. Later, you might look back and realise why, but almost always, there's some kind of lesson to be learned. Some hardship you have to go through to see the bigger picture.*

—It sounds like you've had your fair share of hardship. You've heard what other people have been saying about you, the stories that surrounded you and this case. You've no doubt seen all the tabloids, describing you as a satanist, a devil worshipper, an evil monster. But I'm interested in who the real Caris is.

—*Who is the real anyone? None of us are just one thing, are we? And what's real at one point in our lives might not be reality six months from then. We change. We grow. Our experiences shape us. We evolve. Do they want to know about me now or then? And do they really want to know the truth, anyway?*

—I agree. But I'm sure listeners want to get a sense of what happened to you and why you ended up here.

—*And hopefully by the end of this, they will. I've been trying to decide where to begin. I don't even really know where the beginning is. Did it start with my mum's death? Maybe. If she hadn't been killed in the fire, we wouldn't have ended up in Stoneminster. Or maybe I would have one day. The Universe is the director of every story, so I think one day I would've met Flora anyway. Our life journey leads us on lots of different paths.*

—You've explained what happened with the thrush, but I want to get your side of the story that Rob Curran described, where you were in Blackleaf Forest, stabbing a heart and trying to invoke the devil for some kind of revenge.

—*I did do spells at Witch's Hill. Sometimes alone and sometimes with Flora. But what he said was utter rubbish. I don't know who he is, but I've never used any animal parts in spells. I've never incanted any words to do with the devil or evil or revenge. Because the problem is, if you put bad karma or intentions out into the universe, it comes back at you, magnified. But if you put good out there—kindness, compassion, love—that's what comes back to you. It's a ripple effect. Universal law. The law of nature.*

—So that was yet another false rumour about you?

—*Absolutely. Just like the animal mutilations. That wasn't me, either. I could never do something so cruel. I love animals. They never judge. Never take sides. They love unconditionally. I killed the thrush because I loved it. Because it would be far worse letting it endure agony.*

There were, and still are, so many rumours and lies, it's hard to count them all. People who didn't even know me were jumping over themselves to tell the press what they wanted to hear for their five minutes of fame. And the papers made this big thing out of me not showing any remorse in court, about me looking like a psychopath. But it wasn't like that. It was just that I was... I learned from an early age to never show my pain in public.

People will always believe the worst, though, if they expect the worst from you. And if they assume something about you, everything they see or hear afterwards just confirms it.

—One of the other rumours was about your mum's death.

Maybe we should start with that. Can you tell me what happened to her?

—*My family life before I moved to Stoneminster was what most people would think is unconventional and hard to relate to or understand. We lived on the road, in our caravan, travelling around England, but mostly Ireland.*

Most of my extended family bred horses. And even for Travellers, my family was unique. My mum was a Traveller, born and bred, but Dad came from a totally different background. Although he was of Irish descent, he was an American. He was backpacking round Ireland when he was in his early twenties, and he met my mum at a horse fair, and they fell in love. He knew he could never tear her away from her life so he 'ran away to join the circus', I guess you could say.

I was an only child, which is very unusual in our culture. For a lot of Travellers, having eleven or twelve children is pretty common. But Mum couldn't have any more after me. It just didn't happen. My parents doted on me, though, and of course, I had my extended family—the other Travellers, most of whom were related in some way.

Most Traveller children don't go to school. We moved around a lot, so getting a formal education was out of the question, and it's just not a priority. They're taught about other things. The arts, dance, music, nature, and wildlife.

My parents were both very intelligent people, and Mum homeschooled me as best as she could. She'd buy second-hand textbooks, and I'd do research for projects, the same as any regular educational system.

I wasn't good at maths—any mathematical ability I had came from playing cards. But I loved English—reading and creative writing. I devoured books Mum got from charity shops. I'd read anything I could get my hands on, from the classics like, Jane Austen, Dickens, and George Orwell, to Stephen King, J.K. Rowling,

Agatha Christie, Maya Angelou, Jodi Picoult. And I loved art. Loved the freedom to express myself that way. And I was always interested in history.

Mum and Dad brought me up in a stimulating and fulfilling way where I was free to be me. But it wasn't what she taught me from books that was special to me. It was the other stuff, the things about our ancestors and the travelling way of life that I loved. She taught me about nature, using plants to heal. She taught me about the tarot and reading the stars and about the Universal energy. I loved that. I loved it all.

—It sounds quite liberating. But I bet it could be a tough life too.

—Yes. Life on the road could be really hard. It was a lot of work—fetching water, cooking, looking after the babies in the families. Sometimes we'd get a sale from the horses, but most of the time, we were penniless. I remember one summer a lot of us were working on a strawberry farm, picking the fruit. I practically lived off strawberries for months. Another time, it was picking daffodils.

But the thing I loved the most about our life was being outdoors. Nature was our whole home, really. We played and socialised outdoors, in the woods around a fire, or in fields. Rode horses in wide-open spaces. I hated the bad weather. If it was wet or cold, we'd be huddled in front of a log burner or gas fire in one of the caravans. We had no electricity a lot of the time. We didn't watch TV. But it was my life. It was all I'd ever known. And then Mum died, and everything changed.

—And what came afterwards must've been even tougher. There were rumours of a family feud after your mum's death, and that's why you and Ronan moved to Stoneminster. What can you tell us about that time?

—There was no family feud. I don't know where that rumour came from. Probably the same person who said I'd actually set fire to the caravan and killed Mum. The truth is that Dad's heart was

194

broken. *Every time he looked around, he'd see my mum. They loved each other ferociously, and he couldn't bear to be reminded of her. He was literally broken-hearted. And he sank into a depression.*

Although he'd changed his life totally for her and been accepted into our extended family, I don't think he could live in the same way anymore. So he moved us to the opposite end of the country from Ireland. And it felt like the opposite end of the world for me. He wanted it to be a new start for us both, but life was even harder in a lot of ways. He wanted to get a job and support us, but... we ended up living on state benefits.

—Because of his illness?

—*Yes. He was diagnosed with it soon after we got to Dorset. He had this idea of looking for labouring or roofing work or maybe as a mechanic. He was practical. Could turn his hand to anything. Fix anything mechanical. Or maybe even working with horses again. But it didn't turn out that way. He'd been ignoring the pain for a while. He thought it was just stress or grief. I tried some natural remedies, but they didn't seem to help. And I eventually made him go to the doctor.*

It was a degenerative disease he had, and we knew it would get slowly worse. Nothing seemed to help for the pain, except cannabis. Which, as you know now, I bought for him. But it wasn't just that. It was everything else that happened to me there.

—I'm not sure people in Stoneminster realised exactly how difficult things were for you there. You had a lot of responsibility on your shoulders from a young age.

—*I'd lost everything. My mum. My family. My home. My heritage. I'd never lived in a house before. Never stayed in one place for too long before. Never been to school. It was pretty overwhelming and alien.*

When you live outdoors, you can feel the seasons changing. Hear and see nature all around you. You're in the middle of wide-open spaces and woodland and light. In the house, I felt trapped.

Claustrophobic. I used to constantly open the windows all the time to get the air in. I was woken up by traffic noises or the bin lorries, instead of birds and the sound of the wind. I couldn't tell when it was going to rain anymore, because I couldn't smell it in the air. That's why I always felt better when I escaped the house. When I was outdoors. Then I had freedom again and some sense of openness.

Being stuck in a classroom all day was really hard for me. I used to go to Blackleaf Forest a lot and just wander around, finding flowers to press, watching insects or birds or other animals. Or sit under a tree and just meditate. It was my safe haven.

And I felt alone. Lost. It was hard. Really hard. Moving from one culture to something completely different was a big challenge. And then when people realised we were Travellers, all the lies and rumours started. All the judgement and bigotry. There were a lot of misconceptions about me. About us. It seems like Travellers are the only group that it's still okay to hate. I'm not saying all Travellers are good. I know there are some bad people, just like there are bad people in any society or community. And I know there's racism on both sides. But our community weren't thieving or dirty. We didn't con people or commit crimes. We were just nomadic people who worked hard for what we had, looked after our own, and had our own social laws and rules that we abided by. We always kept our campsites clean and respected the area we were in. We always left it the way we found it.

When I was still living with my family on the road, we had little interaction with other people. But there would be times when we'd go into towns, shopping, or when we were living on the outskirts of a town, and we'd have abuse hurled at us. But we could get away from it afterwards. In Stoneminster, I couldn't get away from it.

—You were bullied at the Stoneminster High School?

—Yes. And those who weren't overtly bullying me were shunning me or making comments or spreading rumours. A lot of people called me names, but Dawn was the ringleader of the abuse.

And it wasn't just words. She bashed into me as I was walking down the corridor, wrote abuse on my locker, that kind of thing. She'd steal my books and the work I'd done so I'd get into trouble. She started as soon as I got there and didn't let up. She used to sit behind me in some classes and stab me with the needle-point end of a compass when the teacher wasn't looking. Or she'd write abusive words on the back of my clothes with Tipp-Ex. One time, she'd made up this Wanted poster with my face on it and taped it up to notice boards all over the school, saying I was wanted for stealing.

And I didn't understand why I was even there. The other kids were interested in things I thought were stupid. They didn't care about anything useful, purposeful. And most of the teachers were teaching things that either didn't make sense or that I thought were inconsequential in life.

But I put a brave face on things for Dad. Even though I wanted to just curl up and die, I kept thinking, No, there's a lesson here that I have to learn. The Universe has brought me here for some purpose. *And when I met Flora, everything got so much brighter. It felt like we were meant to meet. Like she was the other half of me.*

—Tell me about your friendship.

—*Having 'friends' was also a concept I wasn't familiar with. My family was so large that I never felt I needed friends. And when I got to Stoneminster and was ostracised immediately, I just thought I'd never make friends with anyone. Until Flora.*

It started with a rosemary bush at school. One lunchtime, I'd had enough of the taunts coming my way. I think I'd been there about a month, and I was just trying to keep out of everyone's way. I was sitting on the edge of the school playing field, and there was this rosemary bush there, and I was picking bits off it and putting it in my bag. I was going to make a poultice for Dad to see if that helped him, as it relieves muscle pains and inflammation. And I saw Flora walking towards me, across the field. We had some classes together, and I knew she wasn't one of the bullies, so I just sat there, waiting to see what would happen.

She sat next to me and picked some of the rosemary herself then rubbed it in her hands and smelled it. She said, 'Do you know that the aroma from rosemary can improve your concentration, speed, and accuracy? We need to stuff it up our noses before exams'. I just started laughing. And then I told her something about rosemary she didn't know, and then we just started talking about plants. It was an instant connection. From that moment on, we were best friends.

—And apart from nature, you were both interested in witchcraft.

—*Yes, but as usual, that got blown out of all proportion. It was never about worshipping the devil and concocting spells to do people harm or anything evil. For me, witchcraft is a philosophy, a way of life. It's about healing and nurturing. A spell is just a ritual. It's a way of asking the universe to bring you what you want. It's putting your intention out there and letting it manifest itself. It's no different to praying in any other religion. Ignorant people turned it into something completely different in the media.*

—Before we talk about the night Flora was murdered, I'd like to refer back to Jenny's horrific experience and how it relates to you. I know you haven't been listening to the podcast, as you're not allowed the internet in here, but your solicitor, Annabelle, informed me she's been keeping you up-to-date on the episodes.

Are you able to talk about what Jenny told us?

Again, I sense a shift in energy. The room suddenly feels colder. Her shoulders clench up to her ears. Her arms jerk protectively around her chest. Her face twitches. As if the memory of that day has speared through her like a lightning bolt. Caris's eyes dart around the room like a trapped animal's. And she is trapped, literally, inside this prison. But I believe she's also trapped in a life that I don't think was of her making. She takes some deep breaths, as if steeling herself before she begins, and a tsunami of suppressed emotion flashes on her face.

—You don't have to if you don't want to. But I have a feeling this is related to everything that came later. I think what happened when you were fifteen could be the catalyst to this tragedy. The integral thread that leads to the real heart of this crime.

—*It was the end of May, the day of the Stoneminster Fair, which happened every year. They had all these stalls set up in the market square and village green in the middle of the high street. The place was packed.*

It was half-term school holidays, and I'd been working in Willow's shop with Flora. Willow closed up at six o'clock, and we all left. Flora and Willow were going to check out the stalls, but I wanted to get back for Dad. He had Pam coming in every day to help him with things, but I wanted to go back and check he was okay, so I headed in the opposite direction to them.

I'd walked the route hundreds of times. Down the high street. Turn off right into Channing Lane. Then cut through an alleyway that led to the park. At the side of the park, there are bushes and then a small wood on one side, and if you carry on walking through the park, our estate was on the other side. All I had to do is go across the park in broad daylight and then walk through a few other streets for fifteen minutes to get to my house. But that didn't happen.

There was no one else around. I suppose most people were up at the fair. I didn't hear him come up behind me. I didn't... um...

This is where Caris's composure really cracks. I've spoken to people and read descriptions of Caris that say she's cold or arrogant or aloof. But I think it's a front. An act. Or more accurately, a protection mechanism. Whatever it is, it dissipates now, and all that's left is a vulnerable twenty-one-year-old girl with rivulets of tears streaming down her cheeks, struggling to breathe.

At that moment, she's not a convicted killer; she's a victim. Rage simmers inside me as I think about all she's endured in her life. My throat is choked with a rock-hard lump of emotion. I want to put my arms around her and tell her it's okay. But it's not okay. It's far from okay.

As I reach out to touch her arm, give her some comfort, she snatches it back and puts her hands over her face. She doesn't ever want to show her weaknesses to anyone. But maybe, just maybe, if she'd shown this side of her during all her struggles in Stoneminster, people wouldn't have been so quick to condemn her.

Caris asks me to leave the room for a while, and I tap on the door that's locking me in there with her and ask the guard to let me out. I wait outside until she's ready to carry on.

After several minutes, I'm led back inside. I sit down again in front of her, and she tells me the rest. Like Jenny's story, this is very difficult to hear. It's another trigger warning for you here.

—*He punched me in the back of the head. I sort of half fell, half stumbled towards the ground. One minute, I was upright, and the next, there was this almighty pain, and the ground was coming up to meet me. But before I landed, he dragged me by my hair towards the wooded area.*

I was kind of... I was almost bent over double while he was dragging me. I was trying to get away, and I couldn't even scream, because I was just too shocked. It happened so quick.

He threw me down. Facedown. And pressed my face into the dirt and leaves. He had his arm on the back of my head. I could hardly breathe. There were leaves in my mouth and just... I thought I was going to suffocate. I tried to scream then, but the noise was just muffled.

He... He lifted up my skirt, pulled my knickers down, and then... well, you know. He raped me. I was trying to struggle, but it was too hard. He was too strong. I was pinned there. Couldn't move. And he kept saying things to me the whole way through. He was calling me a bitch and a whore and a slag and kept saying, 'You fucking void', just like he did with Jenny.

—I'm so sorry you went through that.

—Thank you. Afterwards... he just ran off. I didn't see in what direction. I never saw his face at all. I think it actually took me a few minutes to realise he wasn't there. Because although he'd gone, it was like I could still feel him on me.

I couldn't move. It was almost like I was paralysed. I stayed like that for maybe ten minutes. And I could hear the Stoneminster brass band playing from somewhere in the high street. It was something so normal. And yet... nothing was normal. Everything was so far from normal.

Eventually, I managed to get up. I brushed the leaves off me and staggered back home. I was in a daze. I couldn't... I couldn't think straight. I didn't know what to do. It took all my mental effort to just get home. And when I got there, Dad had had a fall. I let myself in, and he called out to me from the kitchen. I just felt this intense anger then. I didn't want to talk to him. I just wanted to get in the shower. Get clean. But Dad's legs had given way, and he couldn't get up. He was propped up against the cooker, just sitting there, his legs splayed out. That would happen to him sometimes. He'd lose all feeling in his legs for a while, and he'd just collapse.

I managed to drag him to the sofa, pull his torso onto it and then his legs. And it gave me a few more moments where I wouldn't have to think about what had happened. Concentrating on looking after him, getting him sorted out, meant I wouldn't have to face the rape.

—How did you cope with it afterwards?

—I didn't cope. I tried to push it away. Tried not to think about it. I tried to have denial. But it doesn't work like that, does it?

I... I thought about suicide. I was sick of struggling with everything. Every time it felt like life was getting better for me, something bad always reared its head. It was only Flora who kept me above water. She kept me strong. And the thought of leaving Dad... I just couldn't do it. But it was a struggle. Getting through every day was a struggle.

—You decided not to report it to the police?

—That's right. For the same reasons Jenny didn't. Going through an investigation would be like being raped all over again. I'd never seen the man, so I couldn't identify him. Even if there was DNA evidence, it could still come down to my word against his. If they ever found him, he could say it was consensual. I just couldn't cope with it all on my own. I couldn't tell my dad. He had enough to deal with because of his health. And I didn't think the police would even believe me. People around town already had this idea that I was a no-good, dirty, lying gypsy girl.

—Were the arguments between yourself and Flora that Andrew Strytch heard shortly after that time about the rape?

—Yes. Flora knew something was wrong. I tried to hide it in front of Dad, and that was really hard. I kept it all together at home, but sometimes, when I was out of the house, it would just hit me, and I started crying. I hardly ever cried, though—that was the thing. Of course I cried after Mum. But I learned that crying didn't help. Crying wouldn't change my life. So I kept things inside a lot. Flora was the only one I ever told anything to. She knew about my background, my fears, how I was feeling. But that... the rape... I tried to keep it from her.

Until one day, I was at work in Willow's shop, and I just burst into tears. Andrew had just come in, and I... I just had this big fear that it could be him. I don't know why I thought that. It was probably really irrational. I just... It probably wasn't even him. It was... It was just a feeling. I can't explain it. And I just kept seeing myself on the ground.

—It was a flashback?

—Yes. There was nothing about him that stood out, really. But the worst part, I think, was knowing it could be anyone. That I'd never know who it was because I'd never seen him. I think that's when it hit me that he could be standing right next to me, talking to me, and I'd never know it.

—That must've been incredibly scary.

—It was. I fell apart in the shop. I suddenly started crying and shaking. Flora had been asking me what was wrong for weeks, but I just didn't know how to tell her. Didn't know how to say those words. Then suddenly I couldn't put it off any longer, and I had to get it out. Flora kept trying to get me to report it to the police, but I told her I couldn't.

Over the next few weeks, Flora kept trying to get me to change my mind, but I wouldn't. We argued a few times about it. That was the only thing we argued about. Ever. She was only doing it because she worried about me, but there was no way I could go through with it.

She'd found this rape counselling group through the internet. RASAS. She suggested that if I wasn't going to report it, I should go and talk to other people who'd been in the same situation. So I did. She offered to go with me, but it was something I felt I had to do on my own, because I didn't want her to hear it. And I didn't know until I heard about Jenny's story from Annabelle that he'd done it before. It had to be the same person. He said virtually the same things.

—Did you ever notice anyone following you after that, like Jenny believed he might've been doing to her?

—No. I was more aware by then. I kept alert. Kept watching men I saw. It was horrible. That not-knowing thing. I kept thinking he could do it again. He could come for me again, and I wouldn't know who he was.

I couldn't trust anyone apart from Flora. Living like that is so stressful. And I was trying to get on with school and ignore Dawn and her crowd and earn some money to help with the housekeeping by doing the shop work and spell boxes, and it was just... One day, I snapped and punched Dawn. She'd called me a slag in the toilets, like you heard. Her bullying had been going on for so long then. Usually, I just rose above it. Said nothing and kept my head down. But I couldn't take it anymore. Couldn't take anything anymore. I was a virgin, and I'd been raped, and he'd called me a slag when he was raping me, so her calling me that just made me explode. It was nothing Dawn didn't deserve. But as usual, I got the blame from the teachers. They all thought I was making trouble. Being a bully. I didn't even bother to explain what had really been going on. They wouldn't have listened to me. No one ever listened to me or believed me, so what was the point?

I went to RASAS for a few weeks. We all sat in a circle and listened to each other's stories. And it helped a little, talking to those other women. Helped me feel like I wasn't alone. I wasn't the only one who'd been through it. That I could get through it in the end. And eventually, I started to believe he wasn't going to come back for me.

—But then @InsRule came into your life?

—Yes. Just like what happened to Jenny. And after hearing about what she said, it seems certain it was the same guy—the rapist. At the time, I never suspected it could be him. Because I thought, why leave it months before he started those comments on Instagram? It was a joint page, and the Amethyst Witch had had the same problem with people, so I didn't think it was about me specifically. Now I know different. It had to be him.

—Did Annabelle show you the E-FIT photo of the man Damian saw in Blackleaf Forest the night of the murder?

—Yes. She took a copy of it for me and brought it with her.

—I know you didn't see the rapist, but do you recognise him at all? Do you think he could've been someone you knew?

—Like Jenny also said, there's something familiar about him. I think it could be the eyes. But I don't know who he is. I don't... There's something. I'm just not sure what.

—Okay. After @InsRule stopped trolling you, did you think that was the end of it?

—I thought that was the end of the trolling. But with the rape... It was never the end of it for me. Emotionally or otherwise. It's never been the end. I don't know if it will ever end.

I was trying hard to get on with my life, though, and things were going pretty well. I left school, so most of the bullying I was subjected to stopped. The online spell boxes and tarot readings were doing really well. Finally, Dad and I could afford a few extra things. It was hard living on benefits, and Dad never wanted to live off handouts. So things seemed to be getting better. For a few years, things got better. And then they fell apart.

At that point, the guard enters the room and tells us our time is up. Convicted prisoners are allowed at least two one-hour visits every four weeks, and although the prison governor has been helpful in arranging a more-frequent visit for me for this podcast, he's rigidly sticking to the hour's session. It will be another four days before I can wangle a second interview with Caris again.

In the meantime, before I wrap up this episode, we're going to hear from another witness we've discovered who was near Blackleaf Forest on the night of the murder. Brett Tyler was walking along Lower Street in the village of Westcombe, which is pinpointed on the map up on our website, but to clarify, the village nestles along the northwestern border of the forest. There are miles and miles of locations where someone could enter Blackleaf Forest, and this is just one of them.

—This is so weird. My mate listens to your podcast, and he was talking about it, saying it was round about the time I was in Dorset, so I caught up on the episodes. I'm Australian, but you can probably tell that from my accent, hey? Anyway, me and a group of mates were in the UK backpacking. And we spent a couple of days in Westcombe, staying in a bed and breakfast.

So yeah, I didn't know I actually knew anything until now. I didn't hear about the murder at the time as we left early in the morning on the twenty-second of June in 2017 to go to Thailand. Then we were travelling round Indonesia and Borneo and stuff for almost a year. I don't know if it hit the Australian news, but we were in the outback and jungle a lot and, yeah, I've only just found out.

—What did you see that night?

—It was 'bout nineish, I reckon. Me and my mates had hired these bikes, and we were cycling round the area. I think we'd been up to Lyme Regis that day, but I dunno. Anyway, we all got back to the B and B. We were knackered and couldn't be bothered to go down the pub and get some grub. So I offered to walk down the shop in the village and get some snacks and beers.

I'd just come out the shop and was walking back to the B and B, which was right at the edge of the village, and I saw this guy running out of the woods just a little way up ahead of me. I mean, it was three years ago, and I wouldn't even have remembered it if it wasn't for something that made it stick out in my mind.

He didn't just run out of the woods. He fell over a wooden fence that separates the forest from the footpath. I guess maybe the greenery had grown over it in that part and he didn't see it until it was too late. And he just kind of slammed into it and shot over it.

And I laughed. I thought it was hilarious, but that's my warped sense of humour. That's why I remember.

—What did he do then?

—*I was laughing but I still asked him if he was okay. He just picked himself off the path and mumbled about being fine, then he tucked his head down like he was embarrassed someone had seen that happen to him, and he ran off past me.*

I mean, I just thought he was doing a bit of jogging. Me and my mates had been cycling round the trails in Blackleaf a few days before and there were plenty of joggers and hikers and cyclists. It was still reasonably light so... yeah... it didn't mean much to me.

—Can you describe him?

—*I can't really remember much 'bout him. I think he had dark hair. I think he was wearing shorts and a T-shirt. And he had a bit of a flat nose. Like a boxer, yeah? That bit I do remember because I was laughing to myself, thinking that maybe he was accident-prone and he'd done a face-plant over another fence before. That's all I can really say.*

—Have you had a look at the *Anatomy of a Crime* website and seen the E-FIT picture up there?

—*Yeah. I mean, I think it's the same guy. But, like I said, it was a long time ago. And I only saw him for a few seconds.*

—Was he carrying anything?

—*You mean the bag, hey? Flora's multicoloured bag? I never saw it, but I vaguely remember he might've had something in his hand, sort of scrunched up.*

It's worth noting that if this is the same person Damian saw, it would mean that after he was spotted by Damian running in a southerly direction, he would've changed his direction of travel. Maybe the man did see Damian hiding in that tree and realised he might call the alarm, so he panicked and chose another area to exit the woods. But even though Brett's description isn't very detailed, and he can't be one hundred per cent certain it's the same man, the clothing would match, the features match, particularly the squashed nose, like it had been broken at one time, which is pretty distinctive. The fact that he was running out of the woods matches. With this new sighting of a suspicious man running away from the area of the murder that night, surely this validates Damian's statement to the police? A statement that was ignored. I believe it *was* the same man. And I want to find him.

If you recognise the E-FIT picture on the website or you know something about him or have any other information, please get in touch with us.

Thank you for listening to *Anatomy of a Crime*.

Until next time...

Leonora • 2 days ago
Wow. I'm just gobsmacked. I really feel for Caris. She was a victim twice over. I think there's been a huge miscarriage of justice here. That's 2 people who've seen that man now. He's a violent rapist who stalked and harassed women and then killed one. Why the HELL didn't the police find all this stuff?
^ | ˅ • Reply • Share ˃

Hayter → Reply to Leonora • 2 days ago
No way! It's just a made-up sob story to get sympathy. How do you know it even happened?
^ | ˅ • Reply • Share ˃

typox → Reply to Hayter • 1 day ago
You've got no empathy! Sounds like Caris went through hell.
Everyone was against her from the start, except her best friend. I
don't believe she killed Flora. And this man is still out there
somewhere. He's dangerous.
^ | ˅ • Reply • Share ˃

LawlessState • 2 days ago
The police just took the easy route. Do you remember that big
scandal a few years back where the police and prosecution weren't
disclosing evidence to the defence in many cases that proved they
were innocent?
^ | ˅ • Reply • Share ˃

Justice4all → Reply to LawlessState • 1 day ago
I got sent to prison for a crime I didn't commit. I was in a pub when
someone got glassed in the face after an argument. They charged
me with GBH because witnesses said the man who did it was
wearing a purple shirt. I was wearing a purple shirt, so they came
after me. The police only checked one CCTV camera in the place
that night, and it showed me on it, at the bar, in my shirt. I was
found guilty. Then afterwards, it was appealed because my
barrister finally found another camera! And the police knew it was
there, and they hid it on the disclosure paperwork on purpose!
Surprise, surprise, the other camera showed exactly who did start
the fight. You couldn't make it up. There are so many abuses of
justice going on, but you never get to hear about it.
^ | ˅ • Reply • Share ˃

Wigs&Co → Reply to Justice4all • 1 day ago
I'm a barrister, and this is far too common now. A review by the
attorney general in 2018 showed prosecutors and police were
routinely failing in their duties to disclose crucial evidence. Add to

that legal aid cuts, underfunding that leads to overworked staff juggling so many things they can't possibly prepare or vet everything properly, and some police forces willingly hiding exculpatory evidence. But as long as the government makes loud noises about being 'tough on crime', this is what happens. People don't realise quite how easily they could be accused and found guilty of a crime they didn't commit. I wonder what exculpatory evidence the police failed to disclose in this case?
^ | ˅ • Reply • Share ˃

Lalala • 2 days ago
If @InsRule did kill Flora, why? It doesn't make sense. Why didn't he kill Caris instead, if he was stalking and harassing her after the rape?
^ | ˅ • Reply • Share ˃

Jester → Reply to Lalala • 1 day ago
I don't know. Why don't you ask Ted Bundy?
^ | ˅ • Reply • Share ˃

Colonel Mustard • 1 day ago
She's still guilty!!
^ | ˅ • Reply • Share ˃

DoubleDutch → Colonel Mustard • 1 day ago
Here we go again! Get back under your rock.
^ | ˅ • Reply • Share ˃

X1 1Y3 • 2 days ago
I'm literally crying at this episode!
^ | ˅ • Reply • Share ˃

Mr Whippy → Reply to X1 1Y3 • 1 day ago

Me too.
^ | ˅ • Reply • Share ˃

FlFF67 → Reply to X 1 1 Y 3 • 1 day ago
Who is this man? Someone must know him!
^ | ˅ • Reply • Share ˃

CHAPTER SIXTEEN

POWER

You think it's over now, don't you? You've forgotten about it. About me. Three years is a long time, but I haven't forgotten any of it. Not. One. Single. Thing.

Do you know how many times *I* think about it all? It's something I relive over and over again, feeling the strength rise up inside. *I'm* in control here. Not you. Somehow the secret of it magnifies the experience. Sometimes, it's hard to keep in check. Sometimes, I don't bother to stop it. I take that power and use it again and again. The rush... Wow! It's like nothing else.

You think you're safe now, but you're not. No one is, really. You never know what pleasures or pain are lurking out there in the world, do you? You never know when something's going to strike next.

I know you almost as well as you know yourself. And you still haven't worked it out. You still don't realise. Because most people only see what they want to. Most people never look deep enough.

So you don't know the danger, do you? Don't know what's

going to happen. What I'll make happen exactly when I want to. You can believe in spells and all that sort of shit, but it won't protect you.

I sit in the beer garden of the pub and watch, my gaze following your movements across the shop through the window. I love the way you move—like a wolfess on the prowl. You throw your head back and laugh, the taut sinews of your neck begging to be caressed.

Some guy sits on the next table to me and puts his pint down before pulling out a nerdy book. I want to laugh in his face. He won't find the answers in any book.

I look at him out of the corner of my eye. He's trying to be oh-so hip and cool. All trendy and slick. He makes me sick too. I'd like to smash that book in his face, watch him squirm. He looks up, catches my eye and nods a greeting.

I nod back, picturing myself pouring the pint all over him, and I smile back at him before pulling my phone from my pocket and reading your texts again, one by one, savouring every detail.

After the arsehole on the table next to me gets up and strolls away, I look up and watch you again. Do you know what I'm thinking right now? I'm imagining putting my hands round your throat and choking the life out of you.

How will you look when it happens? I can see it now. Oh yeah, I can just imagine it. Your eyes wide. Astonished. Scared. Terrified. Your essence being expunged. I think about the many ways it might happen and wonder what it feels like to watch someone's life disintegrate beneath my hands. Power surges through me again. Adrenaline mixed with pure, unadulterated force, in an orgasm like no other.

Power. That's my drug. That's the real point to life.

CHAPTER SEVENTEEN

EPISODE 7
FIRE AND WATER

O n the twenty-first of June 2017, Flora Morgan was murdered in Blackleaf Forest. Her friend Caris Kelly was convicted of the crime and given a life sentence, although she's always maintained her innocence. I'm back at HMP Ashmount, talking to Caris, better known by some as the Sleeping Beauty Killer. Finally, we're going to hear about that night in Caris's own words.

—We know you and Flora left Willow's shop at 5 p.m. that afternoon. Then you went to Liz's supermarket and bought wine and a lighter that Flora put in her rainbow-coloured bag. She also had the candles in there. And then you walked along the lane out of Stoneminster to Blackleaf Forest. Can you tell me about the celebration ritual you were going to carry out for the summer solstice?

—People made it out to be this satanic ritual that was a prelude to Flora's murder, but it wasn't. Nearly every society has traditionally marked the summer solstice in some way. It's a time to honour the earth, nature, and the heavens. To find a balance between fire and water. Did you know that stone circles, like the ones at Stonehenge and found on the outskirts of Stoneminster were used to highlight the rising of the sun on the summer solstice?

It's about the battle between light and darkness. Symbolically, it's a time of brightness, sun, and warmth. Crops are growing and need water and heat to keep them alive. Mother Earth is abundant and fertile with life. So it's usually celebrated with some form of fire, like bonfires or candles, and water, like swimming in a river. It's a time to meditate on both the darkness and light in your life and acknowledge the turning wheel of the year, night and day. Being outdoors and celebrating with love spells and candles was how we did it.

—Why did you choose to do it at Rose Hurst's cottage at Witch's Hill? Why not in Flora's back garden, with a paddling pool or bowl of water? Or some other location?

—When I moved to Stoneminster, I heard about Rose Hurst and Witch's Hill. The more I learned about her, the more I could kind of relate to her. She wasn't a witch at all. At least, not in the way the people in the town thought of her. She was a midwife and healer. But in those days, fears of witchcraft were rife. Most accusations were false, but it didn't make any difference. A lot of people were hanged after being found guilty. Things haven't changed much, have they? Rose was convicted based on no evidence other than plenty of rumours and gossip.

Flora was obsessed with her, as well, for the same reasons. But before I was even friends with Flora, I used to go into Blackleaf Forest, to Rose's cottage, and... I saw her. Just like Damian saw her, and the hundreds of other people have seen her over the centuries.

—What did you see?

—At first I heard the creaking sound, like Damian did. By the oak tree. I was sitting under it at the time, and I felt a presence. The temperature dropped, and this breeze kicked up. The birds stopped singing. There was no sound at all.

At first, she just appeared as this black shape. The outline of a woman. Then her face sort of shimmered into being. She had long red hair, pale skin, but her eyes were just dark orbs. She was hovering above the trees off to my right. I was watching her, and I had the feeling she was trying to tell me something. I could sense... I don't know... that she wanted to do something for me. That's when I heard the whispers.

—What kind of whispers?

—It was my mum's voice. She was saying, 'You're okay. I love you, Caris. You're safe. You're okay. Stay strong'.

—Did you feel scared at that point?

—No. I knew Rose wasn't trying to do me any harm. She was giving me a message. Mum's voice wasn't coming from Rose. It was echoing all around me, but I knew Rose was the channel for her. She was saying the same thing over and over again for about five minutes. Then Rose disappeared, and so did Mum.

—Did you tell Flora what you'd experienced when you became friends?

—Yes. And after that, we used to go up there a lot together. Sometimes we'd take a picnic. Or just lie on a blanket under the oak tree, talking. Sometimes we'd swim in the river or do spells there. We were so comfortable with each other that a lot of the time we didn't even need words. We just read next to each other or listened to music. Those were some of the best times in my life, being free and happy and contented with her.

Flora wanted to see if she could get a message from her dad there, but she never heard from him. And I never heard Mum's voice there again. But it was a special place to me because of that. I felt at peace there. So did Flora.

—So who chose that location for the ritual?

—*I did, but Flora probably would've suggested the same thing. There was a good energy there. And I was hoping that, because of the solstice, the protective spirit of my mum would come through again powerfully.*

—What happened when you got to the cottage? Walk me through what you remember.

Caris blows out a breath. She's told this story many times to the police, in court, but the difference now is that people are listening to her this time. Really listening to her.

—*When we got to Witch's Hill, it was deserted. The place usually is. It's off the cycle and walking trails, and the woods are quite dense there, so not many people used to go to that part of the forest.*

Flora put her bag under the oak tree with the wine and candles still inside. Then we stripped off our outer clothes. We were wearing bikinis, and we realised then we'd forgotten to bring towels to dry ourselves with. But it was a hot day, so we didn't care about that.

We walked around the outside of the cottage ruins to the river and got into the water. We were just bobbing in the river, splashing each other, and floating around for about fifteen minutes. It was refreshing after the walk, because it was so hot and humid that day. Then we did the ritual. We both cupped our hands to collect water and poured it over ourselves while reciting a spell.

—How long did the ritual take?

—*About ten minutes.*

—So there was about twenty-five minutes when your belongings, including the wine, were unattended?

—*Actually, it would've been longer than that. We couldn't see our stuff from where we were in the river, either. Someone must've come along and spiked the wine with ketamine. It was a screw top, and it would be easy to undo it, add the ketamine, and screw it back up.*

—What happened after the ritual?

—*There's a bit of a steep bank to get in and out. I went first and was halfway up. Flora was behind me. She shrieked and started falling backwards. I reached out to her with my left arm and grabbed her right forearm. She held on to me, and I pulled her up the bank. That was how I got the scratches. Why my skin was underneath her nails. She caught my skin as she was clinging on to me. It could've been how my hair got trapped in her bracelet, as well.*

Then we stood on the bank in the sunshine to dry off a little. We stood there for about another ten minutes. So it was more like thirty-five minutes where the wine was unattended. And after that, we walked round the side of the cottage back to the oak tree.

—Did you see anyone else around at that point?

—*No. No one. But the oak tree and cottage area is in a small clearing, and surrounding that is the woods. Someone could've been there, watching us, and we wouldn't have seen them.*

After that, we got dressed again and did the rest of the fire ritual. We got some stones from the cottage ruins and put them in a circle. We placed candles inside and outside the circle, lit them, and we recited a spell for healing, protection, love, happiness, and abundance. Then Flora opened the wine, and she couldn't have noticed that it had been tampered with.

We were drinking from the bottle and... and that's it. That's all I can properly remember. Everything after that is just this big blank.

—Flora's body was also surrounded by a circle of stones. Did either of you do that for the ritual?

—*No. We were sitting on the outside of the stones. They must've been moved afterwards. We never drew the pentagram in the dust, either.*

—Willow said you told her you were going to Witch's Hill as

you were leaving the shop that day. She said it's possible someone might've overheard you talking about it through the open doorway. Are you aware of anyone else who knew you were going there?

—*I didn't tell anyone, and I don't think Flora would've done, either.*

—There have been a lot of people who say it's pretty convenient you can't remember what happened that evening. The police and the Crown Prosecution Service, for starters.

Caris blows out air through her nose. She rests her elbows on the desk in the meeting room we're in and droops her head forwards. Her hair falls over her face, and she runs her fingers through it. She stays there for a long minute, just the rise and fall of her shoulders getting faster and faster that gives away her anger. I ask her if she wants to stop, but she shakes her head. Finally, she looks up, sits up. Her jaw tenses, and her teeth grind together. A flush creeps up her neck. But when she finally speaks, her voice is resigned. Hollow. Hopeless. As if her anger, like her tears, are useless in this place.

—*It's not convenient, though, is it? It's very inconvenient for me. They all thought I was lying. They thought I'd spiked the wine and given it to Flora to drink. They thought when she was out of it with the ketamine and alcohol that I killed her. They thought I drank the wine after I'd killed her to make it seem as if I'd been spiked too. Why would I do that? I loved Flora! I loved her. And I don't mean in a romantic way, as some of the stupid tabloids claimed. We weren't having a lesbian affair! She was the only one who understood me completely. Apart from Dad, she was the only one who cared about me. I lost more than my best friend that night. She was part of me. Part of my soul.*

—Ketamine   mixed   with   alcohol   can   produce   severe hallucinations. Is it possible you killed Flora while in that state? That it was, in fact, an accident on your part, due to someone else spiking the wine? Your solicitor mentioned you vaguely remember seeing a shape that you thought was Rose Hurst's ghost that evening, along with a dragon.

—*I've thought about it and thought about it so much. You have no idea. The recollection of a shape I thought was Rose and the dragon is so vague. It's like a fragment of a dream, but when you wake up, you can't grasp it. I can't explain it. The ketamine messed with my head. I don't know. I just don't have any proper memories.*

So, yes, I suppose it is possible I did it and don't remember. I have no answer for that. But it doesn't seem likely, does it, when someone else spiked the wine? There was a reason they did that. It was planned. They must've followed us to the woods. Waited until we were out of sight and then put the drug in the wine. Then waited until we were unconscious and killed her. I think someone must've overheard our conversation that day as we were leaving the shop and followed us. It's the only explanation I can think of.

—When Liz and Bill found you in the woods that night, she heard you mumble, 'It's him'. What did you mean by that?

—*I don't know. I just don't know. I guess I was semi-conscious then, I think. Maybe I saw someone or heard someone. Maybe the shape I saw was real. Maybe it was the killer. But I just can't remember. And if I was lying about all this... if it was really me who killed her and I wanted to get away with it, I would've told the police I definitely saw a man there, wouldn't I? I would've lied to create another suspect. I would've given a fake description of him. I would've said I saw him kill her but couldn't stop him because I was semi-conscious or couldn't move. Ketamine can cause muscle paralysis, too, you know? Doesn't that really show my honesty and integrity?*

—I agree it would've made more sense for someone who's guilty to fabricate a definitive sighting of the man Damian saw. And I don't want to point fingers at your defence team—after all, they did put Damian on the stand—but do you think your solicitors and barrister could've done more for you? Did they do enough to find any corroborating witnesses, like Brett from Australia?

—*I don't really know. All I can say is, I was just eighteen. I didn't know about the law and the way the justice system works. I trusted the people who were supposed to defend me. I was lucky enough to get legal aid, but some people can't even get that now, with all the cutbacks in funding. One of the women in here had to represent herself in court because she couldn't afford a barrister. I know my solicitor was dealing with so many cases. I know my barrister only got the case the morning of the trial. And that's because the original barrister we were going to have was dealing with a trial that ran over, so he had to pass it on to a colleague. Is that really enough time to look through all the paperwork and make essential arguments that could've helped my case?*

And now that Brett has come forward because of this podcast, it proves I'm right, doesn't it? It proves someone else was there. Someone else spiked the drink, like I've always said. Someone else killed Flora.

—Why do you think they didn't kill you too?

—*I don't know. I don't understand it. I've tried to come up with reasons, like maybe he was disturbed by someone before he could kill me. But if he had time to arrange a stone circle around Flora and draw a pentagram, wouldn't he have had time to murder me? Or maybe they couldn't go through with a second murder after killing Flora. Or maybe they targeted Flora specifically for some reason.*

—Again, the motive for me is still a huge unanswered question. We know now about @InsRule targeting your joint business Instagram page, but from what we've discovered since, it was really you he was targeting, not Flora. Jenny believes the E-FIT of the man Damian helped compile is very similar to the man involved in her attack, so if he *is* responsible for the murder, why was he after

221

Flora? Did Flora ever tell you she was having problems with anyone? Was anyone paying her too much attention? Or the wrong kind of attention?

—*No. I don't know why someone would do anything to her. I have absolutely no idea. She had no enemies that I knew of.*

But maybe I do know.

It hits me then—the culmination of stories, the long journey building up to that night. What if this was really all about hurting Caris? What if it was about framing Caris for the murder of her best friend? It's a bizarre, elaborate motive, but it's not impossible. And who would go to those lengths? Many people have described Flora's killer as evil, and they're right. But I'm certain now that person isn't Caris.

Like the original Disney Sleeping Beauty story, I think this whole case has been a fairy tale. But I finally feel like I'm so close to unravelling the conjecture and lies that have tainted the truth from the very beginning.

So I have a message for Flora's killer...

Are you listening to this right now? Are you hanging on every word to see if you'll be named? Are you confident no one will eventually come forward after seeing the E-FIT picture? Maybe you still think you executed the perfect murder and got away with it. Or do you feel the truth closing in on you? Do you realise now it's only a matter of time before we uncover your identity?

Thank you for listening to *Anatomy of a Crime.*

Until next time...

WooLS • 2 days ago
We need to find this sadist! Someone must know who he is.
^ | ˅ • Reply • Share ˃

WTF! → Reply to WooLS • 2 days ago
Whoah! I'm just catching up on this podcast, and I think I might
know who this guy on the E-FIT is!!! :O I'm going to email the
address on this website right now.
^ | ˅ • Reply • Share ˃

Babyboomer • 2 days ago
@InsRule almost cut off Jenny's airway with his arm! Those types
of serial offenders hone their MO. And he progressed to
strangulation.
^ | ˅ • Reply • Share ˃

Roxy5 → Reply to Babyboomer • 2 days ago
Why didn't he rape Flora then if it was the same person? I don't
believe Caris was raped in the first place. It's just a cry for attention
to make people feel sorry for
her.
^ | ˅ • Reply • Share ˃

HGss → Reply to Roxy5 • 1 day ago
Maybe they didn't report it because they knew they'd be ridiculed
by people like YOU! What if it happened to your sister? Daughter?
Mum? Would you believe them?
^ | ˅ • Reply • Share ˃

TTTT • 2 days ago
Anyone know where I can get frog-shaped soap from?
^ | ˅ • Reply • Share ˃

WTAF → Reply to TTTT • 2 days ago
????????????????
^ | ˅ • Reply • Share ˃

Brizzy • 2 days ago
So are there 2 stalkers then? @InsRule, who attacked and stalked
Jenny and Caris, and someone else who wanted to kill Flora? I'm
confused.
^ | ˅ • Reply • Share ˃

WHEE451 → Brizzy • 1 day ago
Dunno. Every time I make up my mind what's going on, something
else changes.
^ | ˅ • Reply • Share ˃

FuzzBalls → Reply to Brizzy • 1 day ago
Might be the same sicko. He's insane.
^ | ˅ • Reply • Share ˃

RapeCrisis • 2 days ago
If anyone's affected by this story who's been raped or sexually
assaulted, don't suffer in silence. There's plenty of support out
there. Please ask for help, even if you don't want to report it to the
police. You're not alone.
^ | ˅ • Reply • Share ˃

Bonzo → Reply to RapeCrisis • 1 day ago
Why didn't they report it to the police if a man raped them? It
doesn't ring true!
^ | ˅ • Reply • Share ˃

Stella3 → Reply to Bonzo • 1 day ago
Oh my God. You have no idea, do you? Only a very small % of

rapes are ever reported. And it's the only crime where the victim becomes the accused!

^ | ˅ • Reply • Share ˃

Tuti • 2 days ago
Now they're trying to blame Kelly's defence team. How ridiculous. She's the one who killed her best friend.

^ | ˅ • Reply • Share ˃

SS10 → Reply to Tuti • 1 day ago
Are we listening to the same podcast here? Nothing stacks up anymore. It's obvious there's been a miscarriage of justice. Everyone needs to share and catch this arsehole!

^ | ˅ • Reply • Share ˃

Twitterz • 2 days ago
Stop going on about rape. It's bad enough listening to it, but reading these comments makes me feel sick.

^ | ˅ • Reply • Share ˃

Poppy → Reply to Twitterz • 2 days ago
Seeing as it affects thousands of women a day, we need to keep 'going on' about it, or nothing will ever change! How 'sick' is that?

^ | ˅ • Reply • Share ˃

CHAPTER EIGHTEEN

EPISODE 8
TWISTED

At the start of this podcast, I had no idea where the investigation would take me. I didn't know the chain of events I'd set in motion when I took on a challenge to find the untold story, and I've been led in a circle. A circle of lies and rumours and evil things that lurk beneath the surface. And somewhere in there was the truth I was desperate to find.

I have to admit this episode nearly didn't happen, but I couldn't leave things hanging. It wasn't enough to expose the serious doubt and questions of Caris's conviction and leave it there. I wasn't intending to find the real killer of Flora Morgan in the beginning. But now I have.

And before this episode goes any further, I need to give you another warning. What you're about to hear is highly disturbing and chilling. It's sick and twisted and has led to a dark place that, although difficult to listen to, needs a light shone on it. In fact, it needs a beacon.

How many of you have heard the term 'incel'? If you haven't, you're not alone. I have to admit I'd never heard it before, and I've investigated some heinous subjects.

In short, it's a dangerous element in our society that has become one of the internet's most vile subcultures. What started as an online forum—a place for lonely, shy, introverted, awkward kids to come together and forge a sense of connection—has rapidly turned into a much deadlier and more insidious community.

The voice you're going to hear next belongs to an investigative journalist who recently did a huge exposé on this very subject and is more of an expert than me. Due to the undercover work she does, she's going to remain anonymous. I think it's essential to get this background from her before we go further.

—What does the term 'incel' mean?

—*In the 90s, there was this online community that began as a place for kids to hang out. Particularly those who had issues about the way they looked or low self-esteem, or problems surrounding dating and the opposite sex. Later, they began describing their romantic problems and lack of relationships as 'involuntary celibacy'. The term was then shortened to 'incel'.*

At that time, it was a friendly place where kids of both sexes could chat—guys who didn't know how to talk to or act around women could get their female members to give advice and vice versa. But fast-forward to the last two decades, and it's turned into a community of somewhere in the region of tens of thousands of men who promote a profoundly sexist, prejudice, misogynistic, and male-dominated ideology that they call 'the black pill'. On a basic level, they reject women's sexual emancipation and believe women are shallow, nasty creatures who only choose the most attractive men.

There are many incel forums out there, and about ninety per cent of the members are under thirty years old. A lot of people share personal stories about how their looks or other personality traits have ruined their chances of meeting a woman. Their experiences are full of isolation and rejection from the opposite sex. Some seem perfectly reasonable, normal guys. But you'll also find a large proportion full of rage and hatred and toxic grandiosity.

The members see themselves as victims of female cruelty. They regularly vent, blaming women for their lack of ability to have sex with them. They teach each other that they can sleep with women by insulting them, manipulating them, or gaslighting them. They have a sense of entitlement that women owe them sex, and there is something seriously wrong with society when a woman doesn't have to give it to them.

Maybe if their beliefs were confined purely to the ranting pages of the internet, it would be tolerable. But these sexually repressed and frustrated beliefs spread over into real life, and on an extreme level of their behaviour, the black pill can, and has, incited violence against women.

—What kind of violence are you talking about?

—*Sometimes this comes in the form of harassment or stalking, sometimes sexual assault or rape, and sometimes murder. On several forums, members and administrators openly praise mass killers of women and encourage members to murder them.*

—I've never heard of any murders in the press with the term 'incel' used. Can you be more specific about how their ideology has led to real-life crimes?

—*Sure. These are documented cases. In 2014, self-identified incel Elliot Rodger killed six people and injured fourteen before turning his gun on himself. Afterwards, there was a posthumous series of YouTube videos, which made his motivation for the attacks clear. He said all he ever wanted was to love women, but their behaviour towards him made him hate them. He wanted to have sex with them, but they were disgusted at the prospect and had no sexual attraction towards him. His angry grievances were laid out in great* detail, putting the blame for his dating problems on the shoulders of women and inciting incels to recognise their strength in numbers and overthrow the oppressive feminist system.

Worryingly, Rodger's actions made him an inspiration to the radical incel community, who labelled him as a saint or hero. Some forums have memes of his face photoshopped onto pictures of Christian icons. For other incels who commit mass violence, or want to, they coined the phrase 'going ER', after Elliot Rodger.

In 2018, Alek Minassian drove a van purposefully on a sidewalk in Toronto and killed eight women and two men, injuring sixteen others. Minassian was an incel, and before the attack, he posted on Facebook, describing himself as basically a foot soldier in the incel war on society. He wrote, 'The Incel Rebellion has already begun! We will overthrow all the Chads and Stacys!' Afterwards, some of the incel community celebrated the murder, inciting other incels to follow up with acid attacks and mass rape of women. Just to clarify, in the warped world of incel-speak, the name Stacy is a term for attractive women, and Chad is an attractive man. Both of whom incels despise.

Then in 2018, Scott Beierle shot and killed two women at a yoga studio and injured five more. He had a record of harassing women and had uploaded misogynist videos comparing himself to Elliot Rodger.

These are just a few examples, but everywhere you look on an incel forum, there are expressions of raw, unabridged rage and hatred directed at women, saying women need to suffer and be tortured. Even if you can stomach it, I wouldn't recommend seeking out any of these places. Women are frequently referred to as whores, bitches, sluts, and often much worse. One member said all women should be fed into an industrial woodchipper. Another said they should all be raped. Another said they should have acid thrown in their faces. Some call them subhuman objects whose purpose is to obey men, spouting male entitlement to own them and female obligation to be a slave to them. They feel entitled to women's bodies. And when they find women don't want to have sex with them, these incels are consumed with hatred for what they see as being denied their birthright.

I'll spare you the rest of the examples I have, because, for one, it's truly disturbing, and two, I'd be here all day. But the bottom line is that a vast number of them aren't just lonely people who want to be loved. They are arrogant, bitter, vengeful, sexist, and narcissistic. They legitimise violence as a good response, a normal response, to the incel's perceived sexual entitlement.

And the sad thing is, that some seemingly normal guys join these forums at first because they want genuine advice about women or their dating problems. They want someone to understand what they're going through, and maybe it feels like a lifeline to them at a difficult point in their lives, but then they get sucked into all this dark negativity and resentment that can shape future behaviour and increase their willingness to actually hurt women themselves. These forums and the internet allow these extreme ideas to spread like a pandemic.

—It also begs the question... how likely are these beliefs to spur on copycats of violence?

—I don't think that's the right question. It's more like, how many of the thousands of attacks on women actually are copycats? With all this glorifying of violence, how many of these people feel more justified in acting it out?

—What are the police doing about it?

—That's a good question. And one I can only partly answer, I'm afraid. Free speech is protected, and people make empty threats all the time. How do you determine which are real and which aren't? Just saying you want to attack or kill women isn't enough for a prosecution. If it's a direct threat to a specific person or a post openly admitting a crime has taken place, then that should be a different matter. But often, these people are either using anonymous web browsers, like TOR, to hide their online identity, which makes tracing them difficult, or they don't openly name names of who they've been violent to.

Stalking, inciting violence, attacks on women, and violent speech should all be investigated, but they're not. In the UK, for example, misogyny is not considered a hate crime. If it was, tackling such incel sites under hate crime legislation would make things easier. The violent fringe of the incel movement should considered domestic terror threats, like any other terror group, but again, that's not happening.

Some law enforcement agencies are working on shutting down sites, but people just move to another one. And any proactive measures police are taking aren't happening fast enough or often enough.

The bottom line is that, worryingly, incels seem to have been dismissed as this odd little internet subculture for much too long. They aren't taken anywhere near seriously enough. But ignoring these places means ignoring the very real danger they pose, because these forums have weaponised misogyny and normalised hateful rhetoric. And for some women, this deadly threat from deranged men won't be recognised until it's too late.

We're supposed to be living in a progressive society, with progressive attitudes, but it's actually regressing to medieval times.

And sadly, like the examples we've just been given, the ideology that exists in these dark corners of the internet hasn't been contained there yet again, and it's on a website called IncLikeMe.com that I tracked down @InsRule. Yes, the man who raped Jenny and Caris. The one who taunted them afterwards by cyberbullying them because it wasn't enough for him to break them once. He had to keep going. He had to keep them scared and tormented. And he didn't stop with cyberbullying them. He went much further.

Just like when he trolled the Instagram page belonging to Caris and Flora, @InsRule logged onto IncLikeMe, which is a shortening for IncelLikeMe, using the anonymous browsing software TOR. TOR is regarded as the best cloak for people who want to hide on the internet. And although it's usually associated with the dark web, there are plenty of legitimate reasons for using it. Journalists and whistleblowers, for example, or people who just don't want Big Brother tracking their every move. Most of us don't realise how little internet privacy we really have. We're being stalked through cyberspace every time we log on and search the web, from our browser and social media accounts to name just a few. And while TOR is very secure, there are a few instances where your IP address, and therefore your real identity, can be tracked and traced.

I'm not a computer or techno expert, so I'll give you the simple explanation of how our technical researchers tracked him down. By enabling JavaScript, cookies and super cookies, and Adobe Flash when using TOR, it can leak your information. And on the twenty-second of June 2017, a day after Flora's murder, @InsRule logged on to IncLikeMe and left a bragging post on the site. Afterwards, he logged on to Instagram, under the profile name of @PowerTrip1, yet another trolling account. But what he didn't realise was that his IP address was visible to all who really wanted to look for him. If you can stomach it, press pause and check out his post on IncLikeMe that we've posted on our website.

Posted by @InsRule Status: Super Member	**I went ER!!!!** June 22nd, 2017, 05:43 am
	I did it! I went ER! Critical mass, guys! Wow. I feel awesome. For years I've fantasised about slaughtering a femoid. Everything is their fault. I'm just a loser, a weirdo, a freak to those Stacys. Well, not anymore. The normies can't kick me down anymore. I've got the real power. We all have. You can do it too. And you know what? I don't think I can stop now. The rush was incredible. I can't describe it. I'm buzzzzzzzzzzzzzzing.

Several people have also now contacted us naming @InsRule from the indentikit picture, and of course, I've turned over everything I've discovered to the police, but I can't leave it there. I want to hear from him. I want to confront him. The evil troll has been hiding in his cave for far too long like the coward he is. He's even been stalking me during my time in Stoneminster. If you've been listening to all of this podcast, then you know him, too, from a previous episode.

When I call the mobile number I have for him, a voice tells me it's no longer in service. When I visit his parents' house, no one answers the door. From inside, I hear a dog barking. The same dog, I suspect, whose hair will be a DNA match for the one found on Flora's body.

After I get no response to my repeated calls and visits, I join and log on to IncLikeMe, even though the posts make me feel physically sick. And as a last-ditch attempt, I send him a personal message through the forum's DM function, asking him to contact me.

I hear nothing and wonder where to go next. Is that the end of the line for me? Can I do no more than wait for the police to investigate what I think they should have before?

No. That's not quite the end of the story. Surprisingly, he calls me on my mobile number, and he agrees to be interviewed. This is the recording:

—You won't find me, you know. I'm one step ahead of you. I've always been one step ahead. You can find anything on the dark web, so a new ID's no problem on there. You'll all be looking for a ghost now, won't you? But before I disappear for good, I'll tell you all what you want to know. Fair play to you for getting this far. The police couldn't investigate their own breakfast, could they? No one believed that village idiot who saw me that night. No one even recognised the E-FIT picture because, well, first of all, it's like a five-year-old did it, and second, women aren't the only ones who can change their appearance.

Caris was right, actually. People only see what they want to. And they only see who they want to. That's the whole point. When you're the fat kid at school, they shun you, ignore you, don't even look at you half the time. Or they bully you. I got bullied at school, too, by that skanky bitch Dawn and her brother, and others. Caris didn't have the monopoly on that.

—That's your excuse, is it? You were bullied, so you raped two women, tormented them, and then murdered another?

—I didn't think you'd understand. You have no idea what it's like to be me. Trapped in this body no bitch would look at. While everyone else is a normie. Getting what they want.

—You mean people you perceive as normal who are having sex?

234

—Of course I mean sex! That's what makes the world go round, doesn't it? Sex and power.

—So tell me why you did this. Was it some warped, evil fantasy that made you destroy their lives?

—You're getting ahead of yourself here. If I tell my story, I'm doing it in my own time.

—Okay. I'm listening.

—So... I was always the fat kid with no friends. You know, the one who always gets laughed at and called names at school? Eventually, my mum started getting worried about me. Dad kept hassling her because he was embarrassed about my size and the fact that I wasn't like him. I wasn't man enough to play rugby like he used to. He kept trying to make me play all these sports to get fit and lose weight, but I was useless at them. I just kept getting hit by all the other kids. They tried to make it look like an accident on the pitch, but they were doing it on purpose. And the more useless I was, the more Dad seemed to hate me. I definitely wasn't his idea of the son he wanted.

He made Mum put me on this diet. I was probably about eleven stone then. I don't remember a time I was ever thin as a kid, really. I kept sneaking biscuits and chocolate and crisps into my room and stuffing them. She gave up in the end. Let me eat what I wanted. But the more unhappy I was, the more I ate. It was a vicious circle.

I remember one time, when it was my eighth birthday. Mum had invited all the kids in my class to a birthday party at the house, and no one turned up. No one. Mum cried her eyes out. Dad just had this look of disgust on his face. I knew then there was not much point trying to make friends. I was different to the other kids.

So after that, I'd spend all my spare time on computer games or internet forums for other fatties. Didn't hardly leave the house except for school.

Before this turns into a big sobfest, I'll spare you the years in *between, getting bullied by that femoid Dawn and her older brothers. But you get the gist, don't you?*

—So you expect people to feel sorry for you? You projected your inadequacies onto women in a way that became more and more violent. You—

—*Do you want to hear this or not? Stop with the judgement. You don't know what you're talking about. They were the cause of all this. They brought it on themselves. They're to blame.*

—How?

—*If you shut up, I'll tell you.*

I noticed Caris round school as soon as she joined. At first, in her lunch break, she'd be sitting at the end of the playing field on her own, with her head buried in a book, and I felt sorry for her. I thought, Yeah, we could be mates.

When Caris came to Stoneminster, she was thirteen. I'd just turned fifteen and was in my last year at school. I liked her straight away. I recognised something in her. Like, we were the same. Social outcasts. Misfits. I knew what people were saying about her. That she was this dodgy pikey. That she was dirty. That she'd killed her mum.

I watched her for a long time, trying to pluck up the nerve to talk to her. Months went by, and I still couldn't do it. But suddenly, she was the reason I wanted to get up in the mornings. Before her, I hated myself and my life. And she made everything better. Just the thought of seeing her every day at school made me happier.

Then, in my last week of school, before I was leaving, I thought, I've got to do it. I've got to talk to her. *She was hanging round with Flora by then, and they were always together. I could never get Caris on her own. But this day, at lunchtime, Caris was on the playing field on her own, eating her packed lunch, reading, and Flora was nowhere to be seen. She was fourteen then. I was sixteen. I probably weighed about fifteen stone. Which, yeah, some people would say is my fault.*

I approached her. I'd already rehearsed everything in my head I was going to say for about a year. How I was going to see if she wanted to be friends. Ask her if she wanted to hang out together somewhere after school and that. We could play video games together and stuff. Because I didn't care what they all said about her. Everyone else believed all the shit; that's why she only had Flora as a friend. But I didn't care.

As I walked over to her that day, I was mumbling everything I'd practiced over and over, making sure it sounded right. And I finally got to her.

She looked up. I'd never seen anyone as pretty as her before. She looked exotic. She was like this little bird of paradise or something. She looked into my eyes. And I felt this twist in my heart. I liked her. Really liked her.

But I couldn't get the words out properly. I opened my mouth, but nothing came out right. It was like my tongue had swollen up. I forgot what I was going to say. And the only thing that came out was, 'Do you want to be my girlfriend?'

I was mortified! Embarrassed as hell. I hadn't meant to ask her that. I just wanted to talk about the friends bit. Take things slowly, you know? I thought if she got to know me as friends, she would really like me. She could love me eventually. But I guess it was what my mind was thinking, and it just blurted out. And do you know what she did?

She laughed at me. She fucking laughed, and then she said no.

—She was only fourteen. How was she supposed to react?

—So what? I'd finally plucked up the nerve to talk to her, and she laughed in my face! But that's what women do. They think they're so brilliant. Think they're so perfect. They lead men on and then embarrass them. They're cruel, lying trash.

I stumbled off, as fast as my fat legs would carry me. She was as bad as slaggy Dawn. And I thought... even the social outcast doesn't *want to know me. Doesn't see me for who I really am. Even she rejected me. You don't know how low that made me feel.*

And as I sort of stumbled away, my face bright red, Flora walked past me, heading towards Caris. I turned back around, and I knew Caris was telling her what I'd just said, because they both started looking at me and laughing. That was crushing. That changed everything. That's where it started.

Have you recognised his voice yet from the interview in episode two? This is Rob Curran, who lied about seeing Caris at Witch's Hill carrying out a devil-worshipping animal sacrifice. And if you recall the story Leanne Welland told us about the fight in the toilet between Dawn and Caris, you'll also remember that Leanne mentioned that Dawn and her brothers bullied Rob at school, when he was known by the nickname, Blobby.

After I edited Rob's story, I went back to see Caris to clarify his version of events on the playing field that day, but Caris only vaguely remembers it. She doesn't remember laughing at him. She told me that she would never have done it to hurt him, as she knew he was also bullied at school. If she did laugh, she says, it would've been a nervous or shocked response to his question. She says she turned him down gently and politely and at no time tried to ridicule him. She says she didn't even know his real name—she just knew him as Blobby—and can't remember any other interaction with him at all.

One of the terrifying aspects is that this incident was the catalyst for something far greater than a snubbed fellow pupil. This conversation, seemingly insignificant to Caris, had the power to mutate into something insidious and deadly. When danger lurks so close to you, you think you should be able to spot it. Look it in the eyes and see it for what it is. But Caris had no clue what Rob was really like. Maybe no one else did, either. Maybe that's why he's so good at hiding his true self. But when you think about it, most people didn't really know what Caris was like, either. They didn't bother to find out.

—*After I left school, my parents moved to Southampton, about seventy miles away. Dad had got a new job there, and I was like, Yeah, whatever, fuck Stoneminster. Nothing good ever happened for me there. Mum kept on at me: 'This is a brand-new start for you', blah, blah, blah. I started an apprenticeship in car mechanics at a garage. The guys there were all right, I suppose, but they still took the piss out of my weight. And I thought, yeah, maybe I should make a real effort to change myself. Maybe if I lose weight, girls will finally start to look at me.*

So I went on this diet and lost loads of weight. And I'd go down the pub with the guys after work and see them chatting up the women and try to watch what they did. See how the women responded. There was one guy there. He had a new bird every frigging week. I thought, How does he do it?

I tried a few times. Tried to chat these girls up in the pub, and they just looked at me like I was a piece of shit off their shoes. They would always start laughing at me with their mates. Again! That's all women ever did—laugh or look at me like I was gross. I tried some more, but I always got rejected and humiliated, ridiculed, by them. They all thought they were so much better than me.

I took a good look at myself in the mirror. But even though I'd lost weight, it couldn't fix my face, could it? I mean, it got rid of the jowls of fat. I could see sharp cheekbones for the first time and a dent in my chin. And my eyes looked bigger because there were no puffy cheeks squashing them up. But I was still ugly. How do you fix that? And I thought... none of those Stacys would ever want me. They want a Chad. Not someone like me.

. . .

239

I'm trying to remain objective and keep the emotion out of my voice when I speak to Rob, but it's hard. It's hard not to let the contempt and disgust out.

—So you joined an incel forum then and started talking with other similar people?

—*Yeah. Someone on one of the fat forums I belonged to had posted a link to it. I checked it out, and it was kind of nice to know there was a name for someone like me. Someone that Stacys hated. When I went on there, it was like I'd found my tribe. I finally fitted in somewhere, because these guys all felt the same. And I could let my anger out on there.*

—But at some point, that anger got too much for you to keep inside, and you brutally attacked the woman I'm calling Jenny to protect her identity.

—*I liked to watch her first. I was eighteen when I first saw her. I didn't go out much with the lads from the garage anymore. I didn't want them badgering me to chat up women and have all the humiliation of being rejected again and again. But I'd go out at night and just walk the streets on my own.*

One night I saw her with her mates, coming out of the pub on a Friday night. I had the same feeling about her as I had when I first saw Caris. [Jenny] was really pretty.

I made sure I was there the next Friday, hanging around outside with the other drunks in case she was in there again. And I saw her. It must've been her favourite hangout. Then the next time I saw her, the next week, she came out on her own. I followed her to the kebab shop. She looked inside; maybe she was looking for her mates. Then she left and started walking home.

And the anger was building again. All the anger I kept online with my incels was just mushrooming. She thought she was too good for me—I could tell. And I was never going to get her to go out with me, let alone fuck me. So I thought I'd teach her a lesson. I wanted her to feel my power, my anger, my humiliation. I wanted to make her pay.

And I did, didn't I? It made me laugh, writing those comments on her social media. I was still watching her afterwards, and I was clever about it. There was only one time when I thought she'd seen me following her. And I imagined her fear. I could almost taste it. I got high off it, I suppose.

Revulsion curdles in my stomach. What I really want to do is hang up. But I don't. If the police don't find him, this may be the only time he ever tells the truth about that night, and it's vital this evidence is used to get Caris out of prison.

—And seven months later, you raped Caris. Why did you go back to Stoneminster and attack her?

—The high only lasted awhile. I kept thinking back to when I was at school and thinking, yeah, they thought I was this useless, ugly, fat kid, but really, I'm the one with the power now. And I kept thinking about Caris. I never got her out of my head. I still went back to Stoneminster every few months to catch a glimpse of her, watch her. I think she was my first love.

—That's not love. That's as far away from love as you can get.

—Yeah, I knew you wouldn't understand. None of you ever do. But look how vulnerable you really are. You think you've got equal rights and equal pay and all that. But you're still just this weak bunch of femoids. We've got the real power. I proved that by breaking into that cottage you were staying at. By following you too. You were scared as fuck because you moved out pretty sharpish, didn't you? Oh, and by the way, I wasn't saying 'Fucking void' when I did what I did. I was saying 'Fucking foid', as in femoid. For those

snowflakes who don't speak incel, a foid or femoid is an abbreviated form of 'female humanoid'.

Anyway, back to Caris. I drove to Stoneminster on my day off and was wandering around the high street for a while. She was working in that hippie shop. Do you know what? I even walked past a couple of kids that were in my school, and they didn't even recognise me. I was probably about ten and half stone then. Skinny, almost. I'd lost loads of weight and I looked way different.

The fair was on. That boring, shitty fair they have every year. I hung around there for a bit, waiting for her to come out of the shop. And when she did, I followed her.

It was easy. She was easy. But I learned one thing with [Jenny]. Don't let them see your face! So I didn't.

—But you weren't content with carrying out a horrific attack. You bullied them both online, as well.

—When the high wore off, I'd look at their bags that I'd nicked and see their ID photos and imagine it all over again. But the power trip... that didn't last as long. Trolling them gave me power again. They didn't know who I was, but I knew them. I knew all about TOR and anonymous software and stuff and was confident I couldn't be traced, but in the end, trolling them got boring. I needed some proper action again. So I moved on to another couple of girls. Never near where I lived, though. I spaced it out. And I even managed to go a year in between them. It's like cigarette smokers who are trying to cut down. You say, 'Just one more hour, and then I'll have a fag. Another hour more, then I'll have one. Another day. Then another. Not yet. Not too soon.' But then, I needed a new challenge. Because the anger just wouldn't stay inside anymore. It was like, when I finally unleashed it, I needed more. It was addictive.

I started weight training then and changed again from a skinny guy to a bulked-up gym rat. That helped with the anger a little bit for *a while. And I had the stupid idea it might make me more attractive to women. But yet again, they just didn't see me.*

—And you bragged about the rapes on the incel forum, didn't you? Under your profile name of @InsRule, like you bragged about the murder on there.

—*Yeah. But I wasn't stupid enough to name names. And it wasn't just me. There were loads of other guys on there talking about what they'd done to Stacys. And that was the time I started seeing posts about other incels who'd gone further than I had. About some who'd actually killed them. And I thought,* Yeah, that's it. That's got to be the ultimate power trip. *That would teach Caris a lesson she wouldn't forget. Because she was with that Flora all the time. All the time! What did Flora have that I didn't have? Why did she like her so much and not me?*

And I started planning it. I was going to make sure there were two less Stacys in the world to hurt people like me. I was going to get rid of Flora and Caris. It was amazing how it worked out, wasn't it?

I know he wants an emotional reaction, but I'm not going to rise to the bait. I want this story told and then over. A sickening sludge has settled in my stomach, just listening to him.

—You intended to kill both women? But instead you murdered one and put another behind bars.

—*Yeah. And that's what you really want to know about, isn't it? Okay, I'll tell you. There was another guy on the forum who was experienced in hacking and stuff. I mean, I knew about TOR and trying to be anonymous, but it looks like I fucked up a bit there, doesn't it? Still, not to worry. You don't know where I am or who I am now.*

Getting back to the story, though. I DM'd him, we chatted, and he managed to find out Caris's mobile phone number. I wanted to send a tracking app to her phone, because I couldn't keep going to Stoneminster all the time and physically follow her. It just wasn't practical, was it, when I lived seventy miles away?

To plan something spectacular, I needed information. So he sorted me out with this app. It was pretty clever. I sent her a text from this anonymous number. It was just a generic text pretending to be from her mobile phone provider. One someone would open and then delete. But the tracking app was attached to it and automatically downloaded onto her phone, so then I knew where she was at all times.

I was trying to be patient. But waiting for the right time was hard. Really hard. Sometimes, I'd go back to Stoneminster and just pretend I was a tourist, or sit in the pub opposite the hippie shop and watch her. But it never seemed like the right time. The frustration and anger were building, and so I thought, in the meantime, I'd just find another girl to take my anger out on.

I was watching her flat, this other girl. And I wasn't concentrating. I should've known, I suppose, because it was in a bit of a shitty area. But there was too much going on in my head, so I made a mistake. While I'm hanging around one day, waiting for her to come out so I could follow her, this guy comes up to me and thinks I'm a dealer on his patch because he's noticed me hanging around. He thinks I'm selling drugs and tells me to fuck off. And I'm trying to explain I'm not a dealer, but obviously, I'm not telling him what I'm really doing. And the next minute, his two mates turn up and start punching me and kicking the shit out of me. And they break my nose. My fucking nose is broken! It was all flat and wonky, and I thought, Shit, *as if I couldn't get even uglier. It was like everyone was conspiring against me. The whole world was. But I knew I'd get my own back in the end.*

• • •

My heart is most definitely not bleeding for him right now. But this explains something. Rob went from being fifteen stone at school to ten and a half stone when he raped Caris and Jenny. As he mentioned himself, with the loss of weight, his facial appearance had changed. Around the time of Flora's murder, he says he was bulked up, muscular, and his nose had been broken. Maybe this explains why the dots in description were slow to connect after the E-FIT picture was released. Maybe this explains how he could go around, chameleon-like, in places where it was possible someone should've recognised him.

—How did you know Caris and Flora were going to be at Witch's Hill that night?

—*Yeah, that's the really clever bit. That tracking app wasn't just a tracker. It was a spy app too. It could also read texts on Caris's phone. Even when I wasn't watching her in person, I was still watching her. You know that text you got recently about winning a holiday? Yep. It's the same one. I've been reading your texts too. Better get rid of that phone now, eh? Ha ha. Yeah. You believed the mysterious witness you went to meet, didn't you? So gullible. Not as clever as you think you are, are you? All it takes is some voice-altering software. You should know all about that from the other people whose voices you changed to be anonymous. You've got no clue.*

Anyway, I'm not here to talk about you. That app on her phone showed a whole stream of texts between Caris and Flora, talking about the ritual thing they were going to do for the summer solstice. Every little detail was in those texts. The location. The time. Swimming in the river. The candles and stone circles and shit. And the wine. I knew then it was my opportunity. I planned it. I planned it so well.

I was already in the woods when they got there. I was waiting near the cottage but off to the right, hidden in the trees. I heard them before I saw them. Talking and laughing and stuff. And I crept closer, through the undergrowth. Watching as they took off their clothes.

Wow. Caris was every bit as stunning in that bikini as I thought she'd be. I'd never seen her whole body before, and it was delicious.

When they went into the river, I spiked the wine with ketamine. Then I slunk off again and watched and waited. Waited until they'd gone through their spell rubbish and were drinking the wine. Waiting until they got unconscious.

It was easy. Flora didn't even wake up. I had my fingers around her throat, and she was completely unaware. At least she went peacefully.

The triumph in his voice makes me want to throw up at this point. I want to hurl my phone across the room and watch it smash. I want to go back to the beginning and erase the whole podcast.

But I can't. I owe it to Caris, to Willow, and to Flora's memory to get the rest of the truth out there.

—What happened next?

—*I was going to kill Caris too. But I realised at the last minute that my plan was flawed. I wanted to teach Caris a lesson. Hurt her for rejecting me. But she wouldn't be hurting if she was dead, would she? Instead of killing her, I just kept imagining Caris waking up and finding her best friend dead instead. I knew how much she loved her. Caris loved Flora the same way I loved Caris. But she couldn't have her anymore. Just like I couldn't have Caris the way I wanted her. Caris would suffer more by leaving her alive to deal with it all.*

I wasn't really thinking about framing her. I wasn't thinking that far ahead. At least... Well, maybe subconsciously, I wanted it to

246

look like that, but I didn't plan that bit in any detail. What happened next was kind of spur of the moment. Improvisation, if you like. And you have to admit, it was pretty cool the way it worked out. I mean, she probably wouldn't have looked at me anyway, even with Flora out of the way, and it meant that if I couldn't have her, no one else could, either. She'd be locked up in prison.

I made a stone circle around Flora. I drew the pentagram in the soil to make it look like all this witchy devil-worship shit. I took Flora's bag as a keepsake. And then I ran through the woods.

I didn't see that Damian nobber hiding in the trees like a nonce. But that worked out for me, didn't it? No one believed him. They all thought he was the village idiot. Ha! I remember seeing that Aussie guy, though. But I figured he'd just think I was a jogger, and as it turned out, that was also stacked in my favour. I'd parked my car on the outskirts of Westcombe and got in it and drove away. The high from the murder was even better than the rapes. It was just mind-blowing!

It was a giant step for the incel revolution, too, eh? Pretty genius when you think about it.

—There are multiple words to describe you and what you've done, but 'genius' is definitely not one of them.

—Ha ha! Funny. Oh, and yeah, I did lie about the heart thing. I never saw Caris in the woods that day with an animal heart. Got you going, though, didn't it? Got you all going! But, hey, I wasn't the only one lying about her, now, was I?

And one more thing—the animal mutilations? That was me too.

So you've got the story now. I hope you're happy with yourself. But don't get too complacent. Because although you use an alias, I can find out who you really are and where you actually live.

When Rob hangs up, I sit for a long time, trying to calm down. I've held off on telling you listeners about him stalking me because I wanted him to make a mistake. Wanted him dragged out into the light. His threat is sinister, and I've been on the incel boards and seen all the violent hatred for myself. But I don't think he'll carry it out. He's got far too much to worry about, keeping himself hidden.

As this goes on air, the police have issued a nationwide alert for him. Interpol have issued international notices. His photo is being circulated in the national press. He looks different again to how Damian and Brett described him. He no longer has a broken nose. No doubt it was fixed shortly after the murder. Please check out a recent photo of him on the *Anatomy of a Crime* website. A cunning, sadistic killer is on the loose, and he needs to be caught, because I don't think he'll stop until he is.

The day after Rob Curran's confession, I attempt to contact his parents again, but unsurprisingly, there's no reply. The press are camped on their doorstep, and no doubt they've gone into hiding. His parents are yet another two lives Rob has ruined forever. But did they know they had a rapist and killer in their midst? Did they know what Rob spent his time doing online? Did they know where all this hatred and anger stemmed from? Are they, in some part, responsible for the way Rob turned out?

Maybe. Maybe not. Often those closest to people are the last to know. And Rob was very good at hiding things. The nature-versus-nurture debate is one that often rears its head and would take up a whole podcast series in itself.

As I turn away from their house and leave their street, jostling through the clambering scrum of media, and conclude this chilling and sickening episode, I hope this isn't the end of the story. Not yet. It can't be. I'm going to take the molten ball of anger I feel for Rob, along with the fury I feel about the injustice Caris has suffered all these years, and use it to keep going. To uncover where and who Rob is now.

The end, for me, will come when Rob is caught. And even though official channels are trying to track him down, don't underestimate the power of social media. So keep sharing his picture. Keep warning your friends. Keep looking for him. He's out there somewhere.

Thank you for listening to *Anatomy of a Crime*.

Until next time...

IncelKing • 2 days ago
Rob's a hero! You Stacys and femoids get what you deserve. We created the world, and you need to remember that. Rob's carried on Elliot Rodger's legacy with style. Incels rule!!!
^ | ˅ • Reply • Share ˃

CDC55 → Reply to IncelKing • 2 days ago
Sick bastard!
^ | ˅ • Reply • Share ˃

IncelHater → Reply to IncelKing • 2 days ago
You vile, evil sicko. I hope you die painfully.
^ | ˅ • Reply • Share ˃

BitsyBobs → Reply to IncelKing • 1 day ago
You are deranged!
^ | ˅ • Reply • Share ˃

56721 → Reply to IncelKing • 1 day ago
You are seriously twisted! I'm embarrassed to be a man. You have no empathy, so you'll never be capable of finding a woman to love

you. Your view of women and the world is completely distorted. You need help. Proper psychological help.

^ | ˅ • Reply • Share ˃

Dwoo22 • 2 days ago

OMG! I'm totally lost for words. What an evil bastard Rob is. I hope they catch him soon. Please catch him and all the people like him!

^ | ˅ • Reply • Share ˃

Faber → Reply to Dwoo22 • 1 day ago

At least Caris can get the justice she deserves now. Fingers crossed she'll be out soon.

^ | ˅ • Reply • Share ˃

WottyPeeps → Reply to Faber • 1 day ago

I hope so too. But how does she rebuild her life?

^ | ˅ • Reply • Share ˃

Chuggsy → Faber • 1 day ago

I'm praying for her quick release!

^ | ˅ • Reply • Share ˃

Grumblez • 1 day ago

I've been sharing Rob's picture on my social media. If everyone shares it, we can reach thousands of people. Come on, keep sharing!!!

^ | ˅ • Reply • Share ˃

OMG • 1 day ago

I can't believe the police aren't doing something about these dangerous websites!

^ | ˅ • Reply • Share ˃

564 → Reply to OMG • 1 day ago

Me too. How can people get away with posting all this hatred against women and inciting violence against them? If they were racist posts, they'd be prosecuted! The government and police need to do something about this RIGHT NOW!

^ | ˅ • Reply • Share ˃

DOld → Reply to OMG • 1 day ago

Women need to come together and organise some protests about the lack of police and government action about these incel terror groups (and, yes, they SHOULD be labelled domestic terrorists!). I've just looked up some of these incel sites, and they are seriously scary.

^ | ˅ • Reply • Share ˃

CHAPTER NINETEEN

EPISODE 9
UPDATE
Media Clip from ITV News

—I*'m standing outside the Court of Appeal in London, where Caris Kelly has had her conviction for the murder of Flora Morgan quashed. Kelly was convicted of the so-called Sleeping Beauty Murder in 2017, after it was alleged she strangled her best friend Flora Morgan in a ritualistic witchcraft killing.*

Today, a judge slammed the evidence against her and the failings of the police to properly investigate the crime. The senior investigating officer involved in the case, Detective Chief Inspector Richard Lewis from Dorset Police, has now resigned.

A sensational new twist in the story was sparked off by the podcast Anatomy of a Crime *when new evidence came to light. Rob Curran, twenty-three, of Southampton, and a former resident of Stoneminster, where the murder took place, admitted on air that he* was, in fact, responsible for a series of attacks on women, including Morgan's murder.

Curran fled the UK and remained at large for several weeks before being apprehended in Amsterdam by Dutch police, using fake Italian documents. A formal extradition was applied for, and Rob was brought back to the UK to face justice.

A search of Curran's parents' house uncovered several women's handbags, one belonging to Flora Morgan, hidden under the floorboards. The DNA of Curran's dog has been positively matched to dog hairs found on Flora's body. After being presented with the evidence and his online confession, Curran agreed to cooperate with the police before entering a plea of guilty to his charge. He's currently on remand and awaiting sentencing.

I'm waiting outside the gates of HMP Ashmount for Caris to be released. The media surrounds the area, jostling for position to be the first to get a direct quote about her newfound freedom. Those same members of the media were so quick to smear her all those years ago.

And then, three years after being fed into a justice machine that took away her freedom and her life, Caris is spat out, crushed and damaged.

She emerges from the gates with Annabelle Sherbourne, carrying a small plastic bag and £46 to her name, a token discharge grant that's supposed to see her through the next few days.

A cheer ripples through the crowd, but this time, it's a cheer supporting Caris. A cheer that says injustice has been put right. A

Twitter storm about this miscarriage of justice has already gone viral.

I push through the crowd towards her. She beams a smile, and we hug. She holds on to me tight and offers her thanks over and over again as the reporters shout out questions. I don't want thanks, though. I want to hear how she's going to rebuild her life. Because although she's free, she's left with nothing. No home, no job, no family. It's like history repeating itself from when she was thirteen.

Caris refuses all media interviews, even though she could earn a fortune for an exclusive. She tells me they didn't care about her then and they don't care about her now. As Annabelle makes an official statement on Caris's behalf, Caris and I jostle through the stream of people, being chased by cameras, to a waiting vehicle that's going to take her on her first steps to freedom.

Until Caris's compensation for wrongful imprisonment arrives and she can get back on her feet, she has no means of financial support. But I have every confidence in her. She's twenty-one years old, with her life ahead of her. She's stronger than she knows. My producers and I have clubbed together to rent Caris an apartment for six months. I hope, by the end of that time, she will be more settled. I think if she started her online business again, she'd make a fortune, and not just because of the infamy attached to her name.

Back at the apartment, I open a bottle of celebratory cognac—definitely not wine, because, as Caris says, she's never drinking it again. It's over this shared drink that I get Caris's final words.

—*I can't believe it. I can't believe it's finally all over. I'm even too happy to be free to be angry right now. I'm sure the anger will come. Later. But maybe anger's a better emotion than pain, than upset, or indignation. Anger's quite a powerful motivator, isn't it?*

—I think it's healthy. As long as you let it out. Channel it into something positive.

—I agree. And I don't want to talk about what happened, either. Everyone knows what happened now. I don't want to go over it. I want to concentrate on the future.

—And what will you do next, do you think?

—I have absolutely no idea. I think I want to try to use this experience to help other people. I have no idea how or what I could do, but I want to try.

—Well, cheers to that!

We clink our glasses in celebration. Then Caris takes a deep breath and stares into the cognac, swirling it around in the glass. The happiness evident on her face from earlier is now etched in a melancholy frown. She looks up at me, her stunning eyes locking on to mine, and I find myself hoping she discovers true happiness in the big, wide world that's been so cruel to her.

—The huge regret for me, apart from the obvious fact that I'll never see Flora again, is my dad. Like Flora, he's gone forever, and I never got to say goodbye to him. Life is going to be a huge adjustment now. And although I've won my freedom—cleared my name—the victory is hollow. Life feels empty without them in it.

—I've been contacted by Willow Morgan. She wanted me to pass on a message to you.

—Really?

—She wanted to apologise for not believing in you. And she wants you to know that she'd love it if you contacted her so you can both meet again and she can tell you that in person. You've both lost someone very close to you and maybe this could be a good opportunity to help you both heal. How do you feel about that?

· · ·

Caris considers this, her head tilted, her forehead scrunched up, deep in thought. When she looks up finally, her face is filled with joy, and I think I see hope shimmering behind her eyes.

—I'd like that. I'd really like that.

—Is there anything else you want to say before I leave you in peace?

—I do. I'd like to say one final thing to whoever's out there listening.

—Of course.

—Nothing is ever black and white. There are always shades of grey that cast their own shadow if you look deep enough. So if you ever see that girl or boy struggling to cope, ask them what's wrong, try and offer them some help. If you see the kid who looks different to you, try to understand them, not alienate them. And even something little that you can do might make a big difference to them.

I've had a lot of time to think in prison about the distressing things around what happened to Flora. What happened to me. And I realised that the commonality between so many bad things that happen is hatred and fear. Whether we're talking about gender rights, equality, racism, gay rights, or animal rights. It's all about fighting against injustice. No one sex or race or species has the right to dominate, control, and exploit another. We need to find more compassion and empathy for each other. We need to make changes. We need to look at the Earth as a whole, not just our own small part in it. We need to grow and educate ourselves to be more loving.

We might all be human, but I think we've lost the essence of humanity along the way. We need to learn to be human again.

Finally, the untold story has been told. Or has it?

Yes, the truth about this case is now out there for all to see. But is the story about a twisted, evil individual who lived out his sick fantasies by preying on others and taking huge pleasure from his theatre of abuse? Is it about racism or prejudice or judgement? About no-smoke-without-fire rumours that stab and scratch and snag everything in their path like barbed wire around a small community? A collective hatred based on pure supposition? Is it about failing vulnerable people in our society? Is it about looking the other way? About not caring what's going on in people's lives when they need help? Is it about the police fixating on an explanation that doesn't really make sense, pushing it into a box where they think it fits? Or the justice system getting things so wrong with terrifying consequences? Is it about sensationalism in the press that sells an agenda like it's a true story?

I think it's actually about all of us, because Caris's and Flora's story could happen to anyone. All it takes is for one false tale to rise up and grow horns, to infuse with lies and conjecture so you can't tell where the truth ever really started, to rage like a bushfire, out of control and unchecked. All it takes is one fake story, one wrong accusation, to ruin someone's life.

Thank you for listening to *Anatomy of a Crime*.

Until the next series...

A NOTE FROM THE AUTHOR

Thank you so much to all the readers out there for choosing my books. I really hope you enjoyed *Anatomy of a Crime,* which was inspired by my love of true crime podcasts, particularly *Serial* and *Casefile.* If you liked it, I would be so grateful if you could leave a review or recommend it to family and friends. I always love to hear from readers, so please keep your emails and Facebook messages coming (contact details are on my website: www.sibelhodge.com). They make my day!

Thank you to Stefanie Spangler Buswell for all the editing suggestions and for catching the things I missed.

And a very big thank you to my lovely beta readers: Karen Lloyd, Holly Christie, Sam Lindsell, Nick Davies, and Teresa Nikolic. It's very much appreciated!

As always, a massive thanks goes out to Hubby Hodge for all your support, encouragement, and chief beta reading duties. You rock!

And finally, a loud shout-out and hugs to all the amazing book bloggers and book reviewers out there who enthusiastically support us authors with their passion for reading.

Sibel xx

ABOUT THE AUTHOR

Sibel Hodge is the author of number-one bestsellers *Look Behind You, Untouchable, Duplicity, Into the Darkness,* and *Their Last Breath.* Her books have sold over one million copies and are international bestsellers in the UK, USA, Australia, France, Canada, and Germany. She writes in an eclectic mix of genres, and is a passionate human- and animal-rights advocate.

Her work has been nominated and shortlisted for numerous prizes, including the Harry Bowling Prize, the Yeovil Literary Prize, the Chapter One Promotions Novel Competition, The Romance Reviews' prize for Best Novel with Romantic Elements and Indie Book Bargains' Best Indie Book of 2012 in two categories. She was the winner of Best Children's Book in the 2013 eFestival of Words, nominated for the 2015 BigAl's Books and Pals Young Adult Readers' Choice Award, winner of the Crime, Thrillers & Mystery Book from a Series Award in the SpaSpa Book Awards 2013, winner of the Readers' Favorite Young Adult (Coming of Age) Honorable award in 2015, a New Adult finalist in the Oklahoma Romance Writers of America's International Digital Awards 2015, 2017 International Thriller Writers Award finalist for Best E-book Original Novel, Honorable Mention Award Winner in the USA 2018 Reader's Choice Awards, and winner of the No.1 Best Thriller in the Top Shelf Magazine Indie Book Awards 2018! Her novella *Trafficked: The Diary of a Sex Slave* has been listed as one of the top forty books about human rights by Accredited Online Colleges.

For Sibel's latest book releases, giveaways and gossip, sign up to her newsletter at www.sibelhodge.com.

ALSO BY SIBEL HODGE

Fiction

Dark Shadows

Their Last Breath (Detective Carter Book 3)

Into the Darkness (Detective Carter Book 2)

Duplicity (Detective Carter Book 1)

The Disappeared

Beneath the Surface

Untouchable

Where the Memories Lie

Look Behind You

Butterfly

Trafficked: The Diary of a Sex Slave

Fashion, Lies, and Murder (Amber Fox Mystery No 1)

Money, Lies, and Murder (Amber Fox Mystery No 2)

Voodoo, Lies, and Murder (Amber Fox Mystery No 3)

Chocolate, Lies, and Murder (Amber Fox Mystery No 4)

Santa Claus, Lies, and Murder (Amber Fox Mystery No 4.5)

Vegas, Lies, and Murder (Amber Fox Mystery No 5)

Murder and Mai Tais (Danger Cove Cocktail Mystery No 1)

Killer Colada (Danger Cove Cocktail Mystery No 2)

The See-Through Leopard

Fourteen Days Later

My Perfect Wedding

The Baby Trap

It's a Catastrophe

Non-Fiction

Deliciously Vegan Everyday Kitchen

Deliciously Vegan Soup Kitchen

Healing Meditations for Surviving Grief and Loss